"Surely it's not someone of aristocratic birth you would want kidnapped?" Brandt asked.

And for the first time, Katherine looked guilty.

"That's frowned upon, you know." He could not believe he was having this conversation. Only his curiosity kept him speaking to her. He'd never abducted anyone. He'd spent too many years keeping his distance from people. The last thing he'd do was capture another person whom he might have to feed and water occasionally.

She nodded. "I said I had a personal reason and I assure you it's a just one."

"Someone in the royal family?" he asked, eyebrows lifted.

"Do not jest. Anyone could have listened to what I've said and figured out who I wanted kidnapped." She interlaced her fingers, letting them rest on the table.

He paused, scowling. In this strange dream he was having, he must have slept through one of the important parts.

She touched her chest and leaned toward him. "Me." She spoke softly. "I need you to kidnap me."

Author Note

Brandt's story began when I imagined a man walking along a street in the early hours of the morning, missing the wife he had lost. The only thing he had as a memento of her was the scent of her perfume.

I didn't feel he would ever be able to move forward into a new life unless someone pulled him out of his grief. A woman barging in on his solitude and tugging him along with her into her life seemed a perfect answer.

Brandt and Katherine's story took me along with them as they moved forward, resolving the past and creating a new journey for themselves. I hope you enjoy their journey!

LIZ TYNER

Saying I Do to the Scoundrel

ISBN-13: 978-1-335-52285-6

Saying I Do to the Scoundrel

This edition published by arrangement with Harlequin Books S.A.

For questions and comments about the quality of this book, please contact us at CustomerService@Harlequin.com.

Printed in U.S.A.

Liz Tyner lives with her husband on an Oklahoma acreage she imagines is similar to the ones in the children's book *Where the Wild Things Are*. Her lifestyle is a blend of old and new, and is sometimes comparable to the way people lived long ago. Liz is a member of various writing groups and has been writing since childhood. For more about her, visit liztyner.com.

Books by Liz Tyner

Harlequin Historical

The Notorious Countess
The Wallflower Duchess
Redeeming the Roguish Rake
Saying I Do to the Scoundrel

The Governess Tales

The Runaway Governess

English Rogues and Grecian Goddesses

Safe in the Earl's Arms
A Captain and a Rogue
Forbidden to the Duke

Visit the Author Profile page at Harlequin.com.

Dedicated to my generous, thoughtful and always encouraging friend Charlotte Schrahl.

Chapter One

The knocking on his door pounded like hooves against Brandt's head, bringing him from ravaged dreams into the summer-baked room. He didn't care where the hands on the clock might be—the hour was too early for him to awaken. He needed another bottle of brandy to cleanse his mouth. He called out to his valet, 'Enter.

'Enter,' he commanded again when he heard no footsteps.

The door swung open.

'Heathen.' The word screeched into his ears as if attached to flying glass. A woman wearing a bonnet the size of a parasol stood beneath the transom. For a moment, he thought he dreamed of a butterfly, the dress fluttered so and bead trim sparkled. A pale face, with dark eyes rimmed in lashes any siren could be envious of, stared at him.

The drunken haze confused him. This was a boarding house—not his home. For a moment, he had forgotten.

Memories returned, anger flooding his body.

He rolled on to his side, and propped himself on his elbow, re-orienting himself, and feeling a breeze waft over his body. Completely over his body.

Everything came back to him. Or enough of it did. He'd shed his clothing when he'd returned from the tavern. He felt beside him for a covering. Nothing touched his fingers but a mattress so thin he could feel the ropes beneath.

'Why did you call for the door to open?' The woman at the door had her hand over her eyes—and her cheeks were flushed. The one behind her seemed to be taking measurements.

'I was dreaming of—' He could not tell her he dreamed of Mary. Of a world of servants and health and sobriety. 'I dreamt of a swarm of annoying bees and I called for the door to be open so they might fly out,' he said. 'Instead one rushed in.'

How had he wronged the woman at the door? He couldn't recall her face, and she didn't look at all the kind he consorted with. She had the look of an outraged wife on her face, but she wasn't his outraged wife.

He took a breath to calm himself and wished the night hadn't been so warm he'd shed his clothing, his covers and the last threads of his dignity.

The female at the threshold looked as if she'd been snatched from Sunday services and plopped in the middle of a brothel.

But no devil had forced her to open his door.

He reached to the side of his bed, ignored his small clothes and went straight for his trousers.

With his body turned away, he pulled his clothing over his legs.

'Perhaps you could introduce yourself.' He spoke calmly to the daft one even as the second woman tiptoed to examine him. He was at a blasted soirée and he had not accepted the invitation. 'You are under the impression we are acquainted. And I am under the impression we are not.'

She sputtered.

'And to what do I owe the pleasure?' he asked, finishing the last button and turning. He would have preferred to have on his small clothes, but then he would have preferred to have drunk a lot more and fallen asleep at the tavern.

The drink had finally destroyed him, but not in the way he had expected.

'Cover yourself,' the young woman commanded. 'You heathen.'

'You can take your hand from your eyes,' he said. 'I've got my trousers buttoned.'

Eyes, which reminded him of sunlight shining through sparkling glass, took a quick look at him. 'A shirt?'

'Oh, let's save that until after we've been properly introduced.'

'We will never be properly introduced.'

She wouldn't be in a tavern, or on the darkened streets. And she shouldn't be in his room. He paid little care to the society folks with their haughty stares. They didn't interest him at all. Never had—even when he'd lived the other life.

'Your shirt.' She waved a finger, pointing at a direction beyond his back, and her eyes appeared to be fixed on his torn window curtain.

He looked around. The peg where he usually put

his shirt stood empty. He picked up his waistcoat and slipped an arm into it, then the other. 'Since you've seen me from top to bottom, this will have to do, Love.' He fastened one button as a kindness.

'Save your words for the lightskirts,' Miss Butterfly Bonnet said.

Calling her *love* had snapped her out of her embarrassment.

'So you are not of that business,' he muttered. 'Pity.'

Her eyes turned to slits. 'Until I opened the door, I was quite innocent. Now I'm tainted for ever by what I've seen.'

He sat on the bed. 'Think how it is for me. To wake up with a shrieking shrew at the door I can't for the life of me remember how I've wronged.'

'Oh, I envy you,' she bit out the words. 'Would that my life was so pleasant.'

They stared at each other.

'You might tell me the nature of your visit.' He examined his mind for a reason for this woman to search him out. 'I truly don't know you or know why you're here.' He yawned. 'Come in.' He waved an arm to indicate the two wooden chairs by the uneven table.

The older woman, peering into the room, gave the girl a push. 'Quick before someone recognises you.' Then the older woman pulled the door shut.

The young one's eyes widened, but she covered her surprise with a tightening of her jaw and squared shoulders.

She took a tiny step inside his room, but she stayed within an arm's reach of the door.

'Sit.' He straightened his shoulders and adopted the look of a coddled peer. 'I will ring the butler for tea.' He let his eyes look thoughtful. 'Oh, goodness, I fear it is his half-day off. We will have to make do with brandy.'

He noticed the overturned glass on the table and looked around for a bottle. He reached down to the edge of the bed and found one still standing with about three swallows left in it—for a small person.

He picked it up, held the bottle in her direction and raised his eyebrows.

Her chin moved, but she didn't open her mouth.

'Speak your business quickly,' he commanded. 'Your bonnet is giving me a headache.'

He relaxed his arm, still holding the bottle. None of this would have happened if his wife had lived. The thought of her stabbed at his chest, and he wished he didn't breathe in the blackness with every breath.

Just the touch of Mary's finger at his cheek had given him more pleasure than he could ever find in a bottle.

He finished the liquid, then flipped the bottle into the corner, enjoying the clunk.

The lady with the overgrown bonnet watched him and her face condemned him. Her nose wrinkled and the corners of her lips turned down.

'Makes two of us.' His eyes swept over her.

Her gaze narrowed as she tried to guess his meaning. He enlightened her. 'I'm not pleased with the sight of you, either, Love.'

The words were true. But, not completely. Something about her stirred his memories. Reminding him of a time when a woman's beauty could touch him.

She wore a matronly fichu tucked into the bodice. Surely she had a body somewhere underneath, but he couldn't be certain. He wagered she double-knotted her corset and wouldn't walk past a mirror unless she had her laces done to her neck.

'I had heard…' She paused, seemingly entranced by the torn curtain. 'I had heard,' she repeated, rushing the words, 'you might be a man of a somewhat, perhaps only slightly, disreputable nature.' When she said disreputable nature, she looked at the floor, then at his eyes. Her hand clasped into a fist. 'That might have been an error. Your nature is less—'

'If gambling and drinking and spending my time in a tavern constitutes, then I suppose my nature could be under question,' he interrupted. Who was this little dash of condemnation, he wondered, to be appearing on his doorstep, discussing his life?

'You, miss—' he speared her with his glance '—seem to be a woman who frequents places where no decent woman would be found and you appear to be looking for a man of impure habits.' He paused, narrowing his eyes. 'Which makes you…'

She stared at him. 'Determined.'

He couldn't believe it. She stepped a bit closer, her hand tight at her side. 'If a bear prowled about me and the only trap I had near was rusty, covered in the stench of ale and might not be able to snap closed fast enough to catch a turtle, I'd use it. If only to sling the weapon at the bear's head.'

He sniffed his arm. 'Ale would be better than the smell of me.'

She tensed her body, near snarling the words into the room. 'Are all men beasts? I had not expected a man such as yourself to have had a father, but I am surprised you have never had a mother either as no one has taught you manners.'

'Ah, milady,' he said with a sweeping bow. He gave her his darkest glare. 'I must retire and you know where you can put your manners. Or lack thereof. Leave your calling card with the butler.'

Katherine tried to take her mind from the sight she had just seen on the bed. The man had been unclothed.

She bit the inside of her lip. She had stepped into a world of wickedness unlike anything she could have ever expected. And the wicked one on the bed—she had chosen him to save her virtue. She had made an error. An error of magnificent proportions. But she couldn't think of another choice and she had so little time left.

'I would like to speak with you as if we are two respectable people,' Katherine said.

'That beetle has already left the dung heap,' he said.

'When you were born,' Katherine said, although she wasn't sure she spoke the entire truth. The rumours said he had fallen from a life of prosperity straight on to the floor of a tavern.

He didn't look as though he spent his life sotted.

The form he had might take some getting used to. His shape had covered most of the bed and his feet had reached past the end.

He wasn't overgrown with hair on his body either, until she looked above his shoulders. She couldn't have described much of him to a magistrate, except for his eyes. They were shadowed into a dark, soulless stare.

His face showed through locks of straight hair,

which hung to his shoulders and mixed with a healthy scattering of whiskers.

This would have been a man she wouldn't have stopped near on the street.

He would have to be harnessed to do her bidding and to save her. But she wasn't quite sure she shouldn't slam the door and run back to her home. His room spoke of his desperate circumstances though, so surely he could be hired to do her bidding?

Only the memory of Fillmore kept her standing firm.

Katherine couldn't let him send her away. Her eyes darted around the room. In the morning light, shadows cloaked the furnishings. The bed was small and the covers fallen on the floor were rough, and worn. The clothing hung on pegs and he had few pegs. The stove stood in the centre of the room, its black chimney crookedly going to the roof. The table was made with the minimum of wood and had two chairs, one missing a rung in the back. Her servants would refuse such a room.

'Don't waste my time.' He planted his feet firmly and opened the door. 'I've got business to get back to.' His smiled crooked at the side. 'My pillow.'

'Wait.' She raised her hand to stop him from closing the door and somehow, she wasn't quite sure how, her gloved fingers alighted on his muscled skin just above his elbow.

All words fled her thoughts. She could feel his strength, almost touch the anger in his eyes. And she could feel the blood in her veins and it moved with such speed it took her breath.

His eyes locked on hers as if she were a blackguard

trying to ravish him. His jaw tensed and scornful eyes seared into her.

She jerked her hand back. 'I got carried away in my quest. I shouldn't, as I've heard you might also be considered somewhat honest.'

She had to take the burning anger from his eyes—or she would be lost. Her stepfather would have won, as he always did. He always won—even choosing the dress her mother was buried in. A dress her mother had hated.

She controlled her voice, softening it. 'You've been described as a decent sort. With clear speech,' she added, hoping to appease him. In fact, he'd been noticed because he spoke with society's tones.

He was a man with an unknown past and the voice of a lord. He'd lived in a fine house, that was certain. And now he was no longer a part of it. People wondered whether he was a wastrel second son, a thief or the bastard child of a wealthy man, and some decided on all three.

'And a kindness to children,' she added softly, her eyes wide to pacify him.

She couldn't remember any other good qualities about him without risking he might realise who'd spoken to her concerning his ways.

'You're good to small animals,' she added, having no idea, but hoping.

He raised an eyebrow, lips firm. 'Continue.'

'You're an excellent judge of horseflesh.' She'd never heard of a man yet who wouldn't agree to the statement.

He tilted his chin down a bit and she thought humour flashed across his eyes. 'Yes...'

The silence was a bit too long and she searched her

mind for things men prided themselves on. 'You're good with your fists.'

A barely perceptible nod of his head and he leaned back, arms crossed, waiting for her to continue listing his virtues. She suddenly lost patience.

'Fine,' she snapped. 'You're a saint. A man of uncommon purity and a sterling reputation about you. Statues should be erected in your honour and placed on every street corner.'

In an instant the veneer of his patience fled and the muscles in his face tightened.

'And you—' His face moved so close she could get foxed from the brandy on his breath and, while his body moved, his head remained close to hers. 'You're a miss who would never leave an embroidery stitch unfinished. You write poetry proclaiming the injustice of a world which ignores its orphans, and on Sunday you say a prayer for those less fortunate who do not have fashionable bonnets, or new cravats.'

'I see we have an astounding awareness of each other.' She pushed her voice to match the strength of his. 'So before we both swoon in awe of each other's presence, might I discuss a matter of a small bit of importance to me?'

'Who sent you to me?' he asked, tone soft but with an underlying bite.

'My sister's governess's sister's husband has a friend who knows you from the tavern.' She forced herself not to step back from those eyes. 'The friend did think you might have honour, though.'

'Yes.' He used both hands to tug at the hem of his waistcoat and disdain pushed his chin even higher. His voice softened, but not his face. 'They would think

I'm honourable. I've never stolen a mug yet from the tavern.'

She stepped closer, almost to his nose, and put confidence into her quiet words. 'You can rest assured that is all they said you had to recommend you.'

'Wise of them.' He crossed his arms, increased the distance between them and leaned on the doorway. 'And, what sort of bear do you wish to trap?' he asked, surprised he found her lips appealing. He didn't know why he even noticed her lips. They weren't overly ripe. Nor thin. They were merely pleasant. But lips? Why would he notice that body part when there were so many others to peruse?

She wasn't sturdy, as Mary had been. She wasn't quiet, as Mary had been and he preferred, but that kind seemed to have disappeared before Eve. Once Eve had started talking, the world had gone downhill quickly. Adam should have made peace with the asp and stayed in the garden.

'I wondered...' she took her time with her words '...if you might consider a business dealing which might be considered to be against the law—although some of it isn't. And it truly isn't unlawful to the conscience.'

He wondered what she wanted him to do. Bad enough she'd woken him suddenly.

'You compliment me to suggest I've got a conscience. But I dare say you should look somewhere else for that.'

He walked to the door, opened it and the woman outside took one look at his face and stepped back.

He paused, stared back at the young wench, pointed

to the door and said, 'Find someone who doesn't mind being awoken before dusk.'

The miss stood nearly a head shorter than he and had more bluff in her face than any card player he'd ever seen, but none of the bravado reached the end of the reticule hanging from her wrist. The beads at the end of the tie were bobbing like—he pushed that image from his mind.

'And what might you be wanting me for?' He spoke before he could stop himself. 'The chore which might interest a magistrate?'

Her lips parted slightly, but she closed them again.

Her lips. When he realised where his mind wandered, he gave a disgusted grunt. His mind had rotted just as he'd wanted, but he wished it had waited one more day.

Her eyes widened as she stared at his face. She tightened her shoulders.

'I can't state my exact needs,' she interrupted his thoughts, 'until I know you'll take on the task.' She waved her hand to the doorway. 'I am a respectable woman, with a chaperon, and it is intensely important that I be able to sneak back into my house soon. I would never seek out a person…' and here she floundered a bit for words '…such as yourself, if I had another choice.'

'I am pleased you're so virtuous.' He lessened the space between them. The soft scent of her touched him—not perfume—but plain soap. The miss nearly reeked with her purity. Forget putting statues of him on corners. This one should have convents erected in her honour. 'You realise your virtue means you might not offer as much as another woman might.'

The narrowing of her eyes pleased him. She should never wake a rusty trap unless she expected to see its teeth.

She stared at him and he could see thoughts flittering behind her eyes. The beads on the reticule clicked together.

'You'll be paid,' she grumbled. 'Then you can buy…' she paused '…whatever services you need.'

He wouldn't need any *services* if Mary had lived.

And as the darkness closed tightly around him, he didn't care to do what she wanted, but he doubted he would be able to go back to sleep in such heat and he had nothing else to do. 'I could be interested in whatever business you might bring to me.' His voice mocked her with a false sweetness. 'Tell me what you have in mind.'

She leaned in so close he could almost taste her soap. Something inside of him froze and then began to unfurl warmth in his body. He bit it back.

'You must kidnap someone.' Her voice vibrated with excitement.

This Miss, untouched as newly fallen snow, wanted him to kidnap someone? He gaped at her. 'I'm guessing it would be someone you find annoying.'

'Not really,' she muttered.

'My skin has an aversion to rope burns—' he touched his neck '—so even though I am honoured to be selected, I decline.' He clasped the door, knowing he would have to send her on her way quickly and not really wanting to.

He just needed to be left alone. 'Out.'

'You must listen.' She held up both palms.

He shook his head and reached for her arm. The

simple touch of her brought back the memories he lived with, blurring his vision. He had to get the woman out of his life. Now. He backed away, not wanting to stir any memories of a woman's softness. Those memories had taunted him, wrapping their dark, nettled cloak around him, until he discovered they would not sting so much if he appeased them with drink.

He stepped around her and touched the door.

'You would get away with it, I'm sure,' her voice pleaded.

He stilled. Before he could stop anything, the soap aroma tangled around him. His throat contracted and, for a second, he couldn't speak.

'Get out and don't come back.' His voice returned with force.

Her eyes widened and he pushed the thought of her fear away.

'Leave,' he snarled, snapping his teeth together on the word. 'You.' His voice spoke with the authority of a hammer on an anvil. 'Must leave.' His arm slashed in the direction of the door. 'Go.'

She stared at him and he realised her cheeks had no colour.

'You must do this.' Her eyes begged. 'I'll die if you don't.'

Chapter Two

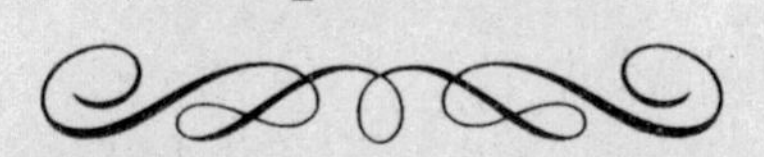

She meant the words. He could tell by her widened eyes. But just because she meant them, it didn't mean they were true.

'Well.' She drew in a breath and crossed her arms, stilling that ridiculous purse with glass beads. 'I understand if you might be too weak to help an innocent lady.' The bravado in her voice ended on a tremble. She pulled in a deep breath. 'After all, you near reek of spirits and I do suppose you could do with a bit of a wash and a shave, and for that matter a good haircut, but might you suggest someone who will do my errand as I have spent a good morning pursuing you and I do not have much time to waste finding someone else.'

'*You* do not have time to waste, yet you are appearing on *my* doorstep?' he asked, quietly. 'Perhaps you should be at—your home—not wasting time there?' he said.

Her shoulders rose and her chin jutted, but her eyes didn't follow through on the confidence. 'I am here to offer you employment.'

'Do I look as though I want employment?' His lips turned up.

'I have set myself on a course and I will see it to the end. Goodness knows it cannot get any worse.' She adjusted her bonnet.

'Whatever that end may be.' He forced the words through his teeth. 'I must compliment you on the bonnet. No one would ever notice you about in such inconspicuous wear.'

She eyed him as if he were untouchable. 'This bonnet was made by Annabel Pierce and is of the finest quality in the world.'

'La-de-doodle.' He leaned forward. 'Do you think she might make one for me?'

'She would not let you step foot in her fine establishment.' She tightened her shoulders ever closer. 'Are you considering the plan?'

He might as well let her have her say. He'd not fall back asleep easily when she left and he'd be lying, looking up at the ceiling and thinking about her, and wondering what she'd wanted.

'How much money is to be made?' Soft words from hard lips.

She appraised him, then she moved to the chair, sitting as if she prepared for a portrait.

He slid into his seat, then gave a twist, making the legs scrape slightly against the floor.

'What's your name, Love?' he asked the woman as she sat across from him.

She slowly blinked and looked at him. 'You'll find out if—if—I decide to hire you.' Her chin dropped. She placed her palms flat on the table, and leaned forward. 'And do not call me *love*.'

'Well.' He clasped his hands behind his head and pushed back. 'You kind of look like a Nigel to me. So you can keep your name secret for ever, for all I care. I'll just think of you as Nigel and, if the magistrate catches me risking my neck for you, I'll be able to say I owe it all to Nigel.'

'Do not call me that.'

'You know my name, do you not? Surely you found out while you were asking questions.' He looked at her and she averted her eyes and a hint of blush stained her cheeks. He grinned.

Her words were stronger. 'Brandt is all I know of your name.'

He looked down, dismissing her, and let the front legs of his chair thump to the floor.

'Do you want to listen or not?' The voice rose at the end, a note of panic in it.

He shrugged, put his elbow on the table and rested his chin in his hand.

She clasped her hands in her lap. 'It's simple really. You'll do the kidnapping in the morning. The footman should be no problem. Try not to kill the older man—very important as he will pay the ransom. You'll handle a ransom note. Collect the blunt. Take a thousand pounds of it, give me nineteen thousand pounds and be on your way.'

'Kidnapping. I could work in a quick nab as I walked to the tavern. Nothing to it.' He smiled, leaning towards her, his eyes shining. 'Aren't you being overly generous?' he asked, pretending puzzlement. 'And—' he raised his head high and put his palms flat on the table '—how greedy I feel. For a woman such as you, a man should risk his life for no coin. A simple kidnapping. How much effort can such a thing take?'

She raised her chin, tilted her head sideways a bit and took in a breath, then looked to the reticule. 'I have the details worked out exactly.' She spread the ties and lifted a folded piece of paper. Then she looked at his eyes and flinched. She lowered her hand, slipping the note away. 'You'll just have to follow my guide. I believe I have the mind of a master criminal.'

'And what crimes have you committed in the past, Nigel?' he asked, his voice softening. She didn't raise her eyes.

'*Surely* you are jesting.' He stood and walked to the bed, knelt on one knee. He felt under the bed and pulled out a shirt, or what was once a shirt, and tossed it into the corner.

He pushed himself back to his feet and frowned, then he leaned down, tossed another garment aside and found an extra bottle, thankful he'd remembered to bring home some breakfast.

He held the liquid towards her, raising his brows. She grimaced and he popped the cork and put the neck to his lips.

He caught her eyes as he lowered the drink, his gaze flickering across a shelf decorated with empty bottles. And another peg with a new coat. He'd forgotten about that coat.

She spoke, her eyes on the wall. 'I'm sincere about this kidnapping. It has to be done. It will be done.' She shrugged. 'There is no alternative.' She pulled at her bonnet.

'Look, Nigel.' He held the cork in one hand and the bottle comfortably in the other one. 'No blackguard worth hiring is going to do all the work and let you have more than half the bounty. You'd be lucky to get a pound. Who are you going to complain to if you don't get a penny?'

'I'll report them to the magistrate,' she challenged him with her voice.

'They hang women as well.' He put the bottle on the table in front of her, keeping his fingers around it. 'Breaks up the monotony.'

Katherine could *not* marry Fillmore. As her stepfather blocked her escapes, Fillmore's long fingers kept inching closer to her.

She had called the one in front of her a beast. But she feared marriage to Fillmore would uncover the true meaning of the words.

Her stepfather had plans for the banns to be read for her marriage—even though she hadn't accepted his nephew. She couldn't imagine any woman desperate enough to marry Fillmore without force.

Fillmore wore the tight buff pantaloons—very tight buff pantaloons—and on occasion those breeches concealed little more than what she'd glimpsed on the heathen's bed. He would sit across from her and sprawl his legs longer, tightening the fabric. And then he'd snicker, and she'd want to leave, and Augustine would make her stay and listen to him talk.

The thought of Fillmore's rolling flesh pressing against her body and his grasping fingers reaching for her, and she never again having the right to move aside…

She'd seen the flash of pleasure in Fillmore's face when she'd stepped away to excuse herself and he'd somehow always managed to be between her and the door. It was a dance of sorts then. He'd grasp her hand to raise it, pulling it near his lips to brush a kiss above, but it wasn't the kiss she avoided—it was the trousers. They always brushed against her skirts. Always. His smile sickened her.

Fillmore would not have turned his back if she'd walked in on him without clothes on. Never.

She'd seen the irritation in this man's face and that had convinced her he was safer than Fillmore. Her jittery stomach calmed and she appraised him.

He didn't know how much she needed him and she didn't think he cared. He kept looking at her as if he had the secrets of the universe and she had nothing but pretty parasols—of course, she did have pretty parasols, but he had no right to sneer at her so because of it.

The man was a scoundrel—but she inspected the fingers clenching the bottle. Normal, sturdy fingers. Clean and trim.

She looked at him and smiled, and she knew, if she had one bit of perfection about her, it rested in the pleasantness she could emit with the evenness of her teeth and the upturn of her lips.

'They don't hang well-born women.' She let her words fall to little more than a murmur. 'We are not smart enough to think of unseemly acts. All our days are spent thinking of ways to beautify ourselves so we may please a man.'

She raised a hand as if she'd just set her tea cup on the tray to be removed by the maid. Her words flowed into the room. 'You would not double-cross me. And, if you did, my tear-stained face as I huddled in the magistrate's office, pouring out my heart—' Her voice hardened. 'I assure you if the money were gone, my emotions would be truly distraught—I would be able to convince anyone of my innocence while I pointed a delicate finger right at you.'

'We can't talk without an agreement on equal shares,' he spoke. 'I can't think why you would go to the rot of kidnapping anyone for a sum as small as that. It's foolish to risk your neck for so little.'

He frowned. The chair was askew from the table and he straightened it and sat, showing no more interest than if he were sitting at the tavern to discuss whatever men discussed when they had nothing to talk about.

'I'm not greedy.' She put both gloved hands on the table. 'And, this is a personal matter as well as a kidnapping.'

When she said personal, his gaze bounced to the ceiling and back. She gave him another of her haughtiest glares.

'Half-share for me, at least. Assuming we agree.' He scratched at his whiskers, his eyes never leaving her face. Even as he bargained, his eyelids drifted down as if he wanted to fall back asleep.

She blinked several times.

He scratched again.

She gave a silent sigh and a condemning glance at his beard.

'Half-shares,' he repeated.

She reached out and delicately tapped the brandy bottle on the table. 'You may raise the ransom another five thousand pounds for yourself. I know you need funds to finance your efforts to keep the tavern owners from starvation.' Her eyes settled on his chin. 'And you do fear wearing out a razor strop so I suppose your coin doesn't stretch for ever.' She waved the words away, letting him know the money wasn't worth a squabble. 'I would hate to see you perish for lack of liquid,' she grumbled.

'My dear well-bred miss.' His eyes half-closed. 'You must learn to snort with your mouth shut. It's more becoming a lady.'

'Perfectly acceptable for a Nigel, though.' She gave a toss of her head.

'And don't worry about me running out of good liquor.' He let his eyelids drop again. 'Or bad.' He looked at the shelf. Various shapes. Ready to be taken back to the tavern to be refilled. 'My hand is never far from a bottle. Or a barrel.'

He didn't plan to kidnap anyone. For one thing, among many others, he didn't see her being able to keep her mouth closed. He could see her at an event, leaning to another flowery sort and whispering, 'Did you happen to read about the kidnapping in *The Times*? Let me tell you, I have quite the criminal mind and I'm such a good judge of character I had no trouble finding a disreputable kidnapper. Would you like his name in case you have need of him?'

He didn't know what was wrong with him, but he didn't want her running the streets searching out someone who would actually agree with her plan and somehow separate her from her chaperon and abuse her. Apparently the drink hadn't clouded his mind as much as he'd thought.

'You know you will have to tell me the particulars.' He rubbed his hand across his eyes, wishing he were rested. He thought it ironic he would always feel exhausted and still have to fight to sleep.

'Are we in agreement?' She stretched her arm out and for a moment he expected her to touch his hand. He tensed. He wanted no closeness with her. Something inside himself warned him not to let her touch him.

'Surely it's not someone of aristocratic birth you would want kidnapped?'

And for the first time, she looked guilty.

'That's frowned upon, you know.' He could not believe he was having this conversation. Only his curiosity kept him speaking to her. He'd never abducted anyone. He'd spent too many years keeping his distance from people. The last thing he'd do was capture another person whom he might have to feed and water occasionally.

She nodded. 'I said I had a personal reason and I assure you it's a just one.'

'Someone in the royal family?' he asked, eyebrows lifted.

'Do not jest. Anyone could have listened to what I've said and figured out who I wanted kidnapped.' She interlaced her fingers, letting them rest on the table.

He paused, scowling. In this strange dream he was having he must have slept through one of the important parts.

She touched her chest and leaned towards him. 'Me.' She spoke softly. 'I need you to kidnap me.'

Chapter Three

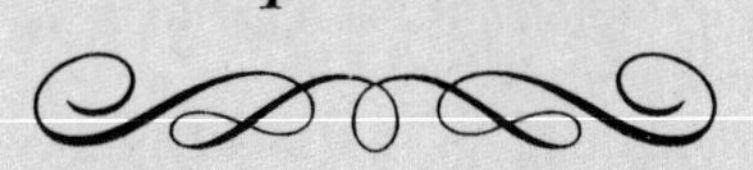

He moved his head sideways, but his eyes remained on her. He stated, 'You're kidnapping yourself for the money?'

He saw the prim set of her shoulders. The clothing she wore, too much warmth for the weather, hadn't been cobbled together by a person saving on expense. The ridiculous lace around the edge of her cloak and her ribbons didn't come without a price.

'Yes. It's only a pittance of what I should have. My stepfather's taken it all.'

'You believe he'll pay the ransom?' He was more than curious. He was interested.

'Yes. He wants me to marry his nephew, Fillmore.' She leaned closer. 'My stepfather does just as his nephew says. They are closer than a father and a son.' She waved her gloved hand.

She shook her head. 'Fillmore believes I should be his bride. I cannot take a step when he is in the house without watching for him and he is getting more and more determined every day. Rooms are being painted for him and furniture reupholstered. When that is finished next month, he is planning to move into the house—as my husband. I must be gone before then.'

He eyed the chit. 'All I need to do is kidnap you—but you will be willingly kidnapped. Secure the ransom. Take my half and we part friends.'

Her eyes flickered when he said half.

'How old are you?' he asked.

She backed away. 'I am old enough.'

'You're on the shelf.' He saw the quick dart of her eyes and the firming of her lips. She adjusted her gloves.

'I have accepted one marriage proposal—' She frowned at him. 'I accepted a proposal which enraged my stepfather. I met a man when visiting my cousin. I thought the man a bit forward when he indicated he wanted to marry me the second time we'd spoken. But he was of decent family and excellent reputation. Bookish. A bit older than I had hoped for, but I saw no reason to decline.' She gave a wistful smile. 'I thought him sweet.'

She shrugged. 'My stepfather wouldn't listen. He refused the match. Refused to let me call on anyone for a year or more. Had a load of manure delivered to the man's door. He only lets me go about now because he's encouraged by his efforts with Fillmore.' She wrinkled her nose. 'This morning I'm buying *hair ribbons* so Fillmore might be impressed.' She gave her bonnet a flick.

Bending forward towards Brandt, she moved the bottle aside with the back of her hand. 'My stepfather is not a kind man. Do not forget. If you have to hit him—'

'It makes me no difference.' Brandt put the bottle back in place.

'It would if you were in my shoes. He expects gratitude on my part for his extreme kindness in allowing me to marry Fillmore. Stepfather says to be Fillmore's wife is the most noble of goals and Fillmore is the best that can be found. I'm sure he's not the best, even when comparing him with slimy things found under rocks.'

'I don't care if Fillmore is a snake or a saint.' He didn't. What she did with her life, or who walked through her memories later was not his concern.

'Nor do I care as long as Fillmore's far away from me. At first, when my stepfather sent a maid to summon me to see Fillmore, I would find him in the shadows outside my room waiting. Now Fillmore summons me himself and he barely knocks before the door opens into my bedchamber. He looks at me and my skin feels tainted.'

Katherine watched as the scoundrel paused, then took a swallow and he didn't speak.

He moved the chair back a bit to stretch his legs and she noticed he was careful not to touch her. She thought he sorted the plan in his mind.

He stood and she looked up at him and placed her hands in her lap. His size overpowered her. Her heart skipped a beat. But, that was why she had chosen him. She needed a man who could threaten with his presence. Who looked capable of violence.

This man appeared suited to danger. The darkness about him didn't stop with his clothes or his face. It seeped from the air he breathed. She couldn't really examine him as she would have liked. If she tried, something tickled in her throat and she felt warmth in her chest, then she had to turn away.

'I would need one more thing, of course, to agree.' He stopped and gave a smile even a mother wouldn't believe.

She waited.

'I would need to know the lady's name.'

'My name is Miss Katherine Wilder.' She aligned her bonnet. 'Miss Katherine Louisa May Wilder.' She waited, the room silent.

'As the one risking so much, on merely a lady's word, you understand if I cannot agree to the methods used in our business, I will respectfully decline and never see or hear you again.'

She made a clucking noise. 'I agree as I do not see how you will be able to fault me in any way. I assure you, I have read many novels and have learned much about crime. I did not lie when I claimed I have the mind of a master criminal. This will be as easy as picking an apple from a tree.'

'I believe a lady named Eve said something similar once.'

'Yes.' Katherine regarded him patiently. 'Since I do want to be tossed out, you've nothing to complain about.'

'No. No complaints at all.' He crossed his bare arms in front of his chest.

She averted her eyes again. The man should put on his shirt.

'Tell me more.' Brandt tapped his fingertips of his right hand against the muscles of his left arm.

She dropped her eyes.

'Continue.' He kept tapping.

She tugged her cloak around herself.

'Are you chilled?' he asked, his voice holding the

innocence of a rector in church. 'Wearing a cloak on such a warm day?'

She didn't answer immediately, but pulled at the edge of her glove. 'I wish,' she continued, 'to be abducted from in front of Almack's on Sunday morning.'

She heard a strange noise from his lips and glared at him. She was certain he tittered. *Men* were not meant to titter.

'Surely Tuesday or Wednesday night would be better. I can't remember which night the lovelies race to Almack's.'

'It would be my preference as well.' She kept her chin high and used the same distance she used when scolding a maid. 'But the carriages swarm the street. They'd block the way as we left.' She leaned a bit towards Brandt and lowered her voice. 'To have a successful plan one must anticipate all possibilities.' Then she stood and her voice regained its command. 'I am only about with my stepfather on Sunday morning. He insists we attend services as a show of our perfection. Besides, it's the only time he doesn't have a weapon at hand.'

'A weapon?' His brows furrowed. 'That's something I might need to take into consideration.'

'I did for you.' She made a fist. 'I want him to be frightened as well. I want him to think that, in one moment, a blackguard could take him away.'

'Why didn't you choose to have him robbed and killed?'

'They don't hang well-born women,' she spoke with a bit of a sniff. 'But I wouldn't wish to be the first and, while I don't love the man, I can't be responsible for his murder.' Her eyebrows rose. 'If you wish to throw in a few punches his way, I would not suggest more than six. He's spindly.' She held up one finger. 'But absolutely no blood. Our laundress has no time for frivolities.'

'How many punches would be the exact number you prefer?'

'Let me see your fists.'

He held up a hand, fingers closed.

She examined his knuckles. 'Perhaps you should not punch him. He's thin, old and, well, I don't know if he could survive.'

'What if he decides to protect you and I must throttle him?' Brandt lifted his eyebrows.

'He will not.' She gently shook her head. She tried not to let her face show Brandt how inept he was in the ways of crime. 'Simply follow the plan. Don't worry about anything else. I will be carried away by you and you will not deviate from my instructions.'

He shut his eyes, waited a few seconds and then opened them.

'This is life or death,' she snapped out the words.

He shook his head and moved back to the chair. He again propped an elbow on the table and rested his cheek on it. 'Continue. I'm listening.'

The raptness in his face didn't fool her. He already overacted. She lowered her eyes and used one finger to touch the table and moved as if following the path of the carriage. 'I'll pretend illness to get my stepfather to stop the carriage. You'll be waiting by the bookseller's with a gig—out of sight.' She indicated an intersection, touching the table. 'When the carriage stops, you'll wrench open the door and pull me out.' She raised her eyes to his. 'My carriage is not attended by anyone foolhardy enough to risk the plan by attacking you, but you may bring a discharged weapon to make sure of our success.'

'I must have a gig and a weapon.' He held out an open palm.

She shook her head. 'You may reimburse yourself from the ransom money. If—' she leaned closer '—you purchase the necessary tools instead of stealing them.'

'I must have blunt.' He waved an arm around the room. 'You see nothing to sell. And I'll not steal a pistol or a horse.' He again put his palm out. 'No one would have a bit of trouble fashioning a rope necklace for me.'

She leaned back and reached inside her cloak. She took a purse from the depth of her clothing, but paused before handing it to him. 'It's taken me four years to get this much.' She raked her eyes over him. 'Don't squander it.'

He took the leather, used a finger to loosen the ties and looked inside. He frowned and raised his eyes. 'I suppose this will buy a knife and a saddle.'

'You'll have to manage.'

'I can cut back on my own costs.' His eyes had an exaggerated mournfulness. 'But the poor lightskirts will have hungry children.'

She reached to snatch the purse from his hands, but he moved the leather pouch aside quickly. She lowered her hand.

'I will contact you soon to give you an exact date and make sure you've purchased the supplies.' She said each word carefully. 'Please be home in the mornings as it is the only time I can easily move from my house without any suspicion.'

'You don't ask much.' He spoke so quietly he almost mouthed the words to himself.

'I will need to be housed somewhere as I await the ransom.' She looked around and shook her head at the same time. 'You'll need to find other quarters and you must always act as a gentleman in my presence.'

He raised his brows and gave one long blink at her.

'I will expect you to be thinking of how best to collect the funds, although I see no great difficulty.' She looked at him, checking to see if he would disagree. 'You'll need to suggest a place not easily ambushed. I'm thinking you could watch my stepfather after he receives the ransom request and relieve him of the purse as soon as he has it and before he expects contact.' She squared her shoulders. 'Be prepared to repeat your plans to me when I return as I want to make sure we both are in complete understanding.'

'Perhaps you should write this down for me.' He raised his chin, his eyes bland.

'Perhaps you should pay attention.'

She barely took a breath before she continued. 'By Sunday, I will bring—' she dropped her eyes '—a few personal items I will be needing and that will not be missed and I will expect them to be stored—safely—' she glared at him '—in your residence until I am kidnapped and the ransom is procured and I can leave. Of course, you will need to spirit me away once we have our funds.'

Then she looked at him. She smiled and her lips parted, and she could already feel the success of her plan. She would not let him ruin it.

'If you should even think of double crossing…' She

indicated the door with a nod. 'The woman outside will turn you in to the magistrate.'

'Are you sure the men in your life would not assist you to leave?'

She clasped her gloved hands in front of her and spoke, stepping back. 'Thank you for your time and I will send someone around with a parcel of soap as a memento of our conversation.'

He picked up the bottle and blew across the opening to make the low, whistling sound.

Miss Wilder captured his attention again as she brushed at her sleeve without thinking, and spoke. 'Sir, I hope after we complete our business you use the money to find an *honest* endeavour.'

With those words, she rose as if leaving her subjects. He didn't even stand as a courtesy.

The door closed softly when she left. Brandt walked to the door, took the key from the wall and locked the latch. That would teach him to come home with enough drink in him to splash up to his ears.

He refused to get bathing water, or his razor.

He settled back in his chair and put his elbow on the table, and made a fist but extended two fingers and put his forehead against them.

Miss Wilder solicited him for a crime, the likes of which he had never even contemplated before, and then chided him to find honest work.

And she made him feel something—something different than a peaceful drunkenness or the black crevasse of desolation. He preferred their companionship.

He took another swallow. Then, he pressed back, again raising the front legs of his chair off the floor, trying to recapture a moment of sitting unconcerned and relaxed. But the image of the woman standing at the door, condemnation in her eyes, would not go away. Anger rolled throughout his body and he could almost hear emotion rumbling in his ears.

He moved, letting the front legs of his chair jar the floor, and stood. Grabbing his hat from the peg, he pulled it on so it covered much of his head. 'Not as much sense as a tavern wench,' he muttered, not knowing if he talked of himself or her. He clutched his frock coat and slipped it over his bare arms. He unlocked the door and buttoned the coat as he hurried, hoping he could still catch sight of the bonnet. He wanted to know where she lived.

He wouldn't let Miss Wilder fashion a noose for him. He'd at least select his own rope for the hangman.

Chapter Four

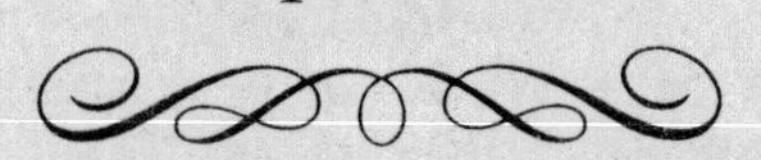

As soon as Katherine turned the corner and knew she was away from the windows of his home, she grabbed the arm of the older woman and pulled her to a stop. She gulped in breaths of air, concentrating on the movement of her lungs. 'You must steady me as my knees are trembling.'

Mrs Caudle put a hand on Katherine's arm, and squeezed. 'All of you is trembling.'

Katherine closed her eyes, straightened her back and then looked into Mrs Caudle's face. 'I will not let Augustine destroy me. I will use him to grow stronger and then I'll use that strength against him.'

'You are as wilful as he is.'

Katherine shrugged away the talk of her stubbornness and they crossed the street, moving towards the cared-for shops.

The older woman kicked at a dried pod of horse dung. 'You've got to move from your stepfather soon or Fillmore will have you in his grasp.'

A carriage rumbled past, drowning the words.

'I know,' Katherine spoke. 'And he is determined that Gussie be sent to a madhouse. As soon as I get the ransom, the very next time he tells you to take her away, do so. I will have a house for the three of us.'

She shook her head. 'Gussie's his own blood and he wants her put away.'

'He thinks she's damaged because she doesn't speak and hides from him,' Mrs Caudle said. 'But since she first toddled about, he would throw something at her or shout when she got in his way. She's much better when he's away, and he refuses to let her leave the house. I don't know if it's because he's afraid someone will see her and think his blood tainted.'

'Or because he thinks I will run away with her.' Katherine nodded, stepping faster to hurry them past the windows. 'We must separate her from Augustine. Otherwise, he'll likely put her in St. Mary's and she'll be locked away.'

'The sooner she gets away, the better,' the governess said. 'Another footman left the house this week because Augustine threw a dish at him.

'If that wastrel doesn't do this...' Katherine tugged at her bonnet ties '... I will handle the kidnapping on my own. I just need someone who looks like a rogue and he does. I'll prop him up if I have to. Augustine has to believe it is true.'

Katherine pushed back a strand of hair which had escaped from her bonnet. She slowed and tried to catch her reflection in the windows as she walked. She wanted no hint showing of where she'd been.

The old woman laughed. 'You have to admit he doesn't wish to kidnap anyone. That speaks highly of him.'

'Yes, but we...' She groaned, increased her speed,

and put a hand to her hip. 'I will just have to do it myself. I can, I'm sure.'

'You need ransom money and a place to hide. And Fillmore has to believe it. The only way your stepfather will pay anything to have you returned is if his nephew says he must.'

'We have to have someone Augustine doesn't know,' Katherine agreed, searching for a hackney. 'That scruff of a man can do it.'

'I wouldn't call him a scruff. If you're going down an ill-got path, he'd be the place to begin.'

'I don't want to go down any paths. I want to hide. Peacefully. In the country. With you and Gussie.'

A donkey and cart awaited them, a young man with obsidian hair holding the reins of the donkey.

Few people were on the street and she didn't want any of Augustine's friends happening upon her. She'd known better than to request the carriage. Augustine would have needed it for some reason or other. Or worse, he might have insisted he would go along. When they were trapped in a carriage, he complained or chastised with every turn of the wheels.

'Child. The lad will kidnap you,' the old woman insisted, helping Katherine into the cart. 'He's got the sight of you and he won't be able to walk away. Remember, when you find yourself alone with him—don't breathe the same air as he does. Men put off an elixir or something. I've thought on it for years and can't get it figured for sure. I think it's the way they breathe and it blinds us. Blinds us. Pulls our senses right out of our body. Makes us forget about all else, but having our way with them.' She shook her head. 'You don't need to be wasting your virtue.'

She raised her voice. 'And do not breathe in when he's close enough to sniff.'

The old woman jumped into the cart with the same spry step as the youth and called to the donkey to move.

She mopped her brow with a handkerchief she pulled from her pocket. 'Lad's rather sturdier looking than I expected.' She mumbled something else, turning her head sideways so Katherine couldn't hear her over the hooves.

Katherine thought back to the man. 'I'd like to see him cleaned up a bit.'

'Ho. Ho. Take my word for it. This one would clean up sparkly as a new guinea. You'd best be hoping he don't clean up none around you, child.' She nudged Katherine's foot with her booted one. 'I've not seen many like him in my life. You be keeping your toes on your hem when he's about or your skirt might be flying over your head on its own.'

Katherine raised her chin. 'I'm not a jade.'

'Don't matter. He's full of elixir. I could tell that the moment I laid eyes on him.'

The house welcomed Katherine, but only from the outside. At the front, filigree bowers for ivy stood almost six feet tall on either side of the door. When her father lived, servants kept the ivy trimmed enough so that visitors could see the metal underneath. But now no one could read the inset of her mother and father's initials in the filigree.

Katherine hurried into the house through the servants' entrance, avoiding the butler, Weddle. He reported Katherine's every move to her stepfather.

Her stepfather must believe the kidnapping.

Witnesses. They would need good witnesses.

Katherine thought of sending a discreet note to *The Times* so an engraver could be present. She would simply curl up her toes and swoon to have the kidnapping on the front of *The Times*.

Her dagger's blade barely stretched longer than her hand, and she wondered if she should take it with her. The knife rested against the base of her bed's headboard so a maid wouldn't see it—although she doubted any would care. Her thoughts caught on Brandt's face. She should have told him not to get near a razor or soap for the next few days. Surely he'd not decide to clean up for the occasion—but one never could be certain what a foxed man would decide if left on his own.

Katherine certainly hoped to savour her adventure. She would be kidnapped in front of Almack's. This was a waltz no one would ever forget. She would scream or screech or whatever was needed to call attention to the deed. Then, she would be overcome with the terror of the moment.

'Where have you been?' The words pounded at her the moment she left the stairs.

Her stepfather glared as if he knew she plotted against him.

The old man had seemed pleasant enough when he'd courted her mother. He hadn't changed the day after, or the week after, but within a year, she knew the man who she'd first met was a sham.

'We were shopping for the ribbons I mentioned last night,' Katherine answered. 'I do want to look presentable.' She tilted her head down, but kept her eyes on him. She didn't want him suspecting anything but obedience. 'I'm to have a suitor tonight.'

'You'd best give him the right answer when he asks you the question.' Her stepfather's brows creased. 'Fillmore's a good lad and I don't want him disappointed. You can't do any better than him for a husband anyway.'

'He does have an adequate nose.' She moved on to the stairs to go past her stepfather. He reached out his hand, gripping her arm.

She couldn't move.

'You'd best not be criticising your future husband.' Her stepfather's gaze pierced her. 'I only tell you this for your own good. He will not take it well to have a disobedient wife.'

His fingers pressed harder into her skin.

'I understand,' she said, head down.

He flung her arm aside.

That evening, she mostly kept her eyes on her food as Fillmore stared across the table at her.

Fillmore's fork stopped midway to his mouth, then he plopped his food between his lips, gulped and spoke. 'I'm pleased to be able to sit and gaze at you.' She could swear his nose hairs quivered with anticipation of their union.

Then he reached up and scratched his head. He was always scratching his head and sometimes other places. She shut her eyes and put a hand over her stomach, telling herself to be calm.

Fillmore clinked his fork against his plate. The noise captured Katherine's attention and she realised the clatter had been on purpose so she would look his way.

'Thank you.' She spoke quietly, unable to look at his glistening eyes.

Her stepfather stood, a servant sliding his chair back. 'I think I'll retire early.' Augustine waggled a finger at Fillmore. 'Why don't you two spend some time in the library after the meal? I'm sure you have much to talk about.'

Augustine turned his eyes to her, threat in his face, and walked by without speaking, leaving the scent of a trunk full of mouse nests in his wake.

She sat proud, kept her face serene, as her mother had taught her. Her mother had been her closest friend. Katherine still ached when she walked by the bare room where her mother had rested while she was sick.

Fillmore smiled across at Katherine, a pink flush on his cheeks and a brief lift of his eyebrows. She glanced away. He moved, standing beside her. A footman pulled out her chair so she could rise and Fillmore offered his arm. She took it and forced a pleasant look on her face as they walked to the study. Her jaw began to ache.

'You're looking extraordinarily beautiful today, Sweeting.' Fillmore pushed the door closed behind them.

'Thank you,' she answered, ignoring the whiff of medicinal which lingered in the room.

Fillmore led her to the sofa and she saw his tongue slide across his upper lip.

She extricated her arm and moved to a high-backed chair near the wall, unable to keep herself from putting as much distance as possible between them.

'Would you sit by me?' he asked, moving to the sofa and patting the blue velvet, then running his fingers along the fabric in a way to make her want to cast up her accounts.

'This chair eases my back.'

He laughed. 'Time enough for that later, I suppose.' His eyes ran down her body. 'I would not want your back hurting.'

She averted her eyes from him. His grey waistcoat strained its buttons so much she didn't see how he could be comfortable and again he wore breeches which revealed more than anyone ever wanted to know.

He stood and closed the distance between them. She looked up at him, feeling an unease. He took her hand in his, the skin of his touch soft, but the bones beneath pinching her hand close. She tried not to think of his ragged fingernails which he loved to savour between meals.

'I've wanted to ask you to become my wife for a long time, but now I can wait no longer.' He spoke each word with precision. 'You should be married and it is time for me to begin a family. I will be thirty-five on the fifteenth of next month and the banns will be read Sunday.'

She fought past the dryness in her mouth. 'Waiting a bit longer might be best.'

'Don't be ridiculous.' He held firm, squeezing her hand. 'You have everything I need in a wife.'

'What would that be?' she asked, truly wondering if he could think of anything to say.

'You're lovely,' he spoke. '*Every night* would be a pleasure.'

His words surrounded her like smoke from a clogged chimney.

'*Every* night?' she asked. She had only thought how repugnant it would be to have him touch her once. To think of him touching her each night was beyond imaginable.

He could *not* be her husband.

'Certainly,' he said the word in such a way she could see the lust pooling in his eyes and his lips glistened with it. 'I've wanted you since you were younger, but I have had other interests. Before you get too old, I want children. And a duke's granddaugher will do.'

When she opened her mouth to tell him no, his eyes shone as if he anticipated exactly what she wanted to say and could hardly wait for the refusal—not because he would be crushed, but because he could crush her.

'Thank you very much. I'll consider your proposal.' She couldn't refuse. He had to have a reason to push his uncle to pay the ransom.

But when she looked at Fillmore's eyes, and saw past them into the darkness beyond, if she had had any doubts about throwing her lot in with the brandy-fogged, unshaven, sadly clothed—but surprisingly well-formed—man, Fillmore's stare cured her reticence.

Fillmore had standing in society—his mother had married some cousin to Wellington and his uncle was married to a distant relation to the King, but she wouldn't have cared if he wore the crown himself.

Brandt, who travelled the ill-got path and covered himself in rags, had more appeal than Fillmore.

Fillmore called her attention back to him. He turned her palm up and rubbed her hand, holding so firm she couldn't pull away, while he caressed the softest part of her palm.

His eyes met hers. 'Our wedding night will be something you never, ever forget.' His other hand now held her wrist and she couldn't pull away. He bent as if to kiss her hand and his tongue snaked out, and she saw the pinkish thing unroll and slide across her palm. A trail of moisture stayed behind.

She turned her face away from him, trying to conquer the bile in her throat, and control her churning stomach.

She pushed her eyes back to him and kept her expression calm. *If the filthy drunken kidnapper doesn't kidnap me*, she thought, *I'll put a dress on him and he can marry Fillmore in my stead.*

'I must think about this.' She stood, putting some distance between them. 'I really must.'

She grabbed a lamp and scurried away before he could fully grasp that she was escaping, and she rushed into the small room where Gussie slept.

Gussie lay asleep on the bed, the puffed sleeves of her gown visible in the candlelight and her cloth doll lying in the floor beside her.

'Sleep well, Gussie,' Katherine whispered, picking the doll from the floor and putting it at the foot of the bed.

Katherine held out the lamp, watching Gussie. She didn't know what it was about the sleeping child that made her so angelic. The chubby cheeks? Innocence in her face? No one with a soul could ever want to hurt a child like Gussie. She could not go to the asylum. The poor child had trouble just being in a room with Augustine.

Gussie rarely spoke more than a word or two, but Katherine knew her sister could think.

Gussie had replaced the purgative in the medicine bottle with water. And she had to have pulled a chair around to reach it. The clear liquid had alerted them when they'd poured some in the glass for her. A remedy the physician had sworn would help her speak, but Gussie hadn't liked it.

And she didn't like wearing shoes, either, and her half-boots had disappeared and had yet to be found.

But it didn't matter what went on in Gussie's thoughts. She couldn't be in a place without her governess or Katherine to watch over her.

Katherine had to get funds. Not only for herself, but for her sister's sake. She needed to be able to give Gussie a safe haven and she would find them a home hidden so far away they could never be found.

Chapter Five

Brandt walked to the Hare's Breath, stepping under the placard with the painted rabbit puffing into the wind. Some men avoided the tavern, he supposed, because it was almost as particular as Almack's. The patronesses were a grizzled sort at the establishment, but you knew by the lift of an eyebrow, the foot easing out to trip you, or the ale being accidentally drizzled down your back if you'd lost your voucher. And if you didn't heed the gentle warnings, you'd lose teeth, or part of an ear, or maybe even the ability to straighten your fingers.

He never thought he'd feel welcome in a place which smelled like dirty feet and bad tobacco, but he did.

A moth flew in front of his face and he swatted it away, then moved to get a mug from the tavern owner, Mashburn. Mashburn never stopped the conversation he had with the gamblers while he got Brandt's drink. Then the owner walked around the table and each man flicked his wrist, tucking the faces of the cards against the table. When the proprietor reached his brother's chair, he leaned forward, squinting. He then reached over his brother's back and tapped two cards. 'Best hand you've ever had,' the tavern owner murmured.

The men laughed, each knowing that his words were a game of their own.

One swallow and something tickled Brandt's lip. He reached up and brushed at it, then looked at his fingers. A hair. Short. Straight. Probably from the dog lying in the corner. He dropped the hair to the floor. The creature could get it on the way out if he wished it back.

He took one more swallow of the ale, but then put it aside. The place was packed for such a night. Four men played cards. The usual group. Another table held the solicitor who received free ale because the tavern owner loved to hear the stories he told when he couldn't remember to keep his silence and a skinny lad sat beside him who was a cousin to a cousin of someone somewhere and now he stopped at the tavern most nights, trying to grow into his trousers.

The moth—or perhaps it was some kind of beetle—returned. He swatted again.

He wished he could swat away the memories of Miss Wilder, with her overgrown bonnet and the smudges under her eyes. He'd followed her to a house that reminded him of the last true home he'd lived in. She'd walked right up to the front door and then she'd paused, and the older woman had spoken and they'd moved inside.

Her face looked pleasant enough, he supposed, but it was hard to see for the bonnet. He'd thought she was trying to disguise herself in case someone she knew was on the street, but now he wondered if she was trying to hide her womanliness.

Her skin glowed with sweetness. He wanted to run his hand the length of her body, reclined beside him. The thought lodged in his mind and he tried to drink it away. But there wasn't enough drink in the tavern.

The skinny lad was speaking too loudly. Brandt gave the boy the one-sided glare that was to tell him to watch his words. The boy ignored it.

'He's tied to his mother's bonnet strings,' the skinny lad made a jest of the solicitor. Everyone laughed, but the solicitor. Solicitors didn't find much amusing.

The solicitor swung a fist and Brandt jumped into the fray to separate them.

The insulted man's gold-tipped cane flew towards Brandt's jaw and the man with the jest ran for the door.

The solicitor swung his cane again and Brandt caught it, twisting it and slinging the man on to a gaming table. The table broke and cards flew. Men jumped from the table and when they stood, all had fists. Brandt stepped back, dropping the cane.

The tavern owner and his brother tossed the solicitor out the door and Brandt grabbed the gold-tipped cane and stepped outside.

He held out the cane to the owner. The man took the cane and he couldn't speak plain for the liquid in him. Brandt asked the man if he remembered where he lived. It took him a while to understand, but he helped him find his way back to his mother's house. Brandt didn't know why he'd done the kindness, but the man thanked him. Thumped him on the back and told him he was a good friend. Brandt told the man if he saw him at the tavern again, he'd buy the fellow enough ale so neither could walk.

The man laughed, offering his services if Brandt ever needed a solicitor. Brandt didn't like the sound of that, but he gave the man a jostle to show he accepted the friendship and they parted at the man's door, but not before Brandt asked the man if he might have some old clothing for sale.

The solicitor had charged twice their worth and reminded Brandt again that he'd be available should Brandt need more assistance.

Brandt didn't want to go back to his room. He knew he wouldn't be able to sleep, so he walked in the cool air, ignoring the scent of coal fires.

He also ignored the scent of the perfumery shop as he walked by it, but then he stopped, turned back and walked inside, the bundle of worn clothing under his arm.

The shop-owner heard the door, raised his head and peered at Brandt, then he recognised him.

'Gardenia,' Brandt said and he stared at the man. The shop owner didn't speak. The older man took two steps to the left and pulled a scent bottle from a case and set it on the counter top.

Brandt walked to the man, took a coin out of his pocket, picked up the bottle and placed the coin in the exact same spot.

Brandt turned, put the bottle in his waistcoat pocket and left.

He stepped outside and for a second his feet refused movement. But he took a breath and strode towards his room.

Then, he stopped again. He couldn't wait any longer. He reached into the pocket, pulled out his purchase, wrestled the clothing under his arm so that he could remove the bottle stopper and took in a savouring breath. Mary's scent.

He wondered what Mary would have advised about the big-bonneted woman. He'd never seen eyes widen so when she first saw him.

He wagered she'd not get that picture from her mind easily. Not from the look on her face. His lips turned up. He didn't think he'd ever shocked a woman so. Well, she shouldn't have opened his door. Not before the sun set anyway.

That was his life now. Nights of drinking. Days of sleeping.

He felt the familiar ache. Felt the anger, the sorrow and the unfairness. Putting the stopper back in the bottle was easier than putting it on memories.

He didn't like the early hours, but couldn't pace the streets at night. Even in the morning, the fog could make his footsteps haphazard.

He'd walked the streets so many mornings until he could collapse into sleep that it had become a routine. Many of the merchants watched for him now, particularly when they needed help lifting something. At first they'd offered to pay him, and occasionally he took payment in goods, and he'd pass them along to someone at the tavern. But everyone knew not to talk with him much.

When the day began to warm and his feet hurt, he turned to his lodgings and let himself inside.

Brandt looked at the wall. He realised he didn't know what day it was and he was not even sure of the month. He had lived like this for—how long exactly he didn't know, but years. He had felt no life in him for such a long time.

And now some haughty high-born near-spinster wanted him to kidnap her from her father so she could take money from the man.

He didn't know why he thought about her. She had a ridiculous *criminal* mind. Indelicate snorts. An uppity little nose. Layers of skirts which fluffed when she walked. Garments not weighted down with street crust. Probably smelled of sunshine from drying in the breeze.

He needed not to think about a spoiled heiress headfirst on her way to ruin.

And if he didn't help her, she would gather speed on her downhill roll. Another man hired to kidnap her might not respect her upbringing.

He let out a deep breath, shut his eyes tightly and rolled his head back, cursing. Rage bubbled in him.

She should not have sought him out. She had no right to ask such a thing of him. Of anyone.

Then he remembered the fear in her eyes and the pause before she stepped inside her house. As if she had to force herself. He picked up a brandy bottle, drank from it deeply, but slammed the bottom on to the tabletop. He could not drink himself into oblivion and he couldn't ignore someone who hated to walk inside such a house.

He stood and the fingers of each hand stretched out of their own volition, almost clawing, and he noticed the twitch.

The drink. No food. No sleep. His memories. He could not care for himself any longer and now this woman plagued him—wanting him to rescue her.

How could he help another when he could not help himself?

Never in his life had he felt so trapped. Those damn lost eyes of hers kept appearing in front of his face.

He put his head in his hands and tried to breathe calmly. Blackness surrounded him and he didn't think he could live much longer as he had, yet he had no wish to change his life. None.

But then he thought of his wife, Mary, and how he'd not been able to save her, and the rest of it.

A few shovels of dirt and life was to go on.

They'd shared their youth, their innocence, and he'd known he had to marry her. Fought hard to marry her. And what had it got her? A few shovels of dirt. And no life to go on. He would have traded places with her. Begged in the night hours to trade places with her, because without her, he was dead. At least one of them could live.

Helping Miss Wilder wouldn't ease his loss.

But he might end with a rope around his neck, he realised, and pictured himself at his own hanging. He almost laughed. A rope would burn, surely, just as the brandy did at first. But he'd got used to the drink quickly. He supposed in the time it took to look at the sky, he could grow used to the bite of the rope, then he wouldn't feel the caverns in his heart any more.

He'd not done much but traverse back and forth from bottle to bottle in the last few years. He'd heard his share of rude songs, and crude jokes and vulgar tales. They would still be there tomorrow. The day after tomorrow and the day after that.

The comfort of the tavern rested in its sameness.

Even if the tavern closed, two more would take its place. He'd always have a bottle to hold him.

He took a coin from his pocket and flipped it up. He grabbed it from the air, slapping it on to the back of his hand, covering it with his palm. Heads, he'd kidnap her. Tails, he'd change his lodgings and forget he'd ever viewed her treacherous—innocent face.

He remembered her with such clarity it seized his thoughts. When her lashes flickered, it was as if feathery fans fluttered above her eyes.

He wondered how she looked when she laughed. If her chin quivered? If she tilted her head, or blushed?

But most of all, he wanted to see the hair she hid under a mountainous hat from a crazed milliner.

It was not right to think so. Not right to think of another woman besides Mary.

He stood there, hand covering the coin.

He slowly moved his palm away and squinted. Tails. *Was it tails to take her, or tails to leave her be?* He took the coin in his right fist and with his left, backhanded the empty brandy bottle hard enough so the glass smashed into the wall.

He took a breath and then flipped the coin again.

Chapter Six

Brandt wore dark clothing and, as dusk fell, he took both horses and went to the woman's house. He'd noticed the sky clouding. He wasn't waiting until Sunday morning at half past eight and fifteen steps beyond the street corner and half a bottle past the refuse in the road. The woman wanted to leave her stepfather. That he could take care of. She could save her blasted instructions for her next kidnapper.

Nor did he want to be hanged if something went wrong. He really was picky about things like that. Tavern floor, fine. Noose, tight. He'd never even tied a cravat tightly. Things went smoother in the darkness. Fewer eyes watched. Usually the people who were about at such hours would go to great lengths to avoid notice and tried to avoid anything which might bring questions their way.

Looking up, windows on the first floor flickered with candlelight and silhouettes of figures moved beyond the curtains. He could take her away. He could hide her. He had the perfect place—waiting, but not for him. She could step over the threshold there. He couldn't, but she could.

He tied the horses near the back of the house. He'd tried to hitch them as if they belonged to a house because if someone nicked them, he was going to be in a bind. Horses irked him. Heiresses irked him.

He noted the dim light from an upstairs window and then the corner ones. He knew the end room was more likely the master's chambers because it received window light from both sides and had the ability to open more windows if the room became stifling. Then, when he saw the curtains being closed, he saw the shape of a valet, not a maid.

He moved to get sight of the other side window and could see only the dimmest of lights behind it. Miss Wilder's room. Earlier he'd stayed long enough to see the outline of her bonnet as she'd removed it. And he'd watched a footman slink out another door, then rush away, possibly going to a meeting with a sweetheart or to finish an errand he'd neglected earlier. In just moments he'd known where to get into the house and where to find the woman when he returned.

Now, he stared up at the house darkened except for shadows near the front entrance.

He went to the back entrance with a bar he had brought along to pry open the door and, when he reached out, the latch was locked.

He put pry marks into the wood, separating the metal from wood, working to get the lock free.

Earlier in the day when the footman had left, Brandt had pretended to ask directions. Then he'd discovered Katherine Wilder was the niece of a duke.

He paused. He had to take care. He knew why she hadn't turned to her uncle. A self-righteous man who refused to let his servants turn their backs on him or raise their eyes when he spoke with them. He doubted Miss Wilder could ever get on well with the man.

Lifting the bar, he slipped inside. He walked the hall until he found a stairway and quickly got to the upper floors. Even if someone heard him, he'd be undetected unless they saw him. Footsteps would be attributed to a servant, or to Miss Wilder herself, or to the master of the house. It would be assumed someone moving about was answering a bell pull.

He found a doorway which he thought paralleled the window he'd watched.

The door opened easily, with only a small click. The first thing he noticed was the flounces. No man could sleep in a room decorated like a petticoat.

He took five paces and stood beside the bed.

His breath caught.

She lay so still. Beautiful. Innocent. And still as death.

Memories flooded back, choking him. He turned to the window, stepped closer, and pushed back the curtain until it stood wide. He felt the burning in his eyes.

He was locked inside his own past.

The covers rustled as she turned away in her sleep.

She'd caused the flood of thoughts. The strength of them. She needed to wake and he didn't want to touch her. But he wanted to shake her, rail at her and curse her. She wasn't Mary and she'd brought the pain back to his mind, and he didn't have drink enough to cover it because he had to be here, with her, instead of sitting at the tavern.

Afraid of what memories would stir if he touched

her, Brandt picked up a book from her bedside table. He nudged her arm with the volume. She didn't move.

'Wake.' He spoke insistently and this time the book was forceful.

She sat up, slapping at him before her eyes were open. He watched as she tried to see in the darkness.

When he saw the mussed look of her hair and the innocence of the white clothing she wore, he clenched his empty hand into a fist. He slammed the book on to the table, uncaring about the noise.

'Come on. Get up. Your chariot is waiting. Her name is Apple.' He reached for Miss Wilder's arm and pulled her to a sitting position.

She jerked her arm away and her eyes flooded with recognition.

'You are trespassing.' The whisper hissed into the room. 'You're in *my* bedchamber, and I am not some *person* who might appreciate a man's night-time attentions.'

As easily as lifting a child, he grasped her arms and pulled her from the bed and to her feet. He stepped back.

He moved away, giving her a graceful bow and pointing to the door.

'It is not tonight, you fool. I have not packed yet. There are no witnesses,' The whisper ended on a hiss. 'He will merely think I have run away.'

Fool, she had called him.

How well she knew. He hadn't controlled his world enough to keep this one out of it with the reminders of another life she forced into his head.

This had been a mistake. He'd thought years passing would give him strength. Would have made him able to face what he was about to do. No.

He'd hoped, *like a fool*, he had strength to look at his past without dunking his head in a bottle.

He wanted to swim to the bottom of a pool of brandy and not return to the surface. He embraced the murky depths and they held him. That would be the only touch he would ever again need. And he'd had to forgo it to keep a clear head so he could keep his feet clear on the direction to her house.

The Miss stood glaring at him.

'Are you listening to me?' She kept her voice low. 'This kidnapping is not so important to you that you're able to put aside the drink for one night and attend to it. You are not following my direction, either. Now leave my bedchamber.' She pointed a finger just as he had done, directing him away. 'This is not how I wish to be kidnapped.' Her whisper hardly sounded, but he could hear her well.

'I could be in a warm tavern.' He gritted his teeth and fought to ignore the soft purity of her skin. She bombarded his senses with the air of womanliness which swept from her to cover him. 'You're not staying in your warm bed.'

Brandt reached for the satchel and pulled out the trousers and shirt. He handed them to her. She had to look like a young man. That would be his salvation.

She stared at him, her arms crossed over the cotton clothing at her chest.

'You simply cannot follow orders, can you?' she whispered. 'And how did you find me?'

She acted as if unaware she was standing in front of a man in her bedclothes. He wasn't. Without the bonnet and the cloak, she seemed half the size she'd been before. Or maybe it wasn't that she was smaller, just that being so close to her caused something inside his chest to feel stronger. His heart beat faster and not because he was scared.

He needed to concentrate on the task, not the woman.

He moved his nose closer to hers and muttered. 'I merely asked people direction to the lady's house who wears disgustingly big bonnets.'

'My bonnet was of no particular size.' She pointed to the door. 'Now, leave or I will scream. You'll be hanged.'

She tried to stare him down.

'You may be right,' he said softly, and grabbed the shirt from the floor. 'But I am here and we are both leaving. A kidnapping in the daylight is too risky.'

He saw the mouth open and knew her next words would be raised.

He covered her mouth with his hand. A sharp intake of breath and she stumbled back, sitting on the bed.

'Don't draw attention to us yet,' he rasped in her ear. 'Or I'll have to return these clothes to the dead man they were taken from.' He slowly took his hand away.

'Vile,' she muttered and slung the shirt at his shoulders, keeping one sleeve in her hand.

He reached to pull it from her, but she scooted back on the bed.

'You're going to wear the shirt,' he said. She tried to wrestle it from his hands.

He moved to hover over her and tried to secure her

hands to keep her from slapping his face again with the shirt.

Both her wrists were locked in his hands.

'Do you wish to be kidnapped?' He put his nose nearly against hers and kept his words low. He released her hands and moved back, sitting beside her.

She glared. 'I'm considering it.'

'I'll leave if you wish me to. I'm sick of this house and I'm sick of you.' He released the shirt. 'Your choice. It's now, or someone else. If I leave tonight without you, I want a promise you will never, ever seek me out again.'

'I'll go.' She held the wadded shirt. 'But you'd best hurry. I do not want to be with you another minute more than I have to be.'

She moved, raising an arm to put it in the sleeve of the garment. And her elbow connected with his shirt and bumped the gun he had hidden in his waistband. She paused, uncertain. 'Do you have a weapon?'

'It seemed prudent.'

'Well, I have a knife. I'll show you.'

'A knife?'

She nodded. 'Of course.'

'You think— Why do you have a knife?'

She leaned even closer, bringing the scent of a woman's soft bedclothes closer to him. 'Because I couldn't get a gun without raising suspicion.'

He stopped. Either she had lost her mind, or she was afraid.

'You don't think Fillmore would come in your room?'

'I've woken when the doorknob rattled.' She moved closer, whispering, 'But I sneaked into my stepfather's study and took the key when he was asleep. He doesn't know I have it.'

'We'll go. Just keep your silence.'

'I want to be married, just not to Fillmore. Anyone but that beast.' She reached up with her left hand and put a palm to his chest. His breath was knocked from him. His entire body warmed. He moved her hand away, but his fingers tightened on her wrist. Neither moved.

He needed out of this mess. He would go out the door and get on his horse and ride far enough away she could never find him and he'd never see her again. But his feet wouldn't move.

Brandt leaned so close to her face he could feel her breath touching his cheek and he mouthed an oath when he felt his body respond. She'd trapped him.

She moved so close he couldn't breathe and her arm brushed him as she tried to reach under the mattress. 'I've tucked it here. The knife. I'll show you.'

He leaned back when she held the blade between them.

His mind registered the knife she had in her hand, but his body registered the woman standing so close without layers of fabric between them, only the softness of the clothes she wore next to her body. He pried the blade from her fingers and stood away from the bed—taking two steps backwards so she couldn't touch him.

He dragged in air through his nostrils. The woman, no sturdier than a stair rail, slept with a knife for her protection. She solicited a governess and a stranger to get her away from the house she lived in. She was either spoiled beyond repair—or afraid.

She righted herself on the bed, and stepped on to the rug beside him, the skirt of her nightrail tumbling to her calves. In one second, he was in a different world, thinking of things he couldn't blame himself for.

She put her hand on his. Fingers over his knuckles clasping the weapon. Warmth on the outside of his hand, the coldness on the inside.

'That is my knife,' she said, 'and I would like it back. I cannot trust you to follow simple directions and I may need it.'

He flipped the knife into the wall across the room. The blade vibrated and so did his body.

Chapter Seven

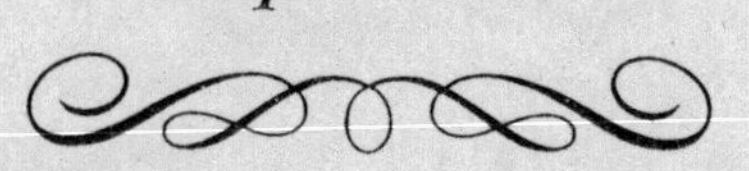

Katherine moved closer and Brandt took a step back. 'Don't toss the weapon away. It's all I have to protect myself.'

'Not any more.'

'I cannot tolerate you in any way, yet you don't make me wish to cast up my accounts as Fillmore does.' Her words were quiet, but forceful. 'Do you understand how despicable that makes him?'

She touched his waistcoat again and held on. 'Do not ruin my plan.'

She could not touch him. And he could not touch her. But he had to.

Gently, he pried her fingers loose from his coat. Slender fingers. He could have crumpled the fingers in a grasp, but he used no more strength than he would have on a baby bird which might fight against him as he moved it back to the nest.

After that he moved her hand away and took her shoulders and back-stepped her to the edge of the bed. 'I will do it as I see fit,' he added. 'Now finish getting dressed in these clothes. You're going to be riding a horse and not side-saddle and we can't have a skirt flapping in the air.' Or riding up to expose her legs.

'I've changed my mind. I'll steal things from the house and sell them and move away on my own.'

Oh, he could see how well that would work out. Her amongst the people who had no conscience. He didn't stop his movements.

'You could be hanged,' she said.

'After days with you, I may buy and knot the rope myself to give to a magistrate.' He moved close enough so a hiccough would have caused their faces to collide. For a moment, even with all the sleeplessness he had suffered of late, he realised he had damned himself again.

Brandt handed her the trousers next. 'Wear these so no one will recognise you.'

'No. They must recognise me.'

'I'll take you where it's best no one does. There is an abandoned house. You can stay there.' He paused. 'Assuming we're not standing here talking this time tomorrow.'

She raised her head and took them. Then she sat on the bed.

Her nightrail brushed the air and filled his nostrils with a scent of femininity. He was thankful the light-skirts didn't smell as hauntingly sweet as she did, or he'd have more than one vice at the Hare's Breath.

'Hurry,' he said. He needed to get her covered as quickly as possible.

She shook her head, her braid whirling against him. 'I am. I've just never—'

'The horse won't care how you look.'

She raised a leg to slip it into the trouser and his

eyes didn't need to see the bare skin revealed as she moved her leg into the clothing. His mind filled in each fibre that brushed against her body.

She put the second leg into the clothing and he turned away.

He didn't need the warmth rushing through him. He didn't want any awareness of her, and yet, even with only sounds behind him, he knew every movement the trousers took as they hugged her close.

He squeezed his lips tight. His brain had rotted.

His movements slowed slightly as he took in her womanliness. If he'd been Fillmore, he would have gained her favour. He would have picked her raspberries, and written sonnets so sweet the ink would have dripped hearts.

But he was not Fillmore.

He could hear her struggling with the buttons. Buttons. Could she not hurry? His mind latched on to each sound, freezing his movement, trapping him closer than any noose ever could clasp his neck. Damn her. Damn her. Damn her.

He stepped back, forcing his legs to move away. Forcing his body into separate parts so he could think about the movements he needed to make next. She was just a human and he was another human and it meant nothing more than that. He was a hired servant to take her to a safe place. It might make up for some of the mucked-up way he had caused Mary to die.

'This waistcoat is never going to fit me.'

He turned. 'Now. Put it on.'

She moved her arms into the shoulder openings. The garment hung from her and she stared at it. 'I can't keep it on.'

'You are paying me to do a job.' He pulled the sides of the waistcoat away from her body and finished the buttons.

He backed away. 'You should never hire a man to do such as you asked me.'

She stumbled towards him, her trousers more sideways than straight and only a part of the front of her nightrail tucked inside the trousers. She put her hands on her hips. 'The clothes are not even from the same person.'

'The clothes...but the waistcoat is mine.'

'Oh.' She reached up, touching the fabric, feeling it, and the touch stilled them both. He could almost feel her hands running along his body.

He had to stop this. 'We must go.' He picked up the hat, held it out.

She looked at it and reached to pull some hairpins from the table. She twisted the braid around and used the pins to secure it. Then she took the hat, fingers brushing his. 'I would not even call this hat worthy of the coal boy.'

He moved his foot from under hers and stepped back. 'I doubt anyone would pay a penny to have you returned. I suppose if I were to try to collect a ransom on you I would find a chunk of coal resting on a few bills from your *modiste*, your hatmaker, your glove-maker, and for slippers, with the request I pay them promptly.'

'I see why you drink. And after being alone with you, I expect I will need something a little stronger than tea.'

'We both will.'

With two fingertips pinched over the cloth, she held

the waistcoat from her body. 'And you should have got a better shirt. It's ripped.'

'It didn't look so well on the dead man either, but he didn't complain.'

She opened her mouth, but no words came out. He won that point.

He moved his index finger to mimic a ball rolling down a hill.

She grabbed the frock coat and waved her hand in the direction of the chest in the corner of the room. 'I'll eventually need a dress.'

He blinked and walked to the trunk, pulling open the heavy lid. She'd packed. *The blasted woman had packed for a kidnapping.*

'It is clothes for the needy,' she whispered when he paused. 'I've told my stepfather I am collecting.'

For a moment he stared forward. He could remember the exact day when he'd last looked at a woman's packed clothing. The memory almost took him to his knees and fuelled a rage churning inside his stomach.

'I must have my blue dress because it withstands rough wear the best.' Soft feminine words.

His jaw tightened and he flopped back the lid of the oversized trunk. He bunched the fabric of the dress she wanted and jerked it out, fighting all thoughts from his head. He couldn't think or he would think of the days when he believed in fairy tales because they came true and the world received more sunshine from his wife's eyes than it would ever need.

He shoved the dress into the satchel which had held the man's clothing. The bag bulged at the seams and he forced the buckle closed.

'I must have…' She was at his shoulder and reaching into the trunk for something edged in a very thin row of filigree.

Lace. Oh, no. That would be unforgivable.

'There is no room.' He moved in front of her, forcing her to step away.

She glared, but she reached for a pair of half-boots by the wardrobe.

She worked the laces of her boots in the darkness. A different blackness raged deeper inside him. He thought of his house and wondered if he had made another grave mistake. He had managed to make only a few rough blunders in his life and, of those few, one had been deadly. He hoped he did not get another innocent buried.

He reached for her arm and tightened his grasp, stilling her. 'You can stay here.' He lowered his voice. 'If you leave with me, your life will be changed for ever.'

'I am of stern constitution.' She two-fingered his sleeve, pulling his hand from her arm. 'I can dress my own hair and—' she walked over to pull the knife from the wood '—I'll need this.'

'Leave it.'

She gave him a glance which looked through him. He returned it.

'Your life will never be the same.' He felt a bit of compassion tug at his heart.

'My life is going to change anyway.'

He brushed a hand across his eyes. When he opened them, even in the darkness he could see the set of her jaw, the firm edge to her face. He wished for more light so he might see her better. Surely he had imagined the dark sweep of her eyelashes? The cheeks so soft fingertips wanted to brush against them.

'If I stay here,' she muttered, 'I am destined to lose my innocence in a horrible way. I will not be rutted every night by a man who makes me want to bathe even when he looks at me. His designs on me are carnal even if they are within marriage.'

'Some of those designs might not be too bad.' He thought of her hair pooled around her shoulders and his hands softly moving down her arms, pushing nightclothes aside.

'You have not had Fillmore's tongue in your mouth,' she muttered, walking to the door and jerking it open.

Well, she had a point.

He reached out, secured her waist and pulled her back against him, relishing her gasp. Warmth tingled in his body and he leaned away from her. 'I beg your pardon, Miss Wilder, but my name is on this dance.'

He reached to her fingertips, holding them—aware of the unroughened skin, the lightness of her grasp.

He pulled back his hand. 'You've cast your dice. Don't complain when they don't roll as you wish.'

'You will see they do.'

He shook his head and moved through the door. 'No, I will see that they roll as I wish them. I am not a governess, or nursery maid.'

He turned back, reached out, snagged her waist with his right hand, then transferred her to his left and kept her close against his body, moving her easily and quickly as if in a waltz.

He gave her a moment to get her feet steady beneath her and then he rushed forward, not giving her time to find words to make him even more upset with himself. Perhaps he should have kidnapped the old man and tossed him on to a sailing ship.

Brandt stopped. A perfect solution to her problem. With much less bother.

But then she wiggled and his heartbeat increased with the feel of the warm skin beside him. He caught his breath. Forget the ship. It had sailed.

The nephew would still be there. And Miss Wilder would be deeper in Fillmore's grasp.

But right now she was in his. His skin didn't go numb when he stood near her like it did with the tavern women. He could feel the wisps of her hair if he leaned his head close to hers and the strands brushed him with the softness that swirled around her.

One strand of her hair floated in the air and brushed across his lips. He blew it away, demanding his body feel nothing. She meant no more to him than a child who might need to be carried out of a rainstorm.

She was a Nigel. Nigel. In men's clothing. Men's clothing that didn't trick his thoughts a bit.

'Show me to your stepfather's room,' he whispered. 'I will let him know I'm an evil kidnapper after the spoiled princess. And then he will shoot me and I will die and it won't be my problem any more.'

'You cannot let him shoot you. I will be stuck with Fillmore.'

'So I must stay alive. How wrong of me not to take that into consideration.'

'He has the weapon in the drawer beside his bed. Don't let him open the drawer. Simple enough.'

'Let's hope it's in the drawer.'

She leaned closer. 'If not, duck.'

Brandt quietly tucked her against the wall after

she'd indicated a door. 'Go out the back door. The horses are ready. Wait for me so we can leave quickly. I'll convince the man easily enough. He'll think I'm on the way to taking you and I haven't got you yet. He may rouse the servants so we need to leave quickly.'

'Do not fail.' She leaned closer and all the other scents of the soiled shirt faded, covered by the scent of her warmth and softness.

She stepped back, the movement a battle march in reverse. 'Watch the drawer. I cannot abide blood.'

'Horses. Outside. Saddle. Backside.'

She turned, a huffy little mouse with her sharp teeth chewing on the imagined words she was slinging his way.

Brandt waited until she moved out of sight, then he opened the door, freezing briefly at the sound of the hinges creaking. A whiff of boots worn too many hours hit his nose.

He heard the bedcovers rustle, then the man in bed sat up. The sleeves of his nightshirt puffed around him.

'Your daughter—' He gritted his teeth. 'I'm taking her. Don't look for her.'

'You…' The old man's voice was drugged by sleep and then his shoulders tightened. 'You and Katherine?' His arm reached to the side fumbling for the weapon.

Moving forward, Brandt's fist closed over the neck of the nightshirt and he pulled the man away from the drawer, both tumbling to the floor.

Augustine's fist glanced off Brandt's chin and another connected with his stomach.

Brandt rolled aside, pulling the man's shoulders

into his rotation, stopping when he had Augustine's face against the rug. Securing Augustine, Brandt moved up enough to keep the old man's face to the floor and curl his arm up. 'I've a pistol,' Brandt spoke in the man's ear. 'And I've no reason to hurt you—unless you fight me. But the woman is not to marry your nephew. It will not happen.'

The man mumbled an answer and Brandt made swift work of pushing the wrists together, taking the thin rope he'd tucked into his trouser waistband and tying Augustine firmly.

When he finished, he pulled the man to a sitting position, propped him against the bed. Augustine swore and Brandt grabbed a bedcover and stuffed the edge in the man's mouth, then pulled the woollen nightcap down to hold it in place.

Then he reached to the drawer and opened it. A duelling pistol. He picked it up, glancing at it. Chances are it would misfire. It was loaded and highly unlikely to have been cleaned recently and recharged often enough to keep the powder from drawing moisture. He put it back beside the powder flask.

He stumbled around until he found the ewer of water for the man's morning ablutions and poured a splash of it into the flintlock's pan. The weapon wouldn't fire any time soon.

Brandt walked out the door. The punch to Brandt's stomach had hurt. Being awake hurt. And not being able to erase the feel of where the woman had brushed against him when she struggled was the most irritation.

He rushed outside and she was standing, the reins

in her hands, and patting the smallest horse's neck. And she was murmuring to the horse.

'I hope you do not mind to ride astride.' He stopped at the horses. Bending, he interlaced his fingers to give her a foot rest to boost herself up.

She took the pommel, rested her foot in his hands and pulled herself into the saddle, surprising him.

At some point, the woman had ridden and she'd not always stayed side-saddle.

He slid on to his own mount. He already regretted the ride ahead of them and knew they would probably both be wishing for a soft carriage before too long. He already did. But they needed the speed of the beasts in case they were followed.

All the slowness left her body and she nudged the horse, taking off before he could get astride.

He jumped into the saddle, pushed Hercules forward, then reached her side. 'The other way.' He raised his voice above the hooves.

She nodded and they turned.

He kept the horses at a steady pace, but slowed them after they'd made some distance. He couldn't afford to wear the horses out. They had a long trek in front of them.

After an hour in the night air, he spoke. 'I know a place where you cannot be detected.' He remembered her sour face as she looked around his room. 'You'll have more freedom to move about. We'll call you something else. A different name. Pick one.'

'Nigel, I suppose.'

'You cannot pick that.'

'Why not?'

'Fine. Pick what you wish.'

She slowed her horse even more, then turned to him. 'Are my clothes really from a dead man?'

'It's best not to know who wore them.'

He saw her inspect the clothing. She pulled the shirt out from her body and wrinkled her nose. She tried to keep the garments from touching her.

'I know you have a laundress.' Her voice was subdued. 'I am sure she wouldn't have minded cleaning these.'

She paused. 'I've not forgiven you from altering my plan.'

'Follow.' He nudged the horse. He couldn't take her from Almack's. *That* would be kidnapping. Best to let her think her plan was going along just as she expected. He didn't feel like explaining anything to the spirited mound beside him. He didn't feel she'd go along as easily if she knew her plan had been altered and he didn't know what a master criminal would think of a simple country life. But once she was in the house Mary had lived in, she could make her choice. It wouldn't matter to him if she left or stayed, but she'd have a chance to make her own decision.

A much better decision than getting him on horseback in the middle of the night. He hated riding. Especially any distance, but it was the best method to get her to the country quickly.

He dreaded the next hours. He knew he would have to care for her a few more days, and he didn't want to play nursemaid—but giving her a new life might take some of the blackness from his soul.

He couldn't leave her at his boarding house. If she stayed at his room, she would find some clever disguise which gave her the feeling she could go out safely—such as an ermine cape and a plumed bonnet.

She would be upset to be so secluded, but he saw no help for it. He had to protect everyone from her criminal mind.

Lightning cracked in the distance. A drop of water hit his face. He stared at the sky and bit back more curses.

Chapter Eight

The rain held, only spitting enough from the sky to warn Brandt the night could worsen.

When the horses began to slow as they tired, he shut his eyes and wished for rest. He'd only slept about an hour in the evening. He'd muddled about getting the horses and supplies. Now the constant slaps of the saddle ripped into his backside and they'd only covered half their distance. Or less.

He heard her horse catch pace with his. 'If this place is not to my liking, you will have to find another.'

He knew he had forgotten something. Why had he not gathered wool to stick in his ears?

From a distance much too close, she continued. 'As you seem to have given my plans great disregard then I graciously submit to your plan—which you cannot have spent much time on—and you smell of spirits and tobacco, and did not even wear a proper cravat as a gentleman should wear.'

His horse jerked his head a bit and he realised he had pulled at the reins. He forced ease into his fingertips. He wished the ride were over. 'Nigel, how remiss I did not bring a cravat for you. Had I known you thought them so appealing, I would have personally fashioned you one to wear.'

'Remember. I can charge you with kidnapping.'

As long as she believed that he would not have to explain anything to her. She could ride along thinking the world was going just as she wished, which was bad enough. He didn't know what she'd do if she found out no ransom would be asked for.

That information would wait until he had her settled.

'I am sure. Do you know my name?' he asked, watching the road. He saw the outline of a house and thought it familiar so surely they were riding in the right direction.

'Brandt...' She thought. 'But, I know your lodgings.'

'Yes. I am certain my landlord is unaware of my full name. And if anyone knows it, it doesn't matter. I'll change it at the next town I live in. My real name could be Nigel.'

'I look more like a Nigel than you do.' She tilted her head to the side. 'You are Brandt.' She leaned a bit closer to him.

He feared she'd topple to the ground. He forced himself not to put out an arm to steady her. He gave a slight nudge of his feet to urge Hercules faster.

'You are supposed to be a man of some honour. When we enquired for your lodgings, the woman insisted.' She kept prattling and she didn't lag behind.

'Who is the woman?'

'The one who does your laundry.'

He nodded. 'I should have known.' He'd never trusted her.

'And why does she claim I have honour?' he asked. She didn't know him. They'd hardly spoken.

'You save her the trouble of carrying your laundry because you bring it to her and pick it up.'

'Because I do not wish for her to knock on the door and wake me.'

'You pay her well.'

He shrugged. 'I pay her the same as any other.'

'You speak respectfully to her.'

'I barely speak at all.'

'When her son brings you wood or water, you are kind to him.'

'I say praises so he will finish quickly.'

'Fine. You are a cad. A lout. A layabout.' She straightened and looked at him. 'How do you make funds for your drink?'

'I let the lovelies ply me with spirits and pay me to look at my body.'

'No woman would do that more than once. I don't care what you claim. Are you a gambler?'

He saw her shadowy movements and knew she tried to soften the saddle's bite on her bottom. He could tell her it wouldn't help. Saddles started out as leather and turned into steel.

'I would starve as a gambler.' He laughed. 'I have no head for it or no real care for it. If I lose I'm angered at myself. If I win, I feel sadness for the one who lost.'

'So where did the money for these horses come from?'

'Did you not notice when I put your jewellery in

my pocket?' he asked, trying to ignore the pain in his head and the jostle of his legs, and the sharp jabbing noise invading his ears.

'No.' She bobbed her head. 'If I had had jewellery to sell, I would not have contacted you.'

'Could you have found someone else?'

'Don't you think I would have chosen someone other than you if I could have? I wished to do it myself, but the governess said it would be charitable to work with you.'

'Save me from a young woman's charity.' He spoke to the heavens.

'You would benefit well from my advice. Otherwise you will spend the rest of your days in the saddened state I found you.'

'I would give Hercules away to be in that saddened state right now. And Apple.'

'You prefer to walk.'

He didn't have to see her face to hear the disdain in her words.

'I prefer to travel distances short enough to walk. I keep imagining bandits jumping from the woods and wearing big bonnets while demanding I rescue them.'

'Oh, we are quite safe. A bandit would look at you and know he would be wasting effort to take from you, and he wouldn't want to listen to your grumbles.'

'I do not grumble. I state loudly.' He snapped the words at her.

'Of course,' she chirped. 'That's what I meant to say.'

But he had only himself to blame. The bonnet should have warned him.

He nudged his horse to outpace hers. She followed.

It was just his luck Apple was as good as Hercules. He should have got her a sway-backed nag.

She didn't seem to notice he had tried to outpace her. And he could understand why she wasn't aware. Hercules kept dragging his tail and Apple kept dancing along. Apple pranced a few steps ahead, showing off her youthful vigour. He was sure Hercules stifled a yawn. The horse was unimpressed by such a ninny.

'I wish the sky were clear.' Nigel shivered delicately, 'But the raindrops were refreshing—although I'm pleased they stopped before dousing us.'

He didn't speak and hoped she would do the same. A flowing stream beside the road gurgled over her words, making him unable to hear her, but only for a moment.

'I wish the stars would peek through the clouds. But I've forgotten my constellations. Are you familiar with them?'

'Only if they are painted on the ceiling of a tavern,' he spoke harshly. Why had he not brought a bottle of brandy?

'You must speak more pleasantly. The night is too lovely to be angry.'

'It's not the first one I've seen and I expect to see about three hundred and sixty-five every year.'

'You are very fortunate to have me along to speak to you.'

'I've not slept as I had a kidnapping to attend to and now the victim has turned the tables on me and is holding me hostage to her chirping. You are… I find your cheerfulness…' He shut his eyes, gritted his teeth and shuddered. 'Abnormally loud, too happy by far and much like a gaggle of crows.'

'I don't think crows are a gaggle.' Even in the shadows he could see a superior tilt to her chin. 'A flock?'

'Or a coven?' he asked. 'Something about you makes me think of a coven.'

'Apparently the lightskirts only need money to be attentive, not wit.'

'I can understand why your stepfather wished you wed. I think he has no affection at all for dear Fillmore.'

'The laundress said you are not married. If you wish to find a wife, you should be able to improve on your appearance with the money from the ransom. You must hide your true manner, however.' She shuddered. 'Well, perhaps that is unfair to women.'

Anger rampaged through him at the mention of a wife. She had no right to mention such a thing to him. Mary had been in his heart from his first kiss to the last time he kissed her, and beyond.

Their last kiss. So much different than their first. A kiss of parting and a bleakness that echoed in him still. The moment he wished he'd stopped living and the moment that had scraped out all the happiness inside him and taken it into her coffin.

'A wife is the last thing I need.' He spoke harshly. 'Do not discuss it.'

She leaned over, reached her arm out and patted his. 'With your long dark hair and scruffy face, you look more like a murderer than a kidnapper. Such a lack of grooming frightens a woman. You make me think of an unshaven animal who snaps creatures beneath his jaws just to enjoy the crunch.'

'I don't enjoy crunching. I prefer liquid.'

'Well. With the ransom, you can improve your circumstances. With respectable clothes, you might find a better occupation.' She paused. 'Then, you might find someone to marry.'

He pulled up the reins on his horse and stopped. When she realised what he'd done, she moved beside him and did the same.

This was folly, he thought. The drink truly had rotted him through and through. He was deprived of sleep and robbed of his mind. And he had a feather-head riding alongside him, babbling about stars.

'Do you not realise we are alone in the middle of nowhere and you are irritating me beyond belief?' he asked, reaching to hold the reins of her horse.

'Yes,' she answered slowly. 'That's why I am so happy. I'm taking my steps to freedom.'

'No. Really.' He would frighten her into silence. He'd had a plan to let her live in his old house, but now she oozed happiness into the air and he wanted silence. At the tavern, when the revelry started he could leave. He had blessed quiet.

'Yes. You've been instructed to do so,' she spoke.

'I have ignored my instructions.' He leaned forward and roughened his voice. 'You can forget about the ransom, Sweet. You'll never see a penny of it.'

'I do not believe you. You have a kind spirit. The laundress said so.' She leaned in his direction. 'You were carefully chosen. It took months to find someone honest enough to do such a deed for me.'

He wished he'd got the horse named Tippy for her. Apple kept easing much too close to Hercules.

'You are saving me from a disastrous marriage to a man with hideous hands.' Her voice sung to the furthest cloud. 'And helping me have a chance to keep my little sister safe.'

'I have captured you.' He drawled the words out, putting an evil sneer into his words. 'I am spiriting you away from your home. Somewhere no one will look for you. Far into the forest. Alone.'

'It is said you fed an orphan who wandered the streets and found him a place as an apprentice.'

'He annoyed me. Always in my path, asking for funds and covered in dirt. I became tired of it and found him a place far from me.' He raised his palm and looked to the heavens, but knew he'd earned no assistance. 'I did not care one bit for the lad. I merely was tired of his chatter.'

'Well,' she said. 'I see a tradition you are starting.' She whispered, 'You are much more gentle than you think.'

'Not any more,' he said. 'I have made the same mistake twice now and I am tired of it.'

'These are my first hours of freedom. Before long, I will have a home of my own.'

'You could have had a home with Fillmore Furry Fingers.'

She shot a look from the corner of her eye. 'I'm twenty-four years old. It is amazing I received even one reasonable marriage proposal when I was younger with the rules my stepfather imposed upon me.'

'Just marry Fillmore.'

'Filthmore. He has more filth in his mind than he can keep locked away. He's unbearable.' The chin went up. 'I chose you over him. Does that not tell you anything?'

She kept her chin high. 'I am not particularly endowed—with charm, with talents or with a tinkling laugh which causes others to wish to join in. I do not even relish the talk of what goes on behind locked doors—unless it is particularly scandalous. But I will have quite the story to tell now.'

'Can you shoot a pistol?' he asked from gritted teeth. He slipped both his reins and hers lightly around the pommel.

'Of course.'

He reached, jerking one of the flintlocks from beneath his shirt, the cooler air against his stomach as he pulled the cloth away to grasp the weapon. He held it to her. 'Put it in your trousers.'

She took it and her hand swooped until she adjusted to the weight of it. 'Thank you. I'm honoured.' She arranged her shirt and put the weapon behind the waistband and he saw the handle easily against the white of the nightrail she wore underneath. 'This is the first time I have held a gun, but I'm sure I can pull the trigger.'

He wished to snatch it back. 'If you are accosted, do not tell them this is the first pistol you've held. Instead, hold it firm and keep your mouth shut. Let the gun speak for you. Do not fire until you are nearly close enough to stick the barrel into a nostril, but not close enough to have it pulled from your hand. Then, ride like blazes.'

'Who do you fear?' she asked, whispering and leaning towards him. 'Do you think I might have to save you?'

He did not wish to tell her it was she who unnerved him. She who lifted his melancholy, but then smashed his misery back into him.

'You have food in the saddle bags. My rooms are empty. Go there. Keep the horse. Handle your own ransom. Get the old woman to help.' He flexed back and reached into his waistcoat pocket and pulled out the purse she'd given him. 'Or get someone from the tavern to find you a man named Leonard. I'm sure he will help.'

Then he pulled his mount closer to her. He leaned and snatched the collar of her shirt and the bodice of her nightclothes, pulled them out from her body and dropped the coins down her front.

She gasped.

He took the reins from his pommel. 'Go back the way we came and you won't be lost.'

Then he kicked his horse and took off.

Chapter Nine

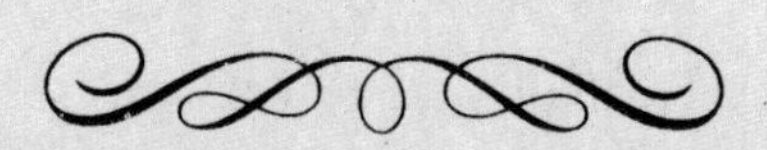

She followed. She could not retrace the way they had come. All dark houses looked alike. One rut in the road bumped the same as any other.

She frowned, unable to recall a time she'd been out of the house after sunset without her stepfather or two chaperons.

She saw him tug the reins. He stopped and, with a swing of his arm, pulled his horse to face her. 'You are capable of finishing the kidnapping on your own. Send a note round to that Leonard fellow who visits the tavern. He's the most boring man I've ever met and is a perfect match for you because you are not nearly tedious enough. You make my head ache. I have business elsewhere.'

'Where?' she asked.

'The first tavern I can find.' His words cut a path through the air.

'Brandt, you should stay away from drink. It gives you a foul mouth and rots your brain.' She put one hand on her hip and Apple stepped sideways. Katherine grabbed the pommel with her free hand and accidentally pulled the reins with the other, causing the horse to take a back step. The movement forced her body forward and bumped her nose on the back of the hairy neck.

Apple looked back as Katherine gathered her balance and tried to get the horse scent out of her face. The creature cocked her head a bit and Katherine turned from the horse's eyes. The beast looked angry with *her.*

'Nigel, Apple thinks you're a novice.'

'It's been a while and you unsettled me.' She huffed from the effort of stilling her mount. 'A true gentleman would never leave a lady stranded in the night.'

'Well, I'm not sure either of us would fit into either of those categories. I don't think a master criminal could be considered a lady.'

'I am both.'

'Not even if I've swigged ale or brandy beyond standing upright would I agree with that and I will put my thoughts to the test as soon as I can.' He pressed his feet into the horse's flanks.

She stayed level with him, ignoring the way the jarring ride bounced her bottom into her hipbones, which collided with her ribs.

Katherine knew she could catch Brandt's horse. She knew it, but she didn't know if Apple deserved such treatment.

But then she looked at Apple's head and the sweet beast had her ears back and a tightness in her neck. Apple understood. She didn't want to be bested either.

'You have kidnapped me and you will not abandon me,' he heard her call out at his side. 'I will follow—'

He heard a squeal and realised she had stopped—both riding and talking.

He reined his horse again and turned to look back at her, expecting to see her in a crumpled mess on the ground.

Instead, she was sliding from Apple and walking, head down, kicking about in the darkness.

Now his stomach was distressing him and he did not wish to hear another word from her. But the sight of her form, small beside the horse, and her slumped shoulders outlined in the darkness, tugged at the heart of the man he used to be.

He went back to her, but before he spoke he reached for the brandy in her saddlebags and took a sip. The warmth slid into him. He took another sip. Then one for good measure.

He hadn't meant to put the brandy in the saddlebag on her horse, but his own. She'd addled his mind even when he selected supplies. And he couldn't place the bottle in the right bag, but had to return it to hers. His had a gown stuffed in his bag. A *blue* one.

He didn't wish to speak kindly to her, but he supposed he owed her such. She was right when she said he wasn't acting as a gentleman.

'I beg your pardon.' He spoke quietly. 'Come with me and I'll see you to safety.'

She looked up at him. Her eyes were tight. Almost shining in the moonlight. She looked to the ground quickly. Hiding tears, he supposed. He'd not meant to wound her.

'Not until I find the pistol,' she grumbled. 'When I was taking aim at you, I dropped it.'

He slid beside her and grabbed her arm. 'You would shoot me in the back?'

The moment he touched her, he knew he had made a mistake. Her skin seared into him. He dropped her arm and stepped back. She was too soft—not the bad kind of soft, but the luscious kind. Even with the disreputable clothes, her womanliness reached out to remind him of what a woman could be. The memories. He shut his eyes and breathed deeply—forcing the thoughts away and returning his eyes to hers.

'I would not shoot you in the back.' Her gaze darted to the ground.

With the horses around them, they were almost imprisoned against each other.

She continued, 'When I caught up with you, I thought I might take your hat off.'

'You've no idea how a bullet can go astray.'

She kept her tone even. 'I merely wished to converse with you in a way you could not ignore.'

'I cannot ignore your voice. It's like trying to ignore a needle sticking into my eye. You are jabbing me. Over and over.'

'Sir, you would desert me in the woods.' She leaned into him and he felt her form push against him. He knew she was being aggressive, but his body didn't understand. It didn't even realise she smelled of horse and grated his nerves. His insides near purred at the closeness of her and kept urging him to forget all unkind words and speak very softly and tenderly to her. His hand called to touch her cheek and his knees wanted to bend and beg her forgiveness.

'Shoot me now.' He raised his hands.

He remembered the warmth of her as he'd tried

to put the trousers on her. The swirl of her clothing around him as she dressed. He recalled the feel of being in her bedchamber. The innocence of her gentle breaths while she slept.

The women at the tavern hadn't caused desire to simmer in him. This woman did. He frowned. That part of him had been buried so long. It had died along with Mary. Why had it chosen now to return? And around this annoying princess who'd been so sheltered she had no real grasp of anything?

She'd felt softer than any flower petal. And her skin—he didn't have to even touch it to know what it would feel like in his hands.

She didn't realise his attention to her words had been lost. She continued speaking and he felt with each word her body drawing closer to his, and he forced his feet to stay still and his arms to remain at his sides. And one other annoying part of him which he had thought had died needed to return to wherever it had been because it kept choosing the wrong moments to resurrect itself.

His damn traitorous body was listening to every move she made with rapt attention. It was no more sensible than she was.

He'd had experienced women trying to entice him to share their beds, but this chirping little bedlamite was making him wonder what it would be like to hold her against him and kiss her softly on to the ground. Would she be shocked, or would she purr and pull him closer?

He'd never tried to seduce any woman. With Mary, they'd been so young and things had progressed comfortably and easily. He'd been tracking dirt on to the floor to irritate her and the next thing he knew he'd been climbing into her window at night.

He'd never courted. He'd just bedded and wedded.

'I think,' she spoke, her voice even more shrill than before, 'I will defend my honour. I will find your pistol and call you out. We can dispense with seconds and we will duel here in the darkness.'

'And you have never held a pistol before tonight? You must be the most absurd woman in the world. And the world is full of absurd women.'

'Could you shoot me?' she asked, her voice timid.

'Not at this moment—' he heard his voice rise '—but that could change.'

'Well, then why would now not be the best time for me to duel with you?' she asked, eyes wide in question and lips firm in confidence. She moved again, little more than a twist towards him.

That twist could have aroused any part of his body it touched. No, he had no desire to shoot her.

'Witch,' he spat out.

Her head turned back to the ground and she searched as if her life depended on it. He hunted with her, his eyes staring at the ruts and his jaw clenched. He couldn't let her test the trigger on the gun. She'd likely blow herself up.

For some reason, he didn't trust she only meant to get his attention. He feared she would miss and kill the horse and he'd be stranded and, while he did like to walk, he didn't wish to walk all the way back to his room.

He looked to the ground, hoping to see the pistol. Kicking the mud and grass and dirt this way and that, he searched.

He heard her sharp intake of breath and she bent quickly, reaching to the ground.

His legs shortened the distance between them in a flash, but she jerked the gun away.

Brandt's arm curled around her waist, pulling her against him so he could reach the weapon, and his fingers locked over hers. He controlled the gun.

But he felt the rise and fall of her breaths and his own almost stopped.

His face fell against her cap, and lower, so he could feel the side of her face as she struggled. He had overdressed her. The clothing was much too coarse, too thick. But he could feel enough. He was caught in the moment.

He realised she stopped her struggle.

'What *are* you doing?' she gasped.

He didn't answer, appreciating her stillness.

'You are sniffing my skin.' She wondered if she might have the tiniest bit of the elixir and he had noticed. She didn't know whether to let a large puff of air out, or slow her breathing, or just wait and decide later.

The cave of his arms closed around her and she relaxed back into the wall of his body. A small twist and they fit together so comfortably.

He touched his mouth to her ear.

Her ear. His moist breath heated her skin and her body awakened at every place they connected. This was not what she had retained him for. She turned her efforts to pushing at his hands. 'If you use your tongue—'

She gasped.

'That wasn't so bad, was it?'

He released her.

She brushed at her face, as if removing his touch, but she wasn't even close to the right area.

He didn't mind. He could still feel her with his whole body. Still feel the warmth she had given him. Ah, the warmth. He'd felt nothing like her skin since before his life had turned to hell. He had not known the feeling could ever again exist for him.

He gave her a courtly bow. 'My pardon, Miss Shrew.'

'Nigel, if you please,' she hissed.

He put the weapon back into his waistband, hoping the cool metal would work as a threat to remind his body its silence was expected. How she had got the gun so far from the road he had no idea.

He wanted to take her from the path and make a bed in the leaves and hold her near. Just close enough to feel her in his arms. To fall asleep holding her and wake with his arm around her, snuggling her against him.

He shook his head, changing his thoughts, concentrating on the situation at hand.

'Follow—' Then he thought of her behind him. 'Beside me and I will get you to a safe place.'

He got back on his horse and heard her struggle on to Apple. Neither spoke. Only the muffled clops of hooves proved their existence.

The night air swirled around Katherine. An owl hooted in the distance, the end of his second call a tapering off with more of a purring sound. Apple moved along as if the night was no different than any other,

her steps interspersing with the whisper of the wind moving through the leaves. When they passed by a stream, frogs serenaded the night.

Brandt had felt like a wall of life surrounding her. The melancholy that had lived inside her so many years that she wasn't even aware of sadness had faded. It had faded the moment he'd taken her from her bed. The world seemed to be holding out its hand and giving her a chance to live again.

She'd always known her mother would not want her wallowing in sadness, but somehow it had lingered inside her. Augustine always waited and then oozed venom into her world. Always. And then he belittled and berated her, and she knew, always, that if she showed emotion or anger he would pick at her harder and longer, and she could not bear that on top of losing her mother.

Being with Gussie had melted away some of it, but only the edges.

Night-time without her mother had been difficult at first, the grief taking over every moment except when she would sit with Gussie before bedtime and Gussie would bounce on the bed or whisper the words *hide and peek*. Then Katherine would leave the room and return for an elaborate search of the entire room, ending with a magnificent discovery of a giggling little girl hiding in the middle of the bed under the covers. Or a cover pulled from the bed and mounded in the corner with a little girl peering out from under it.

The sadness had consumed Katherine so much at first that she'd not really noticed Fillmore moving more and more into their household. Then, during the last year, Augustine had stopped letting her stay with Gussie in the evening and insisted she sit with them. In only a few nights, Katherine had read her fate in Fillmore's eyes when Augustine mentioned it was time she wed.

The smirk on Augustine's lips had twisted into Katherine's stomach, leaving her struggling to keep the horror from showing in her eyes.

His laughter alerted her that she'd not succeeded.

That had been the moment her grief had faded enough so she could see the danger in front of her and she'd known, without hesitation or doubt or wavering of anything within her, she had to get out of the house by any means possible if she'd not wanted to be taken by Fillmore. She'd not known if she'd had the courage, but then little Gussie had hugged her neck that night, and whispered one word. *Love.*

'I can hardly believe I'm leaving,' she said.

Brandt grunted.

She glanced at him, and he stared forward.

'Mrs Caudle warned me to watch my step around Fillmore at first and I didn't know what she meant,' she continued. 'One day, I found her crying. I thought she grieved over my mother. But she confessed she'd been wanting to leave because she hated the household so much. Augustine kept picking at us so, but only the thought of leaving Gussie kept her there.'

Mrs Caudle agreed to stay with Gussie, if Katherine could find them a house to hide in. Gussie could speak their names, though, and they knew they'd have to go far enough and give her time to learn to call them grandmother and mama, and teach her to answer to something else. A family. That's what Gussie needed and Katherine wanted more than anything else in the world.

'When Gussie was born, I thought her a present for me. I had to wait a bit for her to be old enough to sit and then play. Mama was so sick. And she liked Gussie and me to be in the room with her. I held Gussie's hands when she learned to walk.'

Brand grunted louder this time. 'Can you not be silent?'

She let out a huff. 'Watching over my sister was the most special thing that ever happened to me.'

'I know what it is like to watch a baby grow.' The words hit the air with the force of spikes being hammered into the ground. 'I was married.'

She paused. 'I am sorry.'

'Silence is a music all of its own. Play it.'

'Well...' She held her back straight and opened her mouth to speak again. But then she thought of the sadness of losing her mother. And Brandt knew what it was like to watch a baby grow.

She thought of how she would feel if she couldn't return to Gussie. She'd gambled on Augustine being so upset with her being gone that he'd ignore Gussie a little longer. Mrs Caudle had promised to take Gussie if Augustine started talking about the madhouse again. But that would be a true kidnapping and a true risk of Mrs Caudle's life.

Katherine stared at the road in front of her. She had to get the funds and get them hidden. If Augustine ever realised that little Gussie was more than just a stick of furniture that he could toss out, he'd use her against Katherine.

She bit the inside of her lip and twisted the reins in her fingers.

Brandt had moved ahead and she noticed the outline of his shoulders in the darkness. She didn't speak again and the night closed in around her. She let Apple fall back.

A skylark warbled in the distance and then Brandt interrupted her thoughts by saying, 'We're there.'

Brandt saw the bend leading them to the house. He'd not expected it so soon. Too soon.

He swung to the ground and saw his home. In the darkness, the timbers stared at him. The size overwhelmed him. The memories made his heart pound and his mouth dry.

The kidnapping had been a mistake. His life had been a mistake. All of it. He couldn't move.

He realised she was touching his arm and she had been speaking to him.

'Is it boarded up?'

'It's been abandoned for years,' he answered.

The sound of distant thunder emphasised the expanse of darkness.

She led her horse up the road. He made himself follow, each footstep harder than breathing under water.

'How will we get in?' she asked, her voice a cautious whisper.

Brandt had never before seen the structure as sombre, but now it emitted blackness and death.

'The carriage house,' he said simply. He had thought he would be able to enter the house and stay—not in the rooms he and Mary had shared, but at least in the servants' quarters. That he would let Miss Wilder live in the rooms above and bring the house to life again. She could bring the little girl and the governess and have a family around her. She could live the life Mary had expected.

He'd lived a churning lifetime since he had seen his home and the last time he'd stood on this property he'd been married and had a child. He could almost hear his son Nathan's laughter. And see Mary's hands reaching to cuddle the boy. His fingertips remembered the feel of her belly as she grew bigger with his daughter, a child who never got to breathe a first breath.

The breezes ruffling the air taunted him with the family he'd lost. The love he'd had and the love which would have followed had they lived. He'd thought he would have been able to face this. Time healed nothing.

The pleasant memories had faded and turned into ugly reminders of what should have been.

He thrust his hand into his hair, pushing it back from his eyes. He was a coward and he knew it, but no one could be strong who'd suffered his losses.

The road was overgrown with vetch and thistle. A sapling grew between the ruts. Weeds never looked so lush to his eyes. He embraced the overgrowth. Let the land take the house. Let the lying promise of a haven crumble into dust.

A hand pressed his arm.

'Brandt,' she whispered. 'You're... Your breathing is...'

'I'm winded from the ride.' He moved from her touch, knowing she could hear the lie of his words.

Turning away, he heard her footsteps behind him

as he walked around the house. The boards over the windows pleased him even more than the weeds. No one should see inside or be able to touch anything left behind. That world had been sacred.

He knew he could pull the boards from the door and have a roof over their heads.

He refused. Not in Mary's house. He couldn't go to the door. Not and keep breathing.

Walking to the carriage house in back, he led them away from the rooms where his family had lived.

The thunder mocked him, but he ignored the sound and guided Hercules to a stall. His partner in crime followed, strangely silent. From the corner of his eye, he saw her trying to take in as much of the surroundings as she could.

'I don't have a good feeling about this house.' She spoke in a whisper, and her hand brushed his arm.

Lightning rolled across the sky.

Brandt spoke, 'Neither do I.'

Chapter Ten

The carriage house, hidden in the back, didn't have paned windows as the main house did, but wooden shutters and a planked door. It would have to do. He could keep her there. Later, after he put his thoughts away, he could take her to his mother's home.

His mother could claim that she was a daughter of a long-lost friend. Perhaps taken in as a housekeeper. They'd work up some yarn to hide her. His mother could always put a shine on a piece of family tarnish.

A pang hit him in that his mother always claimed her home to be overflowing with family and servants, but she always managed to find room.

Then he took a look at the structure and turned his face away. No. That wouldn't be fair to his mother or to Miss Wilder. He'd open up the blasted house no matter how much time it took him to swallow down the memories clogging his throat.

She deserved a home if she was going to take care of the child and the governess. And if Katherine Wilder was anything like most women he knew, every sad sort with a tale would find a home with her, including every one-eyed cat and every dog with a woebegone wail.

'We cannot stay here.' She stopped, turning to grasp her pommel and jab her foot into the stirrup. 'Surely someone owns the grounds. We'll be found.'

He pulled himself from his memories and watched her struggling to get back on the horse.

She looked over her shoulder. 'Give me a shoulder up. I'm a bit stiff.'

He wasn't putting a finger on her. Especially the part of her she had pointed in his direction. 'We've nowhere else and this will do. Besides, we need sleep and shelter. It's about to rain again. I'm certain of it.'

She turned back to Apple, grabbed the pommel and gave a jump, but slid back to the ground. She kept her foot in the stirrup and put her head against the saddle. 'Give me a hand. I'm too weak from the riding to get astride again and she refuses to kneel.'

'Apple has enough sense to want her sleep.'

After her foot slid from the stirrup she looked at him. 'Brandt, I don't believe in ghosts, but I don't wish to find out I'm wrong.'

He took her reins and stepped back. 'This is the place you'll be staying.'

'I saw your face. You feel an unpleasantness about this as strongly as I do.' She pointed to the house. 'Just because it is abandoned doesn't mean it's safe for us.'

'True.' He turned his back to her. 'Nowhere's safe.' He led Apple and Hercules behind the house, securing them for the night. She followed.

He moved to the carriage house doorway and found it barricaded over. His brother had protected the place well. The solid front door wasn't boarded over because it had a latch from the inside.

He touched the small scabbard at his hip, ignoring the house key, and went around to the back. Wooden shutters covered a pair of windows. There was another set of openings across from these two to let air circulate and remove the heat. The settling of the barn had made the bar crossing the shutters sometimes need a bit of a nudge to free so the windows could be opened. The one he now stood in front of had warped differently. During construction, he'd been annoyed at the unevenness.

'Do you even know where we are?' she asked suddenly from behind him.

'Five miles from the best tavern I've ever seen.' He tapped the shutters. 'A tavern that does not allow women because they spoil the ale and conversation.'

He pulled the blade from his scabbard, and starting from the bottom, pushed the blade into the crack and slid it smoothly upwards until he felt the resistance of the board on the reverse side.

Applying more pressure, he used the knife to lift the bar and, as soon as he was certain it had been released from the clasps where it had been nestled, he slid the blade back a bit and pushed the tip up so it rested against the board and with a nudge, he heard the wood fall to the inside of the house. The shutters slid open as if an unseen hand guided them. Stale air hit his nostrils.

He felt a tap on his shoulder and turned, facing her.

'Wouldn't it be better to break in at the door?' she asked.

He pressed his lips together, then put the blade

away. He would not be able to shove hard enough to push the door open with the board across it. Five men couldn't.

Brandt leaned closer, voice low. 'I want you to have the true criminal experience of climbing in a window.'

'I am fine with doorways.'

'Very well. You may break in the door for us.'

Her eyes darted to the side. 'You'll have to show me how.'

He leaned close, his forehead almost touching her hat brim. 'Through the window. I'll heft you inside.'

'I'd rather not.'

'We've nowhere else.' He raised his brows. 'Nowhere.'

She gave a shuddery shake of her head. 'The reason I wanted that dress… I have a few coins sewn inside for emergency. With it, and what I had in the pouch you gave me, we can hide at an inn. For some time if we need.'

'Nigel. We have no inn and we can't have anyone see us.'

'Surely—'

'Nigel. Thunder. Lightning. Saddles.' He slapped his leg, hitting behind his thigh. 'Saddles.'

She took a few steps from under the roofed stalls and appraised the sky. 'The thunder has faded. And a few sprinkles shouldn't bother us.'

'If our backsides are as tired as they are, think how poor Hercules and Apple must feel.'

She turned in the direction of Apple and sighed.

'Perhaps inside the carriage house won't be so bad.' Marching up to the window, she rested both hands on the frame and peered inside. 'Black as a wash kettle.'

He nodded. 'You and I could sleep here in the horse stalls, I suppose. The hay's old, though. Would be more stick than soft. Probably full of mice. Mice that tend to leave little presents behind.'

Her head turned to him, but then she looked back at the window.

She let out a sigh. 'It's truly dark in there.' She moved backwards and he had to sidestep to keep her off his feet. 'I don't see how you're going to fit through that window.'

'I wasn't planning to go through it.'

'Brandt,' she whispered. 'I believe I heard a mouse. Or a rat.' She looked back at him. 'Rats have sharp teeth.'

'They only bite if you get between them and their food.' He moved behind her and put both hands at her waist to give her a nudge through the opening.

He got several sharp kicks to his shins and stumbled. Her shoulder connected with his cheek and the jaw where he'd been punched at the tavern.

With all the grace of an eighteen-year-old youth, he grabbed the sides of her trousers near her waist, lifting her and giving her a push. He kept a firm hold on her trousers and, before he realised what he'd done, he felt her legs slipping from the trousers as she tipped over and through the windowsill. She was going headfirst into the darkness and he couldn't control her descent. He grabbed tighter, managing to trap her ankles, a bit of her nightrail and her feet near in his face.

'Release me.' She screeched out the word, startling him.

Brandt opened his hands and she tumbled the rest of the way into the other side.

He could not help it. The thump and the little 'eep' gasps made the edges of his lips turn up.

Then, he heard a scream and a sob, and he grasped the edge of the window base and leaned in, his hands reaching to pull her back to safety.

He could make out nothing in the darkness except he thought he saw her flailing arms around her head as she sat on the floor.

'Spiders. Webs. Nose,' she spat out.

He could hear the sound of her spitting and rasping.

'Harmless. The pests have eight legs to run away faster.' Brandt put as much tenderness in his voice as he could. 'The door behind you is barred. Could you make your way to it, so you might get to the pump and wash your face?'

After a few more sputters, she clattered over something, thumped against the door and scratched at the latch. She called someone a foolish addlepate and then opened the door and rushed out.

He led her to the pump, watching as she splashed water on her face and arms. Then he left her so he could unsaddle the horses and secure them for the night.

When he returned to the pump, she said, 'Kidnapping is more heinous than I expected.' She grasped the edge of her opposite sleeve and pulled it to wipe her face. He didn't know if she wiped the cobwebs, water from the well, or, from the waver in her voice, tears.

'I believe we should change our plans and sleep in the main house,' she said.

'We will not,' he spoke more firmly than he intended. 'We are going to sleep in the carriage house.'

'The carriage house,' she pointed out, 'is full of bugs.'

'Whose rest you disturbed. I am sure they will forgive us and share their home.' He turned, wanting nothing more than a soft pillow—or the soothing stench of a tavern—which he'd left behind. He looked at the road. One direction and then the other. A tavern each way. He looked up. A few stars twinkling through the clouds. She still chattered away behind him, explaining her distaste for bugs and mice.

He pushed his hand over his forehead, moving the hair from his face.

He was tired of the ale. Tired of the bawdy jests and the morose faces. The woman's chattering about bugs was of no more or less import than the talk at the tavern and she would still be able to string her words together in the proper order come morning. Even if he didn't want to hear them. He didn't need to shut them away with the drink. He could just ignore them.

He picked up the saddlebags. She'd stopped talking. But then he saw her shadow moving about. Even in the rough clothing, her silhouette shouted to him. She rubbed a hand over her arm, shook out the waist of her shirt and patted back her hair.

He turned away, refusing to look at her.

'Maybe the main house is better. We might find candles.'

'I have some,' he said. 'We can use the stable master's room and the saddle blankets to make pallets on the floor.'

'If you had followed my plans, I would have a mattress.'

'Ah, but this way it's truly an adventure.' He briefly shut his eyes. Adventures were for other people. Not him.

He had to start a fire so they'd have light—something servants always managed before he'd moved to his boarding house. But he'd learned the skill in his youth.

Inside, with a small nest of dried brush, he struck steel to flint, and after the bit of tender ignited, so did a small fire in the fireplace. He then fed it a few sticks from outside.

She sat, her head in her hands, the hat on the table, and he heard another sigh. 'I didn't realise so many duties would need attended to.' Raising her head, she looked at him. 'I cannot even find a chamber pot.'

'One uses the outdoors.'

She put a hand to her chest. 'A true lady could *never...*'

'This is not London…' He mimicked her tone.

She snapped her toes against the floor, before dropping her head back to her hands. 'The governess warned me about life without servants. But she did not mention *that* or itchy clothing.'

He turned to the saddle blankets, leaving her to ponder her plight—of living without servants—except himself.

Brandt went to the saddle blankets and put one on the rope bed, so she would be able to rest her dainty back and his dainty back would have to make do with the floor. He would have groaned, but he didn't wish to give her the satisfaction. No telling how old the mattress was and he didn't know if it had husks in it or something softer, but she would have to make do.

'You want me to sleep there?' she asked.

'I've slept on worse,' he grumbled, thinking of the tavern.

'You don't have to tell me. I saw your bed.'

Compared to this, his bed was royal fare.

Then she sat on the bed and a rustling movement sounded from inside the bed. She jumped up and stepped away from it. 'It's got something in it.'

'Probably a mouse,' he spoke, then paused. He looked around. No sign of mice in the carriage house. 'More likely a garden sn—'

'A snake?' She clutched his arm. 'A snake?'

'Probably a garden one.'

Now she stood behind him. 'Toss it out.'

Looking through husks for a snake didn't seem to capture his imagination, or perhaps it captured it too well. That was a better job done in daylight. 'I'll move the mattress out and we can check it later.'

He pulled the mattress away and looked at the sagging ropes on the small frame. Perhaps it was best she didn't sleep on the ropes anyway. It looked like a mouse had been on the premises and done a bit of gnawing.

He dragged the mattress from the bed. She watched as if a monster snake would leap at her. He took it outside and slung it out of the way. Probably have two snakes in it by morning. He went back to the room. 'You can sleep on the floor.'

'No.'

He paused, watching her. 'Sleep standing up then. I've heard it's invigorating.'

Highly unlikely he would get any sleep with that look on her face. Best to appease since he couldn't put her out with the mattress.

He took her saddle bag and handed it to her. 'Your

pillow.' Then he took the saddle blanket and held it out. 'Your tester bed.'

She took it and raised her eyes to his, and had the same expression he felt if he'd had to get back on the horse. He turned, put his saddle bag closer to the wall the most distance from her and lowered himself.

And he reached his hand out to the side of his bed. He stopped in mid-air. A habit to reach for the brandy bottle at his side. Without thinking, he'd reached for the glass. He put his clasped fingers behind his head and gave a mild shrug. Blazes. He wasn't even thirsty. He was sleepy. Sleepy and tired and somehow relaxed.

'I feel a bit rough after all the time in the saddle. I fear I'm not as strong of constitution as you.' She still stood in the middle of the room.

Air from the blanket brushed against him when she spread it.

'A little close, aren't you?'

'If that snake returns, he's getting the both of us.'

She didn't know their leaving hadn't been an option because he could never have got back on snivelling Hercules. He swore the beast had tried to nip his ear when he'd tied him, then the horse put a hoof too near the toe of Brandt's boot and breathed a particularly heated, damp snort of air into Brandt's face.

Brandt rested his head on his saddlebag and listened to the rustles of movement, breathed in and shut his eyes.

Little grunts, groans and sighs filled the air while she worked getting that blanket on the floor just right.

A blanket on the floor.

She settled and he sat up to see that she'd rolled

the blanket tight and put it as a barrier around her head. A snake detour, he supposed. He settled back to rest his head.

She stilled. 'How long do you think I will have to stay here until I get the ransom?'

'A few days,' he muttered, knowing he lied. But he was sleepy and he didn't want to explain about the house, or get into any arguments. He had a feeling she wouldn't be able to sleep at all and, if she didn't because she was upset about the plan, he could wager the house that she'd even keep the horses awake with her complaints.

He wanted to shut his eyes, doze off and not drink. He knew his muscles would be jittery in the morning. Both from riding and from staying from the tavern. But it was the closest he'd felt to peace in a long time and he wanted to savour the moments of it.

'A few days?' She raised her voice and then he heard an illegible word. 'Do you think there are any dressmakers in the area who might have a current *La Belle Assemblée* for me to use in selecting some new gowns?'

'No.'

'I didn't expect so.' She paused. 'Are any seamstresses in the area?'

'I doubt it. I think the maids make the day dresses and the women make a trip to London for a seamstress for their evening wear.'

'I can manage. I'm planning to live in the country for the rest of my life. I will learn to make do. Perhaps even sew my own clothing. Mrs Caudle says she can teach me.'

Country life would be safer for her. And his mother

would teach her how to run a household, just as she'd taught Mary.

He didn't think anyone at the boarding house could connect him to this estate.

He sat and clamped his jaw while she rustled around twisting the saddle blanket this way and that trying to stretch it again so nothing could crawl over it.

Ladies' maid. Companion. Butler. Groomsman. Footman. At least she didn't expect him to fluff her pillow. But only because she didn't have one.

But she did something to his senses. Made him imagine lace against feminine skin. Lace on underthings floating in the outside breeze on a washday.

He so hated the reminder of washdays.

But then he imagined, of all things, sliding a freshly laundered nightdress over her body. The crispness of the cloth against the softness of her skin and his hands running—

He groaned and turned over, trying to find a comfortable spot as far away from the thoughts of her as he could. Sleep. Was that too much to ask for.

'Is anything wrong?'

'Not if you stop speaking and let me sleep.'

'I wasn't talking, but I won't if it bothers you.'

He didn't answer. She sighed. Nothing more than a gentle breath. And then she sniffed. And then she moved. It sounded as if she put an elbow under her head. Then she breathed in and out a little more loudly than usual. And he lay there, listening to her. Waiting to hear what movement she'd make next.

He didn't know what kind of mire that he'd got himself into. It wouldn't matter, though. He'd left the world around him once before and leaving it a second time would be much easier than the first. He had a life among the tavern folk and he belonged there.

A thumping noise jarred Katherine awake. Her insides clenched with fear. Augustine had found them. She'd told Brandt not to leave the shutters open, but he had. He'd not even been concerned with bolting the door and merely pressed it shut.

Silence followed and she moved only her eyes, pretending sleep, but looking for the origin of the sound.

This time she heard a rustle and, when she looked to the direction of the noise, she saw Brandt moving in his sleep.

Even in the night's darkness she could tell he moved in the grasp of an unpleasant dream. She watched, amazed to see someone so strong unaware of his movements.

Brandt gave short groans from his lips and pushed against the wall, caught up in some imagined world. He rolled to his side, moving as if a rabid animal had bitten him. She couldn't bear the moans, or the sight of him fighting in an imagined world.

Sitting, she reached out and, with only fingertips, touched his shoulder.

'Brandt,' she whispered, amazed at how much warmth flowed from his bare skin. The hint of perspiration and the floral scent he always had about him touched her nose. She rested her other hand on the overheated skin of his side, moving gently to soothe. Within seconds, she felt the tenseness ebb from his body.

'…forgive me.' His words blurred into the darkness. 'Forgive me. I came home without you.'

She touched his tensed hand, then clasped his fingertips. 'It's all right,' she murmured, her words almost lost even to her own ears. 'It's all right.' Her words floated in the night air.

His answer mixed with a rumble of sleep breathing, but his hand held her fingers like a lifeline. She moved, resting against the floor, and put her arm around him. She waited, knowing she'd return to her bed as soon as he fell deeper into sleep.

Brandt's breathing returned, almost becoming the rhythm of a lullaby to her, and she felt herself relaxing. She dozed, waking briefly to snuggle into the warmth around her.

'And I thought you didn't like me.' The voice rumbled into her ear, waking her.

She blinked, shaking the sleep from her mind, then sat as proudly as her shoulders would let her, scooting on her bottom to put distance between them. She met his gaze. 'I sleepwalk.'

He shook his head towards her. 'And I knit in my sleep.' Eyes blinked. 'Once woke up to find a whole shawl in my bed. I had no idea how it got there until I saw the needles.' Voice full of innocence, he asked, 'That ever happen to you?'

She didn't respond.

Enough light seeped from the embers that she could see him plainly. He didn't need to be so unpleasant. She'd spent an hour with her nose buried against his skin and she had no complaints. Before, when he'd been naked, her mind had been overwhelmed and she'd not been able to comprehend much. This time, with only his upper half unclothed, she'd been able to take stock.

Now, she could study him, yet she couldn't. When her eyes rested on Brandt, it wasn't as if she saw him, but felt him. Men didn't even go about with their waistcoat unbuttoned and he had no shirt on. Which, she decided, was acceptable in trying times.

Drunken kidnappers shouldn't wear shirts. If he was a lord, this attire would have been unacceptable. But he was from base society and he had no qualms about a state of undress. She could accept these tavern-crowd rules quite easily. Especially as the rags of his clothing covered something she was sure, even with her inexperience in the matter, was worthy of perusal.

His eyes, half-concealed in the shadows, met hers.

'Is there anything normal about you?' he asked.

Staying on the floor, she pulled her knees up, hugged them with her arms. 'I'm terribly normal and boring.'

'Normal?'

'Yes.' She didn't have to think. 'And quite boring as I have had to be to keep Augustine from noticing me.' She scooted to rest against the wall opposite Brandt. 'If I reacted with any appearance of anything but happy acceptance of what he might do, it was like a mouse dancing in front of a cat. He prefers to sharpen his claws on the skin of those around him, except his nephew. He thinks Fillmore an image of himself. Which is true, only a dark image.'

Brandt leaned back against the wall, staring at her. 'You could not claw back?'

She shook her head. 'Not when my mother was

sick. And he has my sister in his grasp. I must make a home for us before he sends her away. When my grandfather left funds to my mother, he didn't think of what could happen. She wouldn't have wanted me forced to marry Fillmore. She loved Gussie even though Mother was too sick to care for her. Because she doesn't speak, Augustine thinks her mind is damaged. He calls her a little rodent and she keeps out of the way of his feet.'

He sat, filling up her eyes with his shoulders. Looking not a bit like any tavern fare she'd ever heard of. No wonder those fallen women flocked to taverns. It was not all for the ale as she'd thought.

But he had to stop that elixir.

She reached up, touching her nose. It was working too well.

'Are you hurt?' he asked, standing, the covers falling aside. He took a step towards her. His fingers were long, sturdy and one arm reached to her. Oh, he would be breathing all over and touching her, too. It would not be good.

'I'm fine.' She jerked her hand from her nose. 'Just making sure I did not get too much sun on my nose. Without my bonnet it has been a trial.'

He took a step closer, examining her eyes. 'We've not been in much sunshine.'

She took a sideways step. 'My skin. I'm very sensitive to the sunshine in the air.'

'Are you sure you're fine? I truly didn't mean to— I'm not at all used to— And to wake up with your hair tickling my face.' Then his eyes darkened. 'What were you doing?'

'I'm used to sleeping with my cat on the bed. He

purrs. And I must have heard you snoring and snuggled close.'

'Look, Nigel. I don't snore. And you don't sleepwalk.' He groaned.

She tilted her head back. 'Some kidnapper you are.' She arranged the twisted trousers and the too-large shirt, knowing she did little to improve her appearance. 'I would appreciate a little more politeness.'

He looked at her and a lazy grin spread across his face. 'So would I. Keep to your own bed and I'll keep to mine.' He reached for his shirt. 'You've made me most polite. I now wear trousers to sleep in. Are you disappointed?'

'I did not pay any notice to you. A lady does not.'

'No, you don't. You sleepwalk right close to a man. Kind of makes me wonder what you're dreaming about.'

'Not you.' She blinked wide, emphasising her words. 'I could not marry a man willing to live in the sorry state I found you. I wish for someone like myself. A man of honour and good values. An example for others.'

His face took on a boyish look and he seemed to discard an answer. 'I hear the women talk—granted they aren't chaste women—but they do not have their hearts set on the vicar noticing them.'

'Oh.' Some imp forced her to lean ever so slightly closer to him. 'You only know of the tavern women. You must admit, they do not live pure lives themselves. Decent women are different.'

He looked at her and somehow managed to tell her with one little hint of humour on his lips and a tiny movement of his eyes that she had no experience of the world. 'I guess I cannot speak for the women who lust after the saints of the world,' he muttered. 'Those wholesome ones who dream of long winter nights sitting by the fire with their husbands while knitting shawls. But, Nigel,' he said, laughter behind his eyes, 'something tells me you will not be happy with a husband who puts a cosy wrap around himself and falls asleep early. Watching where your eyes roam—waking with you half in my arms, pressing against my private parts, I admit, you've got a rather interesting side to you a man might find quite enjoyable.'

Katherine's thoughts blasted in her head. She'd slept through the most important event of the night.

He moved forward and touched the side of her chin, locking her in place. Her knees wanted to wobble right back to the floor.

'Truly, if you weren't a lady—' One side of his mouth smiled, but the laughter left his face. 'What does it matter? You're—' He stepped back, dropping his hand. 'To touch you is to tempt the fates to bring me more trials and I'm not strong enough to bear what I've already got.'

And he didn't even want to touch her. What a cad to admit that. A low-living, twisted, breathing, kidnapping, naked sleeping man who did not deserve one moment of thought from her.

'I will not sleepwalk again, I am sure.'

'Don't rule it out, completely.' He gave the lightest touch to the back of her hand. 'I promise to wake you gently, should it happen again.' He moved closer, leaned his head towards her and then leaned in even closer.

She felt he was trying to scare her away and she understood.

Being awakened softly by Brandt would change her life. 'I prefer to awaken alone.' She raised her chin. If he believed that, she imagined she could also convince him to buy the Tower from her.

'Well, I shall return to sleep,' he said, settling back onto the floor, and tossing her the blanket she'd used. 'You can join me, or sit there and plan another kidnapping.'

She knew she dared not crawl back beside him. She could barely breathe without his elixir fluttering all around her.

Chapter Eleven

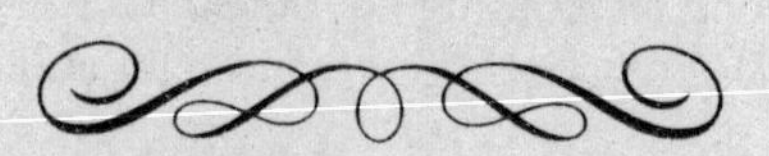

Katherine knew she'd slept little more than an hour—even after Brandt finally quit grumbling at her. Little slivers of daylight brightened the room through the cracks around the closed shutters.

Too much had happened for her mind to rest.

She'd been taken, was housed in a near stable, had the taste of dust in her mouth and could hear the rumble of a man's breathing as he slept.

Other than the moments with her mother, this was the best day of her life.

She looked at the boards overhead. She was in a man's shirt. Her muscles felt stiff. But, she could stand a bit more of it if it meant starting a new life without her stepfather or Fillmore in it.

After her mother passed away, her stepfather never absented a room Katherine was in without telling her how her mother had wronged them all. Her mother had wanted to die—he was certain. If she'd done as he told her and not taken to her bed so easily, she'd still be alive.

Giving her stepfather a taste of what he deserved meant a bit of hardship, but Katherine didn't mind.

She relished it. The discomfort meant she might be able to keep Gussie from her stepfather and keep herself from Fillmore.

Fillmore's eyes darted when he looked at her, reminding her of a lizard she'd once seen in the gardens. At least the lizard didn't drool. She pulled the saddle blanket tight around her. Brandt was so different than Fillmore.

Brandt's arms—they'd locked her in place when he'd held her away from the gun. When she pushed against them, they'd not moved enough to indicate her strength could ever topple him. She caught the direction of her thoughts and the way her body filled with a cosy warmth. The governess was right. She'd got too close to his air.

The soft rumbles he made as he slept sounded pleasant. Comforting. But she supposed she should take care. With each rasp, he sent out a burst of elixir.

Brandt had kissed her ear after she'd lost the gun. And she'd almost shivered when she'd felt a kiss on her neck and he'd followed it with a preposterous tiny lick.

The lick. How odd. And not unpleasant.

She'd been shocked by Brandt's touch—shocked at the warm sensation he caused. Maybe some of the elixir slipped through his fingertips.

Then, he'd kissed her again. The kiss was an odd thing for Brandt to do. He had the tavern women for his affections.

Perhaps he knew how Fillmore disgusted her and he wished to do the same. That was it, she was certain. He'd been trying to disgust her.

His arms had been holding her snug against his

body and he'd not felt at all repulsive. Instead, he'd made her feel buttery. And he'd probably disgusted himself with his behaviour. He'd certainly been more irritable afterwards.

He'd grumbled so much she'd been ready to put a palm over his mouth.

She glanced across at his sleeping form.

Katherine thought of Fillmore. She'd seen too much of him when he was fully clothed. Any more of him and she'd cast up her accounts and throw herself straight into Brandt's arms.

She turned, resting her cheek against the rough fibres of the saddle blanket and ignoring the horse scent.

Brandt's raspy sleep sounds kept tickling her thoughts. Every time he gave a little murmur in his sleep, she felt a warming sensation to her toes. The air was deadly.

His head was turned and his arm was over his face. One booted foot was on the floor.

She had to get out of the room because she couldn't quit looking at him.

Katherine stood, the shirt hanging past her hips. She didn't want Brandt to see her so unkempt.

With a hand holding the trousers in place under her shirt, she tiptoed beside him.

His snores didn't stop. She wondered if sleeping elixir was stronger than the waking one. The air spun around her, sweeping over her, warming her with the same intensity of the sun.

She let her eyes run the length of his body. The drink must agree with him.

Katherine turned, reaching to pull out the dress from the bag. But she paused. She wanted to remain a man for a bit longer. See how it felt. She straightened her shoulders and put a snarl on her lips. Easy to do when wearing clothing made from a brush pile that rested over bunched underclothes.

She went outside to find the water pump she'd seen in the night, giving one last look at Brandt before she left.

Thistle heads popped up from the sea of weeds surrounding the structure, but the horses had tramped a path the night before and the trips to the pump made another trail. No one arriving would think the place ignored now.

The pump handle took both hands and the screech when she raised the lever reminded her of a scream.

She stilled, raised her eyes and looked to the road. Surely no one could have followed them.

The thought of Augustine's eyes, pinched black, lurched into her mind. If he found her now, he would beat her and then turn her over to Fillmore. Another pet had escaped and what he could not control, he would destroy.

She lifted the pump handle again, moving cautiously to minimise the rasping metal.

When she returned to the room, her chemise tucked over her arm, and the borrowed clothes no fresher than the day before, she noticed Brandt's closed eyes.

She stared at the sleeping form on the floor and knew nothing would ever be the same in her life.

They had no time to waste. Brandt had to get the ransom so she could hide herself away. She didn't think the air was truly healthy for her.

The governess had a blind aunt in Warwickshire and, once Katherine received the money, they were to meet there. The funds would secure their safety and from there they would go further north, changing into the family they wanted.

Before she found Brandt, she'd confided in her cousin that she might leave quickly and not to worry about her. It had been a tearful moment, but her cousin had understood. She'd wished Katherine well and even asked if she might visit them later. Katherine had agreed, but told her they couldn't contact each other again until after Augustine died. It would be too risky.

She looked down at the sleeping man. Brandt's closed eyes and rumbling breaths gave him the appearance of a man without a care. And surely he was.

She nudged his calf with the toe of her boot. He mumbled and she wasn't certain the word she heard was suitable for her ears. She didn't know what it meant and she thought she knew all the swear words.

She tapped her boot against his leg again.

His body snapped sideways and, before she realised he'd awoken, he trapped her ankle in his hand.

Her balance wavered, but he held her as firmly as if she'd been shackled.

She bounced a bit to regain her poise, but his fingers didn't lessen their grip, and his eyes were dark and his lips firm as he looked up at her.

'I have waited near an hour for you to wake.' She put her hands on her hips.

Eyes stared up from the scruffy face. 'You could have waited at least an hour and a half. Maybe two.

You should have learned by now I don't take well to being woken early.'

Even though boot leather and trouser fabric separated his skin from hers, the warmth of his hand and the strength of his grip erased all the separations. She stood over him, looking down, but his grasp made her the prisoner of the two.

He didn't release her.

'Are you quite finished with my ankle yet?' she asked.

'Nigel.' He gave her the smallest tug and she had to move closer to him. 'I'd forgotten we dressed you in trousers and shirt. You nearly shocked me out of a year's growth when I looked up and saw a woman inside those clothes.'

She looked at him, one eyebrow raised. 'If you are finding fault with my shirt, you have only yourself to blame.'

'I assume you do not like it because it is not stylish—although it definitely suits you better than those bonnets.'

'This waistcoat is so large I can pull it over my head without unbuttoning it.' She tugged it away from her body. 'And I had to tear a scrap of fabric from my chemise to hold the trousers in place.'

She touched the frayed sash she'd made from the hem of her chemise. 'I'd dress better if I were a thief.'

'Aren't you, though?'

His whiskers near looked a beard he needed shaved so badly. His eyes had smudges, but sparkled with something she'd never seen on his face before. He looked more like an animal about to pounce than a human. Yet, she couldn't seem to pull her eyes away and he didn't seem inclined to release his grasp.

'I'm not a true criminal.' She twisted her foot, but he didn't release her. 'I'm taking what I should have. Or I will soon. My grandfather had made certain my mother was to get an inheritance, but no one made any provisions about what would happen if she were to marry. Augustine took care of that.'

He yawned. His grip on her ankle tightened and he shut his eyes. 'I believe I'll go back to sleep.'

She tried to pull her leg free. She couldn't budge except to put her foot to the floor. She did, leaned down and pinched his nostrils closed. Then she breathed in deeply, trying to judge if the air changed.

His eyes opened, stared at her and he released his grip on her ankle. She stood upright.

'What kind of woman pinches a man's nose?' he asked.

'One with her ankle trapped.'

'One point for you there,' he said. 'And since you are standing, why don't you bring some water so I can wash up'

'Do I look like a valet?'

'No. You look like someone from the tavern. Not one of the finer ones either.'

She turned and gave a hitch to her trousers. 'I'll prepare a meal for you.'

His brow furrowed. 'Why are you not wearing the lady's garment you brought?'

'It is in desperate need of an iron.' She pointed to the garment she'd hung on a hat peg. 'Besides, a criminal must stay in disguise.' She practised a manly swagger and put masculinity into her voice.

She heard his groan.

'Nigel, whatever you do, don't try to convince anyone you're a man. Hunker down and pretend to be a youth, and you might get away with it, but no one's going to believe you can grow a single chin whisker.'

'You've enough for the both of us,' she mumbled before turning her attention to her clothing. After tucking the shirt back into her trousers, she tightened the belt scrap she'd made, and pulled the shoulder of her waistcoat back into place.

She looked at him in time to see him lower his eyes.

She turned, reaching into the saddlebag which had been on his horse. A burst of pride hit her to think he might have some fascination with her appearance. Then she looked down. No, he stared because he'd never seen anyone dressed in a waistcoat with candle wax on it. Neither had she.

Pulling out one of the wrapped parcels he'd brought along, she opened it, looked inside and then folded the paper back. 'Cheese.' She pushed the paper back over the food. She looked at him. 'I've really never cooked cheese before.'

His body moved in one fluid motion as he stood and he held the parcel in his left hand. He used his right to reach into the scabbard at his side and pull a knife out. Then he opened the paper.

Slicing a few slivers of cheese, he walked to the door, tossing the food into his mouth as he moved. Then he went outside.

She didn't like his quietness. He'd not yet told her how he was getting the money from her stepfather.

Katherine didn't let the door close before she had

her hand out to keep it open. She stepped outside, crossing her arms for warmth in the cool morning air.

'You must explain your plans to collect the ransom.' Katherine ran to him. 'This cannot go wrong. I allowed you to kidnap me on the wrong day, and the wrong place and the wrong time. I should have given you my list. But the ransom—that must not fail.'

'I got you away from your stepfather. You should be pleased.'

In the full light, even his face appeared rumpled. His shirt neck had fallen down and he rubbed his hand across one eye. She realised Brandt was the only man she'd ever seen so freshly woken and she'd seen him so several times.

'I am pleased.' She moved closer to him, curious even as she spoke. 'The rest of what I wish—the funds—is of prime concern.'

She wanted to stand close enough to check his breath. She wanted to find out more about the elixir in the light of day and when her mind was strong. No other man had ever had such a powerful flavour of breathing.

Surely he must have something in his breath. Because how could the rags of clothes he wore, such a scruffiness about him, pull her eyes to him? She examined him. Something else had to be at work.

He gently shook his head. 'The ransom is not a prime concern of yours. What you wish is to be free of your stepfather. You are.'

'I want the funds.'

'Then you will have to wait.' He turned, putting the back of his hand to cover a yawn as his elbows stretched.

'Then I will collect it myself.'

He lowered his arms and turned to her. His eyes twinkled. 'And what is the direction to London?'

'I can ask the first stranger I find.'

She heard his quiet laughter. 'First you must escape your kidnapper.'

Chapter Twelve

Katherine could not understand the fascination he had with the fireplace. He kept staring at it.

'Do you cook at all?' Brandt stood, looking at the empty grate, then he appraised her from the corner of his eye.

'My mother would not allow such frivolities. But I would like to learn.'

'I thought not. You bring wood and I'll make sure you don't starve.'

Then he turned away, unaware of the pull he had over her.

She slipped outside and looked at the house, distancing herself from him. She'd needed to walk away.

She walked quickly, struggling through brambles to move away from the house. She wanted to remove Brandt from her thoughts. Something about him reached into her mind and latched on.

Rolling across the floor had been an uncomfortable way to wake—and not how she expected to be treated if she slept near a man. She had been sadly misinformed.

She thought back to the first time she'd seen him. She couldn't get that image to leave her mind. She'd been too shocked to really take all of him in. Pity.

She looked at the house, looming stately among the overgrown hedges. Brandt knew the house. He could have worked for the owner who died. Perhaps the owner had left him a small sum for the good work Brandt did.

She could see how a wealthy man might enjoy Brandt's jests, or how the woman of the house might—Oh, she needed to toss that thought far aside.

She turned back to the carriage house.

Inside, the smell of wood smoke mixed with the scent of food. Brandt stood with his back to her. He had hung a pot over the stove and was now putting dollops of dough on to the lid top to cook.

'Would probably be too much for me to expect you to cook something even as simple as an omelette...'

She raised her brows in question.

'An omelette. My father travelled near Bessières once and when he returned he insisted we have omelettes. Eggs stirred about. Cheese in it. Very tasty. I discovered I had to show the women at the tavern how to make them if I wanted one to my taste.'

'I like my eggs normally prepared.'

'And how might that be?'

'By Cook. And in biscuits and cakes and tarts and things like that.'

'I very much want an omelette.'

'That is probably beyond my experience.'

He leaned forward, blinked slowly and met her eyes. 'I thought so.' He squinted one eye. 'And if we had eggs, I'd make you the best omelette ever.' He frowned. 'But now we'll have to make do with peas.'

'Do you enjoy cooking?' she asked him.

'It doesn't matter when I am hungry if I enjoy it or not. I do not have a club to attend or a cook and by the time I can walk to the tavern I can already have my stomach full.'

'So we are to have peas for breakfast?'

He stopped movement and looked at her. 'I think not. These will take a little longer to cook. We will have bread.'

'Bread?' She instantly thought of Cook's breakfasts. Ham and buttery bread and steaming chocolate—and not a pea in sight.

When she caught Brandt watching her, Katherine put a smile on her lips. 'That sounds very tasty.'

After they finished eating, he stood, grasping the bail of the water bucket, and walked outside.

He turned, trying to get the woman out of his thoughts. He stared at the large house he'd once loved.

The structure stood timeless. Without the boards on the bottom floor, or the overgrown privet growing high, he could see little difference than what it had been years before.

He wanted to see broken window panes, falling shutters, peeling paint. Images flitted through his mind, bringing their bitterness with them.

The world he once held close no longer existed. His mind kept throwing memories at him. Mary's squeals of excitement when she'd moved into the house. The pure joy in her eyes.

'Odd to find a deserted house such as this.' Katherine's voice jolted through him, working like a slap, but he didn't face her. He'd been so lost in thoughts he didn't realise she'd stepped outside.

'How did you know of it?' she repeated.

He shoved his memories aside and answered as if nothing mattered. 'We kidnappers always have a deserted house tucked away.'

She crossed her arms. 'Shouldn't you be drinking?'

'One of us should, I'm sure.' He couldn't take his eyes from the house. He'd loved watching the builders. Loved the way Mary had fretted over the wall coverings. He'd had to cajole her into laughter each time he'd heard the word 'wall' or she would have driven him daft with her concerns.

One night he and his elder brother had laughed themselves to tears, comparing the efforts they made to appear entranced by the selection of fripperies.

Brandt was happy to be the second son and once or twice he'd thought his brother envied him a bit. Brandt could stay with the lands, hidden away, happy with Mary. Forgotten about.

Both their wives had been content—at least Mary had been until, at the end of her confinement, she'd lost the baby girl. He tried to push the memories from his mind.

For the first time he wondered what had happened to Nathan's toys.

'Do you know who owns this?' she asked.

He turned his head to her. 'Kidnapper.' He touched his chest. 'Victim.' He pointed a finger at her. 'You cannot get it through your head.'

'So, you do know who owns it?' She put a hand to shade her eyes and turned away to examine the house.

'A man who lost his mind.'

'I cannot imagine that.'

'Perhaps that is for the best.'

He turned to care for the horses. The animals did not need to suffer any more. He moved to get them water from the pump and a good place to graze where they wouldn't stray.

When he finished with the livestock, he noticed he'd not heard a word from Katherine. He wondered if she had escaped.

'One can always wish,' he muttered, knowing he would gladly give her one of the horses, but he knew he would have to travel with her as it wasn't good for her to be travelling alone and it was even worse for her to be travelling armed if she'd taken one of the pistols. She'd probably shoot her foot by mistake. And limp all the way back to him to explain how he shouldn't have let that happen.

He heard a thump. The sound came from the direction of the house. He walked towards it and found her at the door with a stick in her hands. She had already pried loose one of the boards from the house door.

'Stop,' he snapped. He covered the distance separating them. He pulled the stick from her hands and threw it to the ground. 'Do not go in the house.'

'We got into the carriage house.' She stepped back, eyes puzzled.

'Not the same. We were travellers in the dark needing lodging. No one would begrudge us for sleeping near the horses.'

'You need reminding you are a criminal.' She dared him with her eyes. 'No one would expect more of a man such as yourself. If you are caught, you can claim you were trying to make me comfortable.'

'I see the difference. A magistrate would never arrest a villain who only stole to please his victim.'

'I will gladly accept any punishment for opening this house and taking shelter. It's not proper for me to sleep in the same room as you do. You breathe too strongly.'

He looked at the ground, shaking his head.

She reached up and tugged at the rough wood with her bare hands. Her voice lowered so he could scarce hear it. 'I certainly need gloves for this.'

'You need a keeper.'

She graced him with the broadest smile of disrespect he'd ever seen. 'You were engaged for just such a purpose.' She gave an uppity toss of her head and her hair fluttered.

Her hair. He imagined she'd scream if she could see her hair.

When it had been stuffed under the hat, she'd wound it like a snake coil. Now it looked as if the snake had been struck by a club and smashed about.

She put her hand out, palm flat. 'We made an agreement. As such, I do consider myself your employer and if I wish you to break into this house, I see no reason for you to decline.'

His eyes roamed over her. 'Your hair is a bit—' He wiggled his fingers on one hand, fluttering them.

'If you'll let me...' He'd seen haystacks with more appeal, yet he wanted to put it back together as it should be. It should look soft, touchable... Like her lips.

He should take Hercules and escape while he could.

She tilted her chin down and her eyes lost all humour. 'And I must say, you need assistance more than I ever did or will. You were lost in a sea of depravity and I rescued you—at least temporarily.'

'You—' He realised what she'd said. 'You rescued me?' He looked upwards.

'Would you not consider yourself far away from respectability?'

'By choice.'

She grasped his shirtsleeve cloth. 'This is so faded you cannot even tell what colour it is. No respectable man wears such tatters.'

'So you've decided to be my valet, Nigel?' He met her eyes, 'Then I must say you need a valet as well. I can tell you've never dressed as a man.' Before she could step back, he reached to her, running his fingers comb-like through her hair, which didn't change much.

Then he touched both sides of the shirt top and ran his hands along the back, straightening it. And to linger a little longer, he pulled the drooping shoulders of the waistcoat closer to her neck. He grasped the lapels of the garment and tried to tug it into the right size, but she looked more a street urchin than anything else.

And he refused to let himself pull her close. He contented himself by looking at her.

'You'd never make a proper man,' he said, hands still resting at the lapels.

'I've never seen many proper men. So I should be perfect.' Eyes framed by lush lashes looked up at him and he saw her get a studied look on her face and take a deep breath.

She reached to push his hands aside, but stopped when she touched his skin. Her eyes widened, almost in fright. Her voice whispered, 'The air. It's overpowering. In *daylight* even.'

'It's country air. It doesn't smell. You'll get used to it.' He studied her face.

'Take a deep breath,' she instructed.

He did.

'Breathe out.'

He did.

'Do you feel different?'

He shook his head. 'Only difference is the country air doesn't make you spit tar. It's pleasant.'

She nodded, eyes wide, and studied him, speaking slowly. 'Precisely what I meant.' She stepped towards him. 'But no one has ever done that. Breathed so. I rather like that you do it so well.'

'I've practised since I was born.'

She put a hand to her chest. 'That is why you are so...strong then.'

He shrugged.

'Do you...feel anything...about my air?'

He laughed. 'Your head is so full of nonsense. Air is just air.'

She shook her head and touched the back of his hand. 'No. Really. You feel nothing then?'

He cleared his throat. 'I would not go as far as that.'

She puffed out tiny breaths of air. 'Did you feel that?'

'Am I supposed to?' He raised his brows. 'Are you well?'

She nodded, then shook her head. 'I think I have an illness caused by the air around you.'

'It's not the air.' He ran his hands the length of her arms, capturing her. 'Your shirt's not tucked in at the back. Might I straighten it for you?' And his hands slid around her to the top of her trousers where the garment had loosened.

He splayed his fingertips and only brushed the band of her clothing, not letting himself know the feel of her skin.

She jumped back from his embrace and used one hand to pinch her nose and the other to shove her shirt-tail into her trousers. 'I can care for myself. And you must stop—that thing. That elixir—thing. Breathing it.'

'Elixir?' He concealed his humour at her retreat and his irritation she didn't melt into his arms. 'There's no elixir in country air. It's just air. Without soot.'

'Well, it's not doing me any good.' She tugged at her trouser waist. 'And neither are these clothes. I feel...' She looked at him, eyes narrowing. 'It's the trousers, too. I think wearing them—it makes one feel a little reckless.'

'Nigel. It is not the air. It is not the clothes. It is just the way we humans are.'

Her eyes showed recognition of his words for less than a second but she continued looking away. 'Mrs Caudle explained clearly enough. And I do believe she knows what she's talking about.'

He raised a brow. 'Nature.' He spoke with finality.

'I don't care what you call it. But we must not breathe around each other. Let me in the main house. I'm very delicate and need a proper roof over my head,' she said. 'And you can stay in the carriage house and fill it full of that beastly stuff you breathe out.'

'You're not going inside.' He reached to the ground, picked up the stick she had used to loosen the board, took each end of it in a hand and raised a bent knee and thwacked the stick over it. He gave both pieces to her and she took them. 'Firewood.'

'I cannot believe you would not wish to provide better for me.'

'I gave you a bed, water, an Apple.'

'And saddle burn.'

'I did think I would be able to let you into the house,' he admitted and felt his memories stirring inside him. 'I was wrong.' He turned to stride away. 'Living in the carriage house will fade some of your airs, Nigel. Get used to it.'

He'd never say it to her, but she wouldn't have stepped inside his room if she'd had the notions of society that should have been bred into her. Somewhere along the way, someone had beaten her down and forced her to think more about surviving than soirées.

Chapter Thirteen

She looked at the house, pretending to examine it, but trying to clear her head. She wasn't quite sure what valets did in the privacy of the master's chambers and she wasn't sure she wanted him as her servant. But she wouldn't mind seeing a bit of soap taken to his chin and a razor uncovering the man underneath.

She'd hold his hair out, while she stood at his back, and she'd snip away untidy bits and there were a lot of those. A good valet could tie a cravat, as well. Tying such a knot would be beyond her, but she could try, certainly.

A picture of him jumped to her mind, with tiny red nicks along his chin, his hair trimmed in blotches and a cravat under his chin drooping like a goat's ears. She would do both of them a favour to let him care for himself—but he needed to stop that blasted, tainted, breathing.

His footsteps alerted her he was behind her and she turned. His eyes met hers.

She examined his growing beard, but her eyes

stopped at the beating pulse of his neck. She could never let a rope touch there.

She caught his eyes following hers.

'Nigel, you have *another* blush?' He grinned. 'What *is* traipsing about in your head which shouldn't be there?'

She stiffened her shoulders and bit out the words, 'It's the sun.'

'And I am Wellington.' His voice flowed like treacle. 'But keep your thoughts…' he leaned close '…they surely cannot be sweeter than mine.'

She realised to have those eyes, with some knowledge behind them that she couldn't grasp, staring at her from a man who took care of his appearance might be an insurmountable problem. Especially in a man with an aversion to nightclothes.

She turned her back to him. 'You waste your breath.'

Even with him behind her, she could feel his presence and sense his movements as well as if she could see him.

He leaned in. Her hair fluttered at her ears. 'Some day you'll have to tell me your thoughts.'

'I speak them plainly.' She kept her voice prim. 'You just don't listen.'

'I'm listening—to what you do not say.'

'I'll leave you to your imaginings.' She tightened her shoulders. 'And I'll enjoy mine. But we mustn't think too long.' She moved away from him, to escape his breathing. 'Or else…'

She heard a low chuckle when he stepped back and could tell he turned away by the sound of footsteps.

She moved enough to watch him gather fallen branches for the fire.

She imagined London's thieves eyeing him as he passed and taking note of the sturdy shoulders and legs—and not willing to risk a tussle with him.

One shouldn't expect any kind of propriety from a man of low morals, Katherine decided, moving the opposite direction to gather more fallen firewood. Even men with high morals only used them on occasion.

Men could do tasks of strength without effort, but they never saw further than the end of their nose, or the end of another part of their body, if the governess was to be believed.

She knew she'd never been aware of a man before. Not a man like Brandt.

She could see the lines of his body and the strength in him. Strength he accepted without his own awareness of it.

And when she heard his voice, she knew he wasn't as low born as he pretended. He had been quite meticulous when he'd taken care of the horses, so he might have been a stable man at one time, but if so, it had been at a large house and he'd had underservants.

But he would make a pleasant diversion for a woman who could toss aside her morals.

'What is going on in your spoiled head?' he asked when he returned, gritting out the words. His arms were piled with wood. 'You're not chattering my ears off.'

She forced her face innocent. 'I was thinking of what you might have for us to eat.'

He didn't answer and moved towards the carriage house. She followed, carrying her smaller bundle of sticks and a smile on her lips. She'd employed well. Brandt especially looked appealing from behind. He had legs to spare and, when he walked, his trousers shaped just right.

Inside, she waited as he took the food from his saddlebags. He didn't comment on the missing fruit, but sat smoked meat on the table.

She hitched up her trousers. 'Hungry?' she asked, hoping he might feel the need to prepare a meal.

'Perhaps I was hoping you might prepare something for us?' He stepped closer and raised a brow in question.

'I was hoping you might.' She closed the distance, stopping directly in front of him, and sniffed again. Wood smoke and leather and... She tried to place the fragrance, a light, comforting scent.

He reached out, touching her elbows. 'Stop sniffing.'

'It's not my fault.'

'You don't see me sniffing.'

'Because I don't smell as good as you do.'

He dipped his head near hers and his hands tightened at her elbows, holding her steady. 'I'm not complaining.' Warm breaths tickled her cheek, sending slivers of heat throughout her body.

She moved and, ever so lightly, her palms rested on his waistcoat. The worn cloth turned silken under her touch and she looked at her hands, feeling she'd never seen them before and never seen a man before. 'No one warned me about how you'd feel.'

She raised her face.

His grasp moved from her elbows to her waist, and his head dropped nearer hers and her eyes closed. And in a feather-light movement, his lips rested against hers, only for a moment, and then he moved away.

She blinked and swayed forward, and the kiss started again. He tasted of all the scents she'd smelled before, only now they were alive and unfurling inside her, taking the warmth of the summer morning and easing it throughout her body in a way she'd never felt summertime before.

He stepped back and she almost stumbled as she opened her eyes and returned to the world she'd left for a moment.

'No.' He moved further back. 'I don't need this.' He turned away. 'Not here. Not in this place.'

She stared at him. 'You didn't have to kiss me.'

'Oh, but I did.' Then he turned. 'This is not what I bargained for.' One arm flew out at his side as if pushing all thoughts of her away.

'I thought it was nice.'

'Nice?' He gasped out the word and a whirlwind seemed to erupt behind his eyes. 'You thought it was *nice*?'

'Yes,' she mumbled. 'Didn't you?'

He puffed out enough air that a lock of the hair in front of his face moved, but this time the breath didn't do a thing for her. He gave an undecipherable clenched-teeth response—and brushed by her without speaking and stalked outside.

She followed him, knowing the tension in his eyes marked a decision.

He walked to the back door of the main house and, with both hands on a board and a foot braced against the wall, he ripped the wood from its moorings. He worked at another, twisting and weaving with it until it became loose. He slammed the board on to the ground and looked at her as if it were her fault the house was boarded up.

She crossed her arms. 'Don't tear off the door.'

'I won't,' he said. 'I've got to get away from you.'

'Going in the house isn't very far away.'

'Far enough. Further than you know.'

She watched as he grappled with the boards. He only stopped briefly to brush back his hair from his forehead. She stamped some vetch aside so she could sit, feeling a bit disconcerted to have the fabric of the trousers pulling around her legs as she moved.

But, instead of sitting in the genteel ladylike way, she propped her knees up and put her hands on the ground behind her as she appraised his body. All she needed was a comfortable bonnet to shield the sun from her face.

She reached for a stalk of grass with a dried bit at the end, snapped off the fuzzy part and put the stalk between her teeth. She felt near manly enough to grow a beard.

But nothing about her felt masculine as she watched Brandt working. She should have learned to paint. This, she would have liked to have captured on canvas.

She liked the way his hair moved about when he put his back into pulling the boards from the house.

He turned as he threw aside a board he had extricated and his eyes appraised her. She couldn't read anything in his thoughts and she hoped he couldn't read hers. He had such refreshing movements. This was certainly better than looking at bonnets in shop windows.

She moved the straw aside so she could speak easily. 'What was your trade?'

A breeze ruffled her hair and she thought she sniffed gardenia.

'You smell flowers?' she asked.

He ignored her.

'What trade do you do to earn your living?' she asked.

She pressed the heel of her boot into the ground, eyes still locked on the way the back of his waistcoat pulled across his shoulders. Most men she'd seen wore waistcoats and frock coats in her presence. His lack of proper attire eased her so she felt comfortable asking him any question she wished. If he were a private man, he should have worn more coverings.

He didn't seem inclined to answer. 'I kidnapped you—doesn't give you the right to know the details of my life.'

'Maybe not, but it's not uncommon for two people to have conversation. At least—I would have thought so. But, I guess you might have no interest in *talking* with a woman.'

He turned and reached for another board, putting both hands firmly on it, and the wood groaned as he pulled it free in a single heft. 'My dear Nigel. You are correct.' He looked over his shoulder at her, paused a moment, then turned back to his work.

He tossed the board he removed near the other one, the wood clattering as the boards connected. 'My life is not your concern. But since you so wish to have conversation, I might say, I have had more women try to get in my bed than I have tried to get in theirs.'

He turned back to the board and she heard a

wrenching sound as he battled the lumber and pulled it against the nail. 'I find it tedious my company is considered reason enough for women to push themselves in my face or to expect me to rescue them from whatever trials they have. I try to keep to myself and women do not seem to comprehend I might wish for a brandy, not their petticoats or their words.'

'Are you so enamoured of your drink you think of nothing else?'

'I drank to forget—not be reminded.' He paused, gestured loosely with his hand. 'Just be quiet. And with you about, even brandy is not a consideration. I must keep my wits about me so you don't shoot me in the back, kick me awake, or—' He peered at her. 'Don't steal the horses.'

She stood and brushed the dirt from her hands, using the thighs of her trousers. 'I would not do such a thing. I am a duke's granddaughter, and now that Grandfather has passed, my uncle is the duke.'

He kept his back to her before he glanced at her for half a second. 'The Duke of Carville's granddaughter.'

She was surprised he knew of her. 'How did you know who my grandfather was?'

'When I followed you to your house to see who you were, I asked one of the servants leaving on an errand who lived there. He told me the house had once belonged to Carville's daughter.'

'You followed me?' She touched her chest.

He nodded. 'A daft woman came to my house asking me to commit a criminal act. What if you were a lightskirt leading me into a trap of some sort?' He leaned in and spoke in a loud whisper. 'Not all of the tavern folk are strictly honourable. Like say, a duke's granddaughter.'

She brushed his jest away. 'I never liked my grandfather much. He sat in his chair and talked on and on about how life used to be. Mother made me sit with him when I was young and I read chapters and chapters to him of the most boring books he could find. He'd fall asleep and wake up when I got quiet and make me read some more. Wearing these clothes is much easier.'

He turned his head to her, his hands still on a board. 'As a woman with peerage in your heritage, you should act a lady.'

'I'm ruined. It hardly matters.' She reached a hand to shield her eyes.

'You'll find a way to restore your life.' He put both hands on a board and tugged, the nails screeching against the wood as they pulled free. 'I took you at night so no one knows you're ruined, as you call it, but your stepfather. You can still go back.'

'When I needed a man to dash me to Gretna Green, I couldn't find a single one who'd tackle my stepfather. I want a man who keeps his distance.' She took the board with the nail sticking out and gestured with it. 'I have seen the mess a man can make of a woman's life, more than once.'

'You'll not have much trouble with that, Sweet.' His eyes sparkled. 'Just start shaking that board his way and he'll be backing away.'

She looked down at the nail, then tossed the board on to the others. 'A lot of women remain unmarried and do well. And some marry for security. A home.'

'I will never wed again.' He took the board from

her hand. 'I married young—was too happy in my marriage.' His movements froze for a moment, then continued when he spoke again. 'We had too much. And, then, everything was gone.' He stopped. 'Fate had given me what I asked for most and when it disappeared, I could not stop it.' He laughed without humour.

'Fate.' His voice hammered the word into the air and forced any talk of it closed. The look behind his eyes spurred her to avoid his gaze.

He stacked the boards together, turning the nail side down so they wouldn't step on them. 'Stay near this side of the house. With the carriage house hidden in the rear and my going through the house back door, it's less likely for us to gather attention.'

Brandt turned and her eyes followed him.

She pulled her head back. What was it about him that captured her eyes so? *The man was sweating and she was drooling like Fillmore.*

She shut her eyes and shook her head. Putting her free hand to pinch her nostrils, she took in a breath.

Brandt turned, seeing the pinched nose, and she instantly dropped her hand.

'I do not have an elixir.' He watched her as if he thought her daft. He held the last board in his left hand. He tossed it with the others on to the ground.

He took a step closer. 'Perhaps it's you putting a bewitching spell on me.'

Her insides tumbled to her toes and back to her throat. 'That is nonsense.'

When Brandt looked at her so, she knew they weren't strangers any more. And she couldn't decipher his thoughts, or even her own.

With his right hand, her reached out and held her jaw in a light grasp, and then he moved his face closer.

'Are you sure?' he said. 'I think I am feeling some kind of enchantment. I think you are weaving some sort of charm to pull me close to you.'

'No. I don't know any charms.'

'If you did, would you use them on me?'

'Of course not.'

'My feelings are hurt.' His mouth was so close and she could feel the wisp of his breath against her lips, and the sensation of it entering her body and spreading, covering her from the inside out.

'You are playing a game,' she said.

'I have no more elixir inside me than you have a spell in your pocket.'

She put a hand flat against his chest, thinking to push him back, but she couldn't. He drew in a breath. Her hand connected them, all the way throughout their bodies. He reached up, put his hand over hers, clasped it lightly for a moment and put it at her side. But he didn't move away.

'Elixirs and enchantments are for people much different than we are,' he whispered. 'I've been down that road before and there is no going back. There's only darkness at the end.'

'I've not.'

'And you're better for it.'

He dropped her hand and looked at the house.

He stared at the door, but didn't move. She had to do something—something to take the coldness from his face.

She brushed by him to grasp the knob.

'Locked.' She sighed and looked at the heavy door

and then back over her shoulder at him. 'Perhaps you should try a window next.'

'I'll think about trying a window.' His eyes brushed her face and his crooked smile flashed, moving the conversation they'd had into the past.

An answering flutter grew from her insides. She would never forget him. Even after they'd each moved on.

She hoped they could keep in touch, at least from a distance. She would somehow see he learned a trade after the adventure was over. Perhaps, after she had her funds, if she threatened to expose him as a kidnapper, he could be persuaded to consider becoming some kind of shopkeeper. She couldn't see him inside a simple shop, though. The tavern life had roughened him too much.

She followed his eyes as he kept staring at the house. Apparently, he didn't understand how such a comfortable place could be left empty, either.

This dwelling should be open. Should have the bustle of life around it. She thought she could see a barn in the distance which would have kept the smaller livestock needed for the family.

'It's a sin to let a house ruin like this.' She spoke softly, more to herself than anyone else.

His head turned quickly to hers and his eyes flashed. 'There are worse sins.'

'Yes,' she mused. 'But this manor should have a family.'

'Who are you to speak of a family?' He put a hand to the door and she noticed he clenched his fingers. 'You detest your stepfather. Did not like your grandfather. And you talk of a marriage only as a means to produce a child.'

She stared at him, her voice quiet. 'I have an aunt and cousins, but my stepfather refuses to let a carriage driver take me near my family.'

He moved a half-step towards her and she forced herself to stare back.

'I have my sister, Gussie.' She held her chin high. 'And some day Gussie will have suitors and she'll find a man who can love her. She is my sister, half by blood and whole by heart. I would not change that.'

She sensed his rage, controlled but deep. She didn't feel the same as she had with her stepfather's anger. She knew Brandt wouldn't strike her.

'I will be able to have people to tea. And I will invite cousins to see me. I have some who have been ruined and we can all be ruined together and talk of our own adventures instead of the debacles of others.'

'Can you be so sure?' Some inflection in his voice convinced her his feelings were inward. Directed at himself.

'I have no bargains to make with the devil or creator to give me a life of sweet contentment. But I'll have the best I can have.'

He nodded, picked up the last board he'd dropped and strode to the carriage house. She heard the plank crash into the outside wall and fall to the ground as the door closed.

Brandt didn't stay inside more than the time it took him to turn around. She saw him striding to the manor's back door again. When he walked abreast of her, she saw a key in his hand. He put the key in the lock of the door and the barrier creaked open as if pulled by spirits.

He stared ahead, then turned back to her. 'Stay here,' he commanded.

She took a step forward, but the door shut in her face and she heard the sound of a latch closing. Pushing against the wood with both hands did no good. Locked from the inside. This was the cut direct.

She stood and stared, wondering if the house was his. But it couldn't be. He was from the tavern.

In a few minutes, the door opened and he shoved two pillows into her hand. 'Take these to the carriage house.' He thrust them at her and again she heard the turning lock.

She flopped the pillows against each other as she walked, trying to keep the dust off her face and coughing when the efforts failed.

When she returned, the door was again closed and he'd set out a bucket with a pan, two cups and other supplies from the kitchen.

She smiled and took them quickly back to the cupboards in the carriage house. Cups—and a bucket to carry water in. She felt quite regal herself.

By the time he'd finished, the little carriage house had two comfortable-looking mattresses side by side making a pallet on the floor, a small looking glass, a bit of cookware and even several flannel washcloths.

But then he'd taken a hammer and nailed the boards back in place even stronger than before.

She sat at the table in the darkening light, leaning back in her chair, her fingers interlaced at the back of her head, and sighed a sigh of contentment. 'I quite like this place now. You're finally getting a decent criminal mind.'

He stared at her. 'I have no more a criminal mind than you do.'

She shut her eyes, secure in the knowledge she'd done much to help him. He hadn't used his razor—the one she'd noticed while looking through the saddlebags—but he had dampened his hair and brushed it back from his face. She'd wait to offer him suggestions on buying new clothes with the coin he received from his share of the ransom.

Perhaps she could get him to secure paper and pencil for her and she could make a list so as not to forget anything.

She sat straight and looked at him. She'd been too happy with the supplies to think of asking earlier. 'Where did you get the key?'

'Perhaps I do have a bit of the blackguard in me after all.'

At the moment, he looked nothing like a blackguard. He sat in the chair, but his eyes were closed.

'Where did you get the key?' she repeated.

'I am acquainted with the man who used to live here.'

'How?'

'I grew up near here. Lived a few miles away all my childhood.'

'Is he still alive?'

'Do you wish to know the stream he washes his small clothes in?' he asked, one eye open.

'Simple questions.'

'Which I simply will not answer, Nigel.'

'I find that discourteous.'

'The same as he would find your questions.' Both eyes stared at her. 'Tomorrow will be better to discuss...

your questions,' he added. 'After sleep. I'd just returned home when you barged in my door, then I spent the day trying to talk myself out of taking you while I got horses. Then I waited until your house was quiet. Only a few hours of sleep last night. You keep a man awake.' He touched his stomach 'And hungry.'

'You will collect my ransom. You have not given me the details.' She leaned forward, feeling the success of her plans.

'The less you know, the better.' Dark eyes twinkled with a teasing gleam. 'Should you be tortured, I would not wish for you to be able to give away my secrets.'

She caught herself mid-nod and stopped. 'No one would torture me.'

'You're right. Perhaps I have not figured out how to collect the funds and have not told you yet.'

She felt a flutter of unease and stood, taking the dishes they'd used so she could take them to the well. 'Tomorrow I will go back to London, hide in your room and see the ransom is collected. I will arrange for it.'

'You can't retrieve a ransom and you needn't get anyone else involved in this.' He moved beside her.

She hurried to leave, trying to keep the plates from falling as she reached for the door. 'You wish to keep it all?'

His hand snagged out and he pulled the door wide for her to leave. When she stepped back, he stood so close behind her she could feel his presence through her clothing. 'Nigel. You cannot depend on me for much, but I would never take your funds.'

'Not…' She paused. 'Not even your half?'

'No.' He shrugged.

She realised she'd paused a moment longer than she should have while she contemplated her awareness of his body as he remained behind her. A flush of embarrassment replaced the pleasant warmth she'd felt a second before.

'I must have my share. I need to buy food, clothing and shelter and take care of Gussie.' She tried to brush away her actions.

His hand went to the small of her back and he leaned in, so close at her ear she could feel each whisper of breath as he spoke. His voice rumbled against her with the strength of an outside fire blasted with a burst of wind. 'I hope you use the funds to find an honest endeavour.'

Words escaped her mind, but the effort she used to find them went straight to her feet and she kept her head high and moved quickly out of his reach.

Katherine didn't worry because he had a plan of his own, but she hoped it good enough.

She knew if he were caught, her stepfather would not rest unless Brandt dangled from a rope and she dangled from Fillmore's tongue. She would wish to trade places with Brandt.

Augustine knew so many influential people. She should have told Brandt her stepfather had already had a man transported for theft and she had suspected his only crime had been to anger him.

At first she wouldn't have cared if Brandt might be caught. His nimbleness in keeping ahead of the magistrate was his responsibility. But now—now she couldn't see him killed.

If they were discovered she would have to admit she willingly left with Brandt. Sacrificing the remains of her reputation would be no great hardship, but sacrificing herself to Fillmore would.

And she knew her stepfather would not rest until he had her married to Fillmore and Fillmore would not be a kind husband. Once she'd tried to rush from the room after they'd eaten and he'd taken her arm to prevent her from leaving. She'd had bruises in the shape of his fingers.

His courting methods left much to be desired. Even Augustine had not left bruises on her mother.

Katherine bit the inside of her lip and watched Brandt from the corner of her eye as she filled her cup with water from the bucket.

Perhaps the safest thing would be to get the bed ready so she could sleep. They'd slept late into the morning because of staying up most of the night, then he'd collected the things from the house for her and mostly stared at the manor house.

She looked across at the mattress he'd thrown out in the night and walked to inspect it. Definitely worse in the daylight. The ones he'd brought in would be much better and, while he'd put them close, she didn't feel she had to escape from a snake or from Fillmore.

In fact, Brandt had tossed her from the bed the night before.

'Will you promise not to toss me across the floor if I sleep close to you?'

'If you sleep next to me, you do so at your own risk.'

She looked at him and at the shadows beyond his eyes. She would take the risk.

Chapter Fourteen

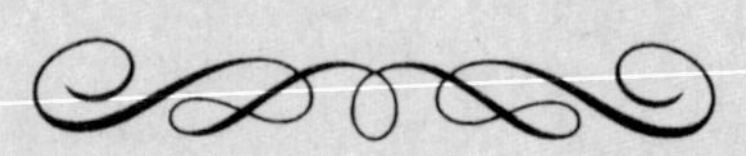

The door crashed open, waking her from the light sleep she'd finally managed, and her mind wouldn't work fast enough to sort out the details. She blinked and looked into the barrel of a gun. A rifle the size of a carriage was held by a man who looked the size of a house.

She blinked again, expecting the barrel to disappear, but it didn't. She felt Brandt's hand clench at her stomach and she stiffened against him.

Three men, seven feet tall, with staring eyes and holding weapons, moved into the room. An army.

'I did it,' she shouted the words. 'It was my plan. My idea and I kid—'

Brandt's hand clamped over her mouth and he held tight.

'Adam, could you not knock?' Brandt drawled. 'And I think the weapons have scared my lady.'

The men lowered their guns, standing stone still, staring. The one in the front barked a startled laugh and gave a quick bow, backing up. 'I will wait for you outside.' He chuckled again. 'Welcome home, little brother,' he added as they left and he pulled the door shut.

'Welcome home?' Brandt muttered, removing his hand from her mouth and sitting up. He raised an eyebrow. 'My brother. The eldest. He's always been a bit irritating.' He studied her a moment, then said quietly. 'I would prefer you do not tell him I kidnapped you.'

'I thought he was a magistrate who had followed you,' she whispered, looking into his face.

'If a magistrate arrives, I would prefer you not mention a kidnapping to him—especially.'

'I said it was my idea.' She put a hand on his chest and could feel his heart beat, and she realised he didn't have a shirt on. For a moment, they were alone in the world and he was the one person she wished to be with.

And she was a fallen woman next to a man who obviously had no idea what to do with a newly ruined lady.

Katherine saw no reason to move her hand away from him. She was quite pleased with the way his chest felt. 'I would not have you take all the blame.' In fact, she would take it all if he would keep his shirt discarded. She would even take responsibility for the fall of any empire.

'I appreciate your consideration. I'm sorry he frightened you,' he said and brushed a brief kiss across her forehead as casually as if he'd done it a thousand times. 'I do not know what I will tell my brother, but I think it best if any person of law might happen upon us, we answer questions as they are asked and do not blurt out all.'

She thought she didn't deserve such an insult to her

criminal ways, but didn't challenge him and moved to stand beside the bed. She saw a brief smile touch his lips as he buttoned his waistcoat and walked to pick up the beaten-down boots.

She scurried to put on her half-boots and the waistcoat.

He sat in the chair, slipping on his footwear. Pausing, he looked up and smiled. 'So how did it feel to be caught in bed with a drunken kidnapping tavern rat?'

'I look beyond repair,' she said, scowling into the mirror he'd brought from inside the house. 'I cannot speak with them looking like this.'

'My brothers will understand.' He stepped out the door. 'They are family. It's their lot in life.'

Family. The word settled into her mind like a soft cover falling over a bed. A family. She would get that, somehow. She would find a proper family for Gussie. Gussie had never had real grandparents, or aunts or uncles and no cousins. She could not bear to see her grow up so alone.

Outside, he found Adam and Harlan at the front of the house. Adam leaned against the railing and Harlan sat on the steps, scratching the ears of a bull terrier. His cousin, Jefferson, moved about at the edge of the weeds, but turned to join the others.

'I didn't expect such a memorable greeting.' Brandt walked to the men.

When he'd last seen his younger brother, he'd teased him that he could shave with a flannel cloth over his chin. They looked just like his family should look, only a little older. The same darker hair from his mother's side of the family, but in all else, he and his brothers were marked well by his father and Jefferson looked more like a brother than a cousin.

Harlan and Jefferson had been at university when Mary died. He was the only one of his father's sons who didn't go to Oxford. The others didn't have the same reason to stay home that he did. He'd invented an illness to keep from leaving, and the apothecary's mixture his mother insisted he take hadn't cured the pretended affliction, but had made him sick. The whole house felt the argument afterward between him and his father, but he'd been allowed to stay.

'I didn't think you'd sneak home. But you've been known to prowl quietly about in the night.' Adam grinned at his brother.

Brandt was surprised to feel no defeat at the mention of his past night-time travels. He reached out and thumped the younger two on the shoulder and then feigned an attempt to knock off Adam's hat.

Harlan yawned, sitting on the steps, and propping the rifle across his knees. 'Who's going to tell him?'

Adam turned to him. 'A man was looking for you this morning. Said he wanted to talk with you.'

'What did you say to him?' Brandt asked.

'The truth. Hadn't seen you in years. Didn't expect to see you any time soon.' He shrugged. 'Then when he left, we decided to check on your house.'

'What was he like?'

Adam's lip curled. 'About my age. In a carriage. Said his name was Peavey Fillmore.'

'The man still around?'

'We don't think so. We made sure his carriage had left before we came out to check on you. No one in the village will tell a stranger anything, anyway.'

'The man thought to marry her. He's not going to. I just haven't informed him yet.'

'He didn't look too happy with being sent away. Had a couple of his friends with him, but then, we had the advantage of surrounding the carriage so that calmed him down a little. Particularly as Harlan had the terriers with him.'

'I'll find him and talk with him.'

'Want us to go with you?'

Brandt shook his head. 'And don't tell her about the man. I don't want her to worry.'

'Want to tell us about it?' Harlan asked.

'No, but I will soon.' Another concern stopped Brandt. 'And Mother is well?'

Adam brushed it off. 'She is fine. All her little chicks are close by, but you.'

'She needn't be concerned.'

Adam looked heavenward as if expecting to see lightning bolt from the sky. 'No. We have seen you but two times in recent years, and then only because I met you in London. Your letters to Mother—she keeps them by her chair.' Adam's eyes, one brow cocked, raked over Brandt, 'She believes that rot about you staying at Albany and conversing with Wellington.'

Brandt looked at him. 'I merely tell her I speak often with one of Wellington's relatives. The man pretends to be close to him and I pretend to believe it.' He shrugged one shoulder. 'I give advice and tell him to pass it along and he assures me he does.'

'At least you've returned now.'

Brandt shook his head and looked to the road. 'I don't know if I'll be staying. I just wanted to see the house again.'

'Appreciate your honesty, Brother.' Adam adjusted his hat, tucking his hair under it. 'You could have easily lied and said you wanted to see how your family is.'

'I am pleased to see you.' Brandt smiled. 'But don't ever expect to hear me say that again.'

'It sounded so strange to me the first time I have not been able to comprehend it,' Adam said. He turned his head to look at the younger two. 'Do you think he just got lost and ended up here?'

'Yes.' Harlan nodded. 'He was always bad with directions—except with windows in the darkness.'

Adam gave Harlan a small shove towards the horses. 'His courtship methods haven't changed. His first courtship was mostly done under the bedcovers from what we could tell.' His eyes challenged Brandt to disagree and his smile said he knew Brandt couldn't.

'This isn't your concern.' Brandt knew Adam never listened. 'I'm not marrying Katherine.'

'And you took this one from her bedchamber in the middle of the night and she is not married, either to you or anyone else?'

'Could we not keep this among ourselves until I discuss it with her?' Brandt asked. 'I plan to have Mother tell everyone she hired a new housekeeper for my house. I'm going to open it again.'

Adam frowned. 'Mother will never believe she's your housekeeper. You'd be better off telling her she's your sister.'

'This is my house. My land. You should keep quiet about what happens here.' Brandt knew his words were wasted.

'And she's your woman, too,' Jefferson added.

'She is not my woman.'

'You didn't have to reach far to put your hand over her mouth when we woke you.'

Harlan looked at Adam. 'Wonder what he was keeping her from saying?'

Adam looked at Brandt's face. 'I don't know, but it probably wasn't "Good morning".' He tapped Brandt on the shoulder. 'Stop by the house and see the family.' He gave him a serious look. 'I would like it if you came by. We'll make things comfortable for you both.' He looked at the home behind him. 'And we can help you get this house ready so you won't have to stay in the carriage house.' He shook his head. *'Housekeeper?'*

Brandt agreed with a quick upturn of his head. 'I won't be here. It won't matter.'

'You could marry her. You married—' He caught himself and stopped when he saw the warning glance in Brandt's eyes. 'You married Mary. You don't care about a person's station in life.'

'Nor do I care to marry again.'

'Out of curiosity, have you ever courted a woman in the expected way?'

Brandt rubbed his arm as if he slowly rubbed warmth into his body, but the day wasn't cool enough to need the motion. He met Adam's eyes.

'I can't let anything happen to her. I couldn't save Mary and Nathan—and this one's been so sheltered…'

Adam spoke and each word had the weight of his whole being behind it. 'If you need to leave her here and go—we'll take care of her. And we'll send anybody coming along on their way.'

Brandt shut his eyes and gave an internal blink before he opened them. 'She's a high-born woman who's never had to make do on her own. I will have to find a way to get her settled.'

Jefferson spoke quietly. 'I'd say you had her settled pretty firm on that bed.'

'Her stepfather intended to force her into marriage with a man she doesn't want,' Brandt spoke. 'And this is one woman who shouldn't be forced against her will. Her husband could let his guard down at some point.'

Adam expelled a breath. 'Brandt. I swear you couldn't carry on a normal courtship if your life depended on it.'

'I am not courting this one.'

'No need,' Harlan said. 'She's sleeping so close to him in the night he can't roll over without bumping her out of bed.' He appraised Brandt, frowning. 'I swear I cannot get past the tips of a woman's fingers and you and Jefferson cannot find a woman who will say no. Life is not fair.'

'This is just a business arrangement for her.'

'Even you cannot make me believe she is paying you—' Harlan looked heavenwards.

The look on Harlan's face irked Brandt. His younger brother needed to show more respect.

'Well...' Brandt gave a look of smugness, mixed with a leer, determined to shut Harlan up '...she has offered a few pounds. Nothing overly substantial. Certainly not my worth.'

Adam snorted. 'Brandt. Your words fall so smoothly when you lie. That has not changed. "Oh, Mother,"' he mocked. '"Please send for more books. I so love to spend my time reading."'

'It's the truth,' Brandt decided not to be so smug. 'The woman with me has offered me coin.'

Adam's eyebrows rose and his chin moved forward. 'She is paying you for what?'

'Just to keep her from her stepfather. Although it is a bit more than merely a run to the country for the air.'

Adam's lips almost disappeared, but the sides moved up. 'At least this time, I suppose we will not have to listen to Father rattle the windows with curses.'

'He calmed.'

'I regretted telling,' Adam admitted, his head moving to the side. 'I thought I'd have to live with Mother forever blaming me because the two of you had killed each other.'

'Good enough for you.'

Adam gave a grunt. 'We will do our best to see that only family is aware of your movements—if that's what you wish.'

'Will you both be here tomorrow to watch over her? I want to go to London to make sure Mr Fillmore stays away. And I don't want to risk taking her with me.'

'Certainly,' Adam said.

He looked to the road, knowing he had to leave to make sure Katherine wasn't discovered. And knowing, just beyond the turn in the road, one could take a few steps to the side and be standing at a cemetery.

Mary and Nathan's last home. And the baby's.

The door opened, and Katherine stepped out.

'Katherine, my brothers Adam and Harlan. My cousin Jefferson.'

She stopped for a half-breath and stared at him, then she greeted his brothers.

'And this is Chaser,' Harlan spoke up. He looked at the dog. 'Welcome her, Chaser.' He held his hand up and clasped his fingers several times, and the dog barked once for each flash of Harlan's fist.

'That's a well-trained dog.' Katherine admired the animal.

He reached over and scratched her behind the ears. 'Pick of several litters and brings me my hat every morning.' He took off the hat and put his fingers through the holes in it. Then plopped it back on his head. 'And like having the brother I'd always wanted.'

Katherine interrupted and indicated Adam and Brandt with her hand. 'You are brothers?'

Adam and Harlan nodded.

'And your last name is?' she asked.

'Radcliffe,' Adam spoke easily.

'Is Brandt's the same?' she asked.

'Of course. We prefer to think otherwise, but our mother insists she didn't find him abandoned by the side of the road and take him in because he looked so pitiful.'

'Will the two of you be visiting Mother today?' Adam asked.

'Certainly,' Brandt said. He knew he needed to discuss his future plans with his mother. His mother would need to help Katherine set up a household.

'We will be happy to introduce you to our mother as Brandt's betrothed.' Adam smiled in Katherine's direction.

'No.' Brandt shook his head. 'Out of the question. It is ridiculous.'

'You can both decide to part directions later. This

way it will set her mind at ease about you.' Adam glared at his younger brother. 'Could you not do this one thing to make Mother happy as you have caused her a bit of grief over the past few years?'

'She's not going to live for ever,' Harlan added, shaking his head.

Brandt ground his teeth together before answering. He checked Katherine's eyes.

'Oh, I will be so happy to call it off later.' She looked at his brothers and smiled.

'Tell Mother. But tell her she must keep it a secret we're in the area,' Brandt said.

Adam gave a bow to his brother as he turned away. 'I'll send the carriage and make sure the path is clear of servants except the most trusted.'

Katherine watched the little dog bound away behind the men as they rode away.

The more she thought about it she was fairly certain Brandt owned the manor house and planned to let her stay there. His brothers hadn't asked him one question about it while in her presence. No one had mentioned it to him while she was in the room.

So everyone knew.

'You own the carriage house. Don't you?'

Eyes turned to stone. No one had ever looked at her with such distance in his eyes. 'Yes.'

'What was your wife like?'

The air changed. The elixir left.

'Alive.'

He opened the door to the carriage house. 'After you,' he said, holding it open.

She went inside and watched as he heated water to

shave. The steam rose from the bowl as he sat it on a stand. He gave her a glance before unbuttoning his shirt and she turned her eyes modestly away, moved out of the reflection of the mirror, and watched him.

'Would you like me to help?' she asked.

'Take off my shirt, or shave?' he asked, a smile crinkling his eyes.

He glanced her way, holding the wet cloth to his neck. Warmth flooded her cheeks.

'Taking off your clothes seems easier for you than keeping them on.'

'And not shaving is easier than shaving. But the blade's sharp. I would have let you heat the water, but I think this is a job for someone who has done it before. Why don't you just watch?'

He stood as if he were alone and moved the blade with a flick here and a flick there, the razor sliding across his skin, never pausing, never wavering as it navigated the contours of his jaw.

'Well?' he asked, turning when he finished shaving, still holding the razor. 'Do I look presentable?'

'You clean up very well.' She wasn't surprised to see a strong jaw—a strong pale jaw as it had not been touched by much sun. 'You shave so quickly, I'm surprised you don't do it more often.'

He put down the blade. 'The barmaids. You ask for a mug and they bring it and think they can give you an opinion on the length of your hair. I left the whiskers to irritate them.' He picked up the towel, looking in the mirror, wiping a few spots on his face. 'Shaving almost reminds me of the past. Of the house. I preferred the tavern look, particularly when it irked Rose, the barmaid.'

'Did you like the women at the tavern?'

'I suppose. Annie lives in the back and she's got a big heart that's always getting broken. Rose has no heart, but she has to walk home. So on nights when she didn't leave earlier with a friend…' he paused, letting her know it was a male '…I'd stay until she was ready to leave and see that she was home safe. The ale was always free after everyone left and on a slow night Mashburn would let them cook whatever they wished.'

'It sounds pleasant.'

'Not Rose's cooking. She liked everything overdone.' He touched his chin again. 'Surprised she didn't figure out a way to burn the ale.'

She stepped sideways, leaned around and studied his hair.

He pulled her hand to his face and her palm went out, and he held her wrist and moved her arm so her touch caressed his cheek.

'Smooth as a babe's bottom.' His eyes sparkled.

She smiled. 'Looks a bit like a plump rump to me, too.'

He breathed again and breathed strongly. She felt it cover her—the elixir—slipping down her body, cloaking her with a sensation so strong her whole body reacted.

'I thought of how you sneaked to my bed in the night. And, if it happened again, I did want to look better for you while you pushed yourself closer.' His voice and eyes held exaggerated innocence.

'Sir, you forget…' she forced herself to look into those teasing eyes, even though she thought she saw something more intense behind them '…I may have been asleep in your bed, but I was tossed from it. That's not something a woman forgets easily.'

'I was asleep.' He winked at her. 'A mistake and one should never repeat mistakes.'

She looked away from his face. 'In your sleep, you show your true feelings and I respect them.'

'My true feeling is that you're not much better with your hair than Rose is with her cooking.'

Her lips parted.

'You do not have to look at me quite so amazed,' he said. 'I can twist it up for you.'

'You're willing to—' She raised her hand and brushed it over her hair. 'The maid always did it for me.'

He frowned. 'It doesn't seem that difficult. Easier than shaving.'

She waited, hoping he'd say something more, but he didn't. 'There's no brush.'

'I've a comb. I'll twist your hair into a knot. I've seen it done.'

She sat, back straight in the chair. He walked behind her, took out the pins, moving slowly so it didn't hurt her.

He slipped the ribbon from the braid. Gentle tugs let her know he removed the plaits, taking his time, as if he were memorising the strands, and then, with his fingers spread, he started at the temples and threaded his fingers through the hair, while he brought the comb behind his movements, sliding his hands above her ears and down the length to her back. With each slow touch her heart sped. Her breathing heightened and his fingers held her in a waking dream.

'A bit more,' he said, his voice rough to her ears.

He held her head, tilting it down. Sliding his hand up the back of her neck, he gathered the hair in one hand and wound it around itself, moving to tighten it at the top of her head. She felt the pin glide against her skin, holding the hair in place, and another traced her head, before securing the locks. He dropped one and put his hand lightly on her shoulder. Then he leaned down to lift the clasp and his breath heated the back of her neck when he stood.

'I let a wisp out,' he said. His hand skimmed her skin and he nestled the lock against the bun he'd made.

'There,' he said. 'See how you like it.'

She looked around and up at him and touched where his hand had heated her skin. 'It'll do.'

'Does it feel better?'

'Much,' she said, her fingers still resting at the back of her neck.

'Good. Then we can be on our way faster.'

Brandt walked into his brother's house. The sofa fabric had changed. The arm no longer had the mend spot from the candle burn. But, the portrait Thomas Lawrence had rendered of his father still gazed over the room with a wistful look in the wise eyes. The paint had barely been dry when his father passed away and Brandt believed his father had wanted the canvas done so when he was gone, he could be in their midst.

His mother sniffled when she hugged Brandt and he thought she felt frail. His sister cried on his shoulder and then looked him up and down and said, 'My tears have obviously ruined your clothing.'

Then, a moment later his sister darted away with Katherine and Adam's wife to get the children so they could see their uncle.

'Are you going to marry again and return home?' his mother asked and he saw the hope in her eyes.

'I've really no plans to marry again, Mother.' He gave her another hug. 'I just didn't want you to have the wrong opinion of the woman I'm with. She doesn't deserve it. I was hoping you'd tell everyone you've hired staff to set my house in order and that she could be in charge of the duties there, as Mary would have if I had died.'

'Mary would understand if you married.' She brushed her handkerchief across her nose. 'And… well, you don't seem to be alone. She looked at him closely. 'And this woman?'

'We have only recently met. And she needs a home.'

'You're sure—certain—' he saw the hesitancy in his mother's face '—certain you would not wish to *stay*?'

He shook his head and his eyes met hers. 'I can't, Mother. I can never again live there.'

She opened her mouth to speak—to argue, he knew. But she closed it again and leaned forward. 'Son, are you rescuing a fallen woman?' She rotated her hand. 'You do tend to like… I mean, Mary, who was a dear, dear, woman, wasn't exactly of our social standing.'

Fury spiked inside him, but he kept his words even. He wanted no disagreement. No memories that might cause him to need to make amends. 'I did not rescue Mary. I loved her.'

'I know. I know you loved her. I do not doubt that.'

He shot a look at Adam, who shrugged as if to say it wasn't his fault he'd raised her hopes. But then, Adam had never been as quiet as Brandt would have preferred.

'I always have you close at heart as well, Mother.' He took her hand and brought it to brush a kiss over her knuckles.

Then his sister-in-law returned with his infant niece and he saw his nephew again, surprised to see the lad sprouted tall and lean.

And all the happiness he felt around him showed him what he had lost. Katherine seemed so fascinated with the children. She discussed the little girl, Gussie, with his sister, making it sound as if she spoke of her own child.

The sight of his brother's children and the way his sister-in-law tended her family brought back to his memory the times Mary and Ione had sat at the table and compared babies while the men talked of tenants and crops and horses.

Before, Mary would have made sure Nathan did not get too lively with his cousins and she would have told Ione about Nathan's latest escapade and listened at the mischief of his cousins and they would have probably whispered about 'our rascals' and they would not have been talking about the children.

He didn't even remember the first time he saw Mary. He'd paid no attention to her. Another female servant.

Usually, Mary had done the scullery work while her mother cooked. He didn't remember when he noticed her. And he wished he could remember what he'd done to her on the freezing day he'd walked outside and she'd taken revenge by dousing him from behind with a glass of cold water. Then she'd dashed inside and hidden in the servants' quarters. He'd known his father would have had a fit to catch him there, so he'd had to be careful.

It hadn't been long after when he'd begun sneaking down the stairs, outside and around to her window in the night. Going straight to her room involved too many hallways with too many doors.

And now Mary lay in a grave while he sat with his family—and wished he'd never returned.

He knew he cared for his mother and brothers. Knew it. And he wanted to be happy to see them. But everything reminded him of what was gone.

He smiled, feeling each jagged edge of the place where his heart had been.

He loved his mother. No question of that. He loved his brothers, no question of that. At least his mind told him he did. But his heart had been buried with Mary. He'd thought time would soften the memories and he thought it had. But he'd seen the empty house and it was nothing more than a shell that had once held his wife and child close.

He wanted to return to the tavern—not to the house. Not to the rooms which held the last traces of his happiness and now mocked him. But to his world which gave him a diversion and stood filled with people drinking to the demons which haunted them and laughing at the scars they carried.

But, he had to get Katherine taken care of and then

he would go back. He would drink and laugh and curse at the daylight.

He'd never again crawl into a woman's window or kidnap one.

Adam's shoulder dipped to one side and his head followed the tilt when he asked a question. 'So—should we get the fatted calf and the worst ale? I seem to remember that Brandt could drink the worst swamp water and call it fine.'

'I've got the worst brother and I call him fine,' Brandt muttered. 'And I am not talking about Harlan.'

'I knew that,' Harlan spoke when he and Jefferson stepped behind Adam. 'But we are pleased you returned—so you must count us as a bit off in our thoughts, I suppose.'

'Boys,' his mother interrupted. 'Please try to show a good example for the children. Pretend you are no longer in leading strings.'

'Have we reached that point yet, in your mind, Mother?' Adam asked.

She shook her head, then reached to pat Brandt's arm. 'Every day—I hope it will happen.'

'It might some day,' he said. 'Just don't count on it.' He gave her a kiss to the cheek, told them goodbye and walked out the door with Katherine.

'You seemed quiet at your family's house,' Katherine said. 'As if you didn't feel at ease.'

'I don't,' he said. 'I don't belong there any more. I'm not a part of them.' He stopped. 'Now that I think back, I never was. I didn't want to go to university. I felt more comfortable with Mary's family.' He paused. 'Perhaps the way I feel more comfortable with the people of the tavern.'

'I'm sure they wish for you to be a part of the family.' She put a hand on his arm.

'They don't know. They think it is all grief for my wife. I hope they always believe that.'

Chapter Fifteen

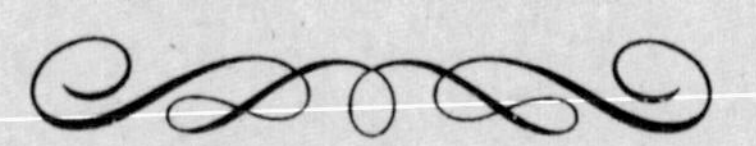

By the time they returned to the carriage house, Katherine would have liked nothing better than a warm bath and a well-made bed.

'I'll be outside,' Brandt said.

'Are you sure?'

'Yes. Bar the windows and doors. If anyone is searching for you here, I'll be there to see him. I'll be watching the door from outside with my back against a tree. Besides, they would think you're in the main house. My brothers discovered us too easily. I don't want anyone else doing the same.'

'You can be inside with me.'

He acted as if she'd not spoken for a second, then he said, 'It doesn't seem safe to me tonight.'

She remembered the way he'd touched her hair and the kiss, and she didn't think it was only the chance of someone finding them keeping him outside.

'My brother Harlan will be bringing his dogs and we'll all be keeping watch. Nothing can get by his dogs without us knowing.' He stood at the doorway, his hand on the frame. 'Remember, bolt the door behind me.' He closed the door as he finished speaking.

She walked to the door, putting the bar over it as he'd asked. If he was that determined to stay on the outside, she'd let him.

He wanted to live the rest of his life alone. He had no idea how fortunate he was to have a mother and brothers, a sister-in-law and nieces and nephews. No idea.

The only way she could have such a family around her was to have the ransom. Fillmore's family was no better than garden slugs and she couldn't bear the thought of having them in her life.

She'd asked Brandt about fifty different ways the simple question of how he planned to get the ransom and he'd told her the same answer over and over. She wasn't to concern herself with it.

And she really wasn't concerned about it for herself. But she had to think of Gussie and Mrs Caudle.

She couldn't have the family Brandt did, but perhaps it would be best for her. She'd have a family she'd chosen. Her half-sister. Mrs Caudle. She'd find other people without families and together they'd manage just fine. But first, she had to secure something more for them. Families had to have shelter and food.

The next morning, a quick slap to the outside of the door woke her. Brandt stood there and he had the reins in his hand. Hercules stood behind him, chewing grass as if all was right with the world.

'Remember,' he said the word distinctly, 'Adam is watching the road. No carriage can get this way without him seeing. Harlan will be spending most of the day in the woods and will have his two dogs with him. Since he's been a lad, he's always trained those dogs to do just as he wants. No one can get near the house without you knowing.'

'No one could find me, could they?'

'I'm about to find out. I'll go and see how Fillmore and Augustine are faring.'

He wore the old hat she'd worn before. 'Don't expect a hearty welcome. You could not look more disreputable,' she said.

He scratched his cheek. 'Yes.' He swooped closer to her ear. 'The first time you saw me.'

He was on the horse in a flash, leaving a soft trail of laughter behind him.

Katherine watched him leave, the carriage house suddenly seeming dark, dusty and nothing more than a forgotten stack of boards.

When the horses disappeared, she took a moment to take stock of herself, and feel the strength she had inside. For the first time in her life, she had no one to answer to. And no one to hide from—at least in the carriage house.

She'd been hiding since her mother became ill. Hiding from Augustine so he'd not notice her and take out his rages on her. Then hiding from Fillmore so she would not have to pretend she could tolerate him.

This was the first week of a new beginning. She would be dead to her old world. Now, she would need a different name and history to go with her tragic widowhood. She would miss Brandt. Miss him terribly. And when anyone asked about her husband, she would think of him and it would be easy to be melancholy. Loneliness seeped inside her, causing an ache in her heart.

She'd never missed a man's company before. Never.

She walked around the house, a hand shading her eyes while she inspected the walls. Very little actually stood between her and the inside of the house. Surely if she trespassed she'd only find empty rooms and rugs faded by window sunlight. What harm could there be in seeing forlorn and forgotten walls and floors?

She walked forward, tramping down the purple vetch with light-deprived stems. A dragonfly lit on the door frame. Then the insect flittered away, drawing her eyes upwards, to the windows.

She could find a way to get in. No one would have to know.

Brandt had said his brothers were near. She called, 'Mr Radcliffe.' She waited. 'Mr Radcliffe.'

Finally, Brandt's brother and two dogs stepped out of the woods. 'I'm feeling nervous with Brandt gone,' she said. 'I just wanted to know I'm not alone.'

He shook his head. 'Adam's watching the road at the front and the dogs and I have been enjoying the trails around the house.'

'It must be tedious for you to sit and stare at this place.'

'Not at all. I'm mostly walking around the house, letting the dogs have their way. They'll let me know if anyone approaches. We're enjoying the cooler weather.'

Katherine nodded and they talked about his pets for a while, then he tipped his hat and moved back into the woods.

She doubted he'd ever look her way again because he was so aware of the woods.

At the rear door of the house, Katherine tried the latch again, just to make certain. Locked.

She moved to the front door, admiring the porch, and noticed that if a person were not too particular, the boards over the windows just to the side of the porch could become a haphazard ladder, especially since the windows on the lower floor were tall, majestic ones. She could pry a board loose to give her extra space for her toes, but it could work. Above that, she saw a ledge to leverage herself on to the porch roof. Then two windows—just the right size to open.

She took off her boots to give her more flexibility in her feet. And she got a knife from the things Brandt had collected and stuck it in her waistband.

Testing her foot on the lowest board, she began her climb. Without a thought in her head except where her toes might go next or her hand might go, she moved upwards until she found herself on the ledge.

Walking on the porch roof was easy, but she only had two windows to try. The first did her no good. When she slid the knife into the casement of the second one and pushed up against the pane dividers with her fingertips, the glass moved.

She worked harder, feeling the sweat on her temple as she bit her lip and worked her fingers under the base of the window. When she had enough space to push her hands on to the sill, she held her breath and ratcheted the glass up.

She truly did have the mind of a criminal, she thought, as she straddled the ledge and then ducked her head and went inside.

Dust blanketed the room, but she didn't see the bare chamber she'd expected. The house looked as if the owner had left for the season and hadn't returned. All the furniture and trappings were arranged for living. A candle near the window had wilted sideways, melting from summer heat, but not enough to puddle in the holder. A ghost would be quite comfortable.

And with more stealth than a spirit, Katherine began exploring.

First, she found a library smelling of dust and, perhaps, mildew.

She walked the room, trailing her fingers over the spines, moving a book here and there, dusting a bit to see the books better. Reading *The Parent's Assistant* on one spine, she gave the book a tug, pulling it from the others. The book had an ink splotch on the cover as if someone had accidentally dropped a full pen on to it.

Her own mother had read the tales in this book to her when she was young and the memory gave Katherine the only warmth she'd felt in the house. She opened it and heard the creak of its bindings. But she could only read a few words before feeling loss.

Shutting the book, she held the volume almost as a talisman, walking to the other rooms.

She saw the master's chamber, the sitting room and the table where the mistress of the house did her *toilette* and she'd left behind a perfume bottle with rust-coloured rings in the bottom.

A miniature of a beautiful woman sat on a tabletop. She walked near it. A sketchpad caught her eye. She picked up one dusty edge of the cover, and opened it. Drawings of a boy's face smiled back at her and she immediately released the cover.

In the nursery, Katherine thought it odd to see a child's room neglected, still with clothing and toys. Little soldiers stood in one corner as if waiting for a boy to take them to war. She saw a wooden bear lying on its side, with a soldier toppled at the animal's feet. She picked up the bear and man, placing them straight.

A carved, round rabbit, bigger than the bears, sat on the bed. He looked a bit lopsided in the eyes. His ear had tooth marks on it and she could imagine an infant catching the rabbit and sputtering over the creature.

At the thought of the child, she took a step backwards.

The house felt as if it were a shrine, even though it appeared the owners had merely left and forgotten to return. A shrine to happiness that showed through the dust on the window curtains and tabletop scarves with flowers embroidered on the edges.

She'd begun to feel as base as the people who took their meals at a hanging.

Families didn't leave so much behind. Even the very wealthy. And a house might be closed up for a season, but the saplings in the yard told her this house had been boarded for quite some time.

The dust of the house clung to her, but it wasn't only dust. She felt remnants of the family's remains. If she searched the grounds, she expected she'd find a cemetery. She didn't want to see the graves.

She brushed her hands over her arms, trying to wipe away the feelings. Before she could take another step back, she saw a framed drawing.

She'd never seen a drawing of a man holding a child. Never.

She stepped closer. 'Brandt,' she whispered. For a moment, she couldn't look away. The drawing wasn't perfect, yet it was. Because where skill lacked, heart had replaced it.

Quickly, she rushed to the open window, trying to get to fresh air before the house suffocated her.

Gasping, Katherine thrust the book under her arm and slid through the window. Even holding the volume, she managed to slam the window shut from the outside.

But then she realised she still had *The Parent's Assistant.* She reached to open the window, but this time her luck didn't hold. The window stayed in the casement. Standing on the roof, she felt like a target for evilness.

Tucking the book inside her waistband, she ignored spears of fear as she backed down from the roof, moving with all the speed she could muster.

She'd trespassed, not just into Brandt's house, but into his heart, and she'd discovered his memories.

As they approached the Hare's Breath, Hercules sighed and Brandt patted his back. But it didn't change things.

The horse hated him. The beast lunged for every uneven surface and added as much bounce as possible.

Brandt thought of the home where he'd lived. Going inside the house hadn't been hard after the first few steps, but he'd stayed in the servants' quarters and they held few memories for him. As long as he'd kept his mind directly on his tasks, he'd felt no pangs of regret.

Above stairs, though—above stairs would be entirely too unsettling.

He continued on and swore never, ever, ever again

to go to a woman's aid if she approached him for anything more than a simple handkerchief. Rescuing Katherine had taken some of the barbs from his conscience. He would not add more by staying too long with her.

But he knew he could not let her down. He'd let Mary down. He'd have to find a way to take care of Katherine. From a distance.

He didn't need more temptation. He had not been able to resist more than five minutes of desire with Mary and, even though he was no longer a youth, he didn't think he'd changed that much.

From the first time he'd lain with Mary, he'd known he wanted to spend the rest of his life with her. From the first time he'd kissed her.

He'd never expected to kiss her goodbye.

Everything in his life had to return to the way it was. There wasn't enough of him left to settle into the house again. He belonged in his boarding house room and the Hare's Breath. He just had one problem to take care of first. He would get Katherine settled.

The horse stopped in front of the tavern as if he'd known exactly where Brandt was going. Brandt dismounted and Hercules slung his head, almost pulling the reins from Brandt's hands. Brandt tied him to a post anyway.

When Brandt walked into the Hare's Breath, no one looked up or sideways or any way but the same way they'd been perusing before he entered. But then, he'd only been away a few days—not a truly unusual occurrence.

Yet, everything seemed different to his eyes—much as if he'd been gone years.

And he knew his appearance wasn't ignored. After a while, he'd hear *Brandt's Buttons* from the piano player. The man made up a song for everyone.

Rose brought him an ale before he'd taken a seat. 'Man came around asking about you. I didn't tell him nothing and thought he left, but he stayed around outside and asked questions of that bag of wasted bones, Toady, about you. Toady told me about it the next night. Said he told him to go north like he was going to Cambridge and he thought your family has land about a half-hour's ride before he got there.'

'How'd he know?'

'It's where your wife's buried. When you first came here, you'd talk about her grave sometimes.'

'I'd forgotten.'

After he thought of what she'd said, he stared at her. 'You weren't working here then. How'd you know?'

She gave a one-sided shrug and brushed some crumbs from the table onto the floor. 'You might have only mentioned it once or maybe twice when you were sotted, but a man like you, who doesn't talk much—well, makes us wonder. Gives us something to do if we puzzle you out. We remember things you say and share it.'

'I've never once asked any questions of anyone here.'

She rubbed her hands together, dusting away the specks from the table. 'And couldn't you still tell most of what's happened to us to bring us here?'

He paused, then answered, 'I suppose.'

She leaned over, putting a casual arm around his shoulders and giving a small squeeze. 'And it didn't hurt that one night while you were here, a key slipped out of your pocket. Remember that time I sat in your lap and you pushed me out?' She winked. 'And then later Annie left. Well, your key must have fallen on to the floor while I was on your lap trying to hang on. So Annie took it to your room and looked inside the box under your bed where you keep papers and letters and such that you pick up from the bank.'

'You should be in the workhouse.'

She shook her head. 'You kept too much to yourself. Wanted to know what sort of fellow you were.' She pulled back and gave him a big smile. 'Just making sure a bad sort wasn't walking me home. And that, my friend, is how I've kept out of the workhouse.'

He wondered how much he'd missed when he assumed no one paid any attention to him.

He'd really had his head deep in the bottle and misery.

The memory of Katherine tucked away in a carriage house kept poking at him. He had to finish what he'd started.

Reaching into his waistcoat pocket, he extracted a coin. He held it between two fingers, raising it so Rose could see.

Rose did a double take when she saw the coin, then she snatched it from his fingers. She smiled and took his hand to pull him up. 'Finally,' she said.

He didn't let himself be moved, but slipped his fingers around hers and nudged her back to the chair. 'No. Sit. This is for conversation.'

'Brandt.' She shook her head and fell into the seat. 'I'm too tired to talk if I have to make sense.' She propped her elbow on the table and shut her eyes. 'But let me try.' She took a breath. 'You're a stallion. A warrior. Whatever. Whatever. Best I never had.' She opened her eyes. 'So why'd you want to talk to me?'

'Any news of a woman being taken against her will?'

Her eyes widened. 'You didn't.'

He gave a firm shake of his head. 'I didn't.'

'No. No one's been discussing such a thing. The man looking for you didn't mention that.' She raised her brows. 'And I'm takin' it personal that you won't give me a try.'

He stood and took her hand, raising it to brush a kiss over it. 'Told you, Rose—you wouldn't be impressed.'

She chuckled. 'Prob'ly wouldn't.' She looked at the piano player's back. 'I like a man with a lot of talents.' She shrugged, never taking her eyes from the other man. 'He's a poet, too.'

Brandt heard the first notes of *Brandt's Buttons* and watched Rose stare at the back of the piano player's head.

'You know, Brandt, death-bed promises don't count.' Rose kept staring at the piano player.

'I've not made any death-bed promises.'

'Yes. You did. Maybe not out loud. But you sure did.' She reached across and took a sip from his drink, and kept the mug in both hands. 'Men are my work. I see all kinds. And you're normal enough and you've not married again. You made a vow strong as any marriage promise when your wife died. Just not normal for a man to be alone as much as you.'

'I lost more than just a wife.'

'All the more reason for you to marry again.'

Then a stranger entered the tavern—a hulking man whose overlarge shoulders seemed to collapse in on to his body. He took a seat at the other side of the room. Brandt hardly gave him a second glance, until he saw Rose's mouth open and she stared.

'That's him. The one who asked about you,' she whispered, her back to the stranger.

Brandt took the mug from Rose's hands, stood and moved to the other table. He handed the drink to the newcomer. The man raised his eyes to Brandt, 'Should I know you?'

'If you're looking for Miss Wilder, then perhaps it's best you don't.'

'Don't know you, or don't look for her?' He smiled and put the ale to his lips.

'Both. I have her.'

Fillmore put the mug onto the table, splashing some liquid from it. He raised his head and his nostrils widened. His eyes turned into narrow slits. 'Bring her back or Augustine will be telling everyone she was forced away.' His voice rolled like smoke under a doorway. 'You'll hang for this. I'll pay the man who hangs you myself, so he ties your hands, but goes easy on the rope around your neck so it don't slide. No quick snap. You'll strangle. Slow and sweet.' He took a drink from the mug and cold eyes looked into Brandt. 'I'll be there to watch, in front, with my wife, Katherine, by my side. And then I'll take her home to celebrate, in bed.' He smiled. 'A wedding present. From me to her.'

Brandt leaned closer to his face, forcing himself to ignore the fetid air surrounding Fillmore. 'She's already celebrated getting away from you and if you touch her, I will put you alive in a crypt. One no bigger than a dog would fit in.'

'You best not have touched her,' Fillmore said, jumping to his feet. 'She'll pay dearly for it. And so will that scrawny gnat of a sister she has.'

'She's not returning to you.'

Fillmore smiled, the kind that would make the hair on a dog's back stand. 'Tell her that her sister will be in a madhouse, if Katherine doesn't come home to me.' Then he smiled, let out an ale belch and said, 'When her father tells the magistrate his daughter's been abducted, Katherine won't be able to defend you. Not if it means her little sister pays for it—in one form or another.'

Katherine would never let the child be put in a madhouse. And Brandt couldn't either. He couldn't let a child Nathan's age be locked away.

Fillmore strode to the door. 'Tell Katherine to return now and she can have the gnat. I'm a generous man to those I care about, and those I don't care about I'd like to roast on a pit. Sadly, there's laws against it and we have to make do with a noose.'

'We'll be talking again soon.'

'I'm looking forward to it.' Fillmore eased his shoulders through the doorway.

Brandt told Harlan he'd returned and Harlan had faded back into the woods, letting the dogs keep watch.

'Open up, Katherine. It's me.' The moments ticked into an eternity while he waited for her to unbar the door.

The door opened, a lamp behind her making her hair halo into frazzles around her face, and sleepy, innocent eyes stared at him. His throat caught. He took the bar from her hand and put it back into place on the door.

He touched her arm, moved inside and took her fingers.

Brandt waited, spending this last moment with her before everything changed. 'Fillmore still plans to marry you.' He couldn't tell her about Gussie or what Fillmore had said. She'd sacrifice herself for her sister.

Her hand tightened on his.

He put his other palm to his forehead. 'I felt concerned—leaving you so long.'

'All is well,' she spoke, the words a mix of statement and question while she studied him.

'No. It's not. Fillmore knows you're with me and he knows where my family lives.'

The words fell into the air.

'I'll go somewhere else.' She moved back, touching his shoulder. He froze in place. 'I just need funds. Money does everything a person needs. And Mrs Caudle will bring Gussie. You can help her get to me. Or I'll hire someone else.'

He turned his head so she couldn't see his face.

She sat on the edge of the bed, putting her feet on the floor. 'When will I have the funds?'

'Funds?' he asked.

Katherine couldn't think of what to say. She had to have the money. *Had to have it.*

Another man had misled her. The suitor who'd proposed had wavered, but remained firm when the manure was delivered to his door, but when she'd said she couldn't leave Gussie behind, he'd laughed in her face. And now, Brandt—perhaps her last hope—had failed her.

'You can stay here,' he said.

'I do not want your charity. I want a life away from my stepfather and I want my sister. I will pay you and I will need money to do that and to live on. You could marry again. Your next wife will not take well to a woman living in her house.'

'I am not going to marry.'

Holding out her right hand, she used her left forefinger to tap her palm. 'Ransom. Here. I want to take the money my stepfather married my mother for. My grandfather's. It's rightfully to take care of Gussie and me.'

Only the width of a cloth separated them.

He spoke as if he hadn't heard her. 'You must give up your so-called criminal mind. And no plans to murder anyone, ever again. Or kidnap your sister.'

'Brandt. I cannot promise such. I've too many years left in front of me.'

Determination flashed from the set of Brandt's jaw, the lift of his eyebrows as he looked at her. 'You don't need his money.'

She did. Death had taken her father when she was young. Her mother had been in the grave for four years and she still missed her. Even Gussie had not filled the void completely, but she'd helped.

For her, the world lay in front of her. For Brandt, everything shadowed behind him and each day took him further from the memories of his loved ones. And he refused to release them.

Katherine knew she would have a family. A family of her own making, but none the less people who cared about her. She would make friends with dowagers and women who had no prospects, and maybe she would find an orphan to raise. She would find some skill to augment it and take care of Gussie. It didn't matter to Katherine whether Gussie would speak much. She could talk. She just wouldn't around Augustine. She hid from him and he knew it. And he would make Mrs Caudle bring her to him sometimes in the evenings, question Gussie and rage at her for not speaking.

'I'll make sure your father can't get near you.' He touched her arm in reassurance. 'I'll be there to keep you safe and get you married.'

She took in a breath and held it, so she could move forward enough to look into his face safely. The shadows were coming back. He'd been back to London and it showed on his face. She was certain he'd been at the tavern. She could sense him pulling away and taking himself back into the life he'd had.

She reached up, an excuse to touch him, and let her fingertips brush down the unruly bit of hair just curling at the side of his neck.

Katherine swayed closer, inhaling. 'You've done so much for me. So much, Brandt. And I want you to know I appreciate it.'

His hand reached to her waist, stilling her, and holding her back from him. This time, she felt her insides tremble at the contact, fighting the swirls of warmth and the awareness of him which radiated out from his touch.

'I have to return to London and convince Fillmore I'll never marry him,' she said.

'I'd planned to get my brothers and go back and discuss it with him.' Brandt sat at the table, twisting a shred of hemp in his hands, the strands of rope invisible in the darkness. 'It will be no sacrifice to risk the noose. If that is what it takes to save a woman and a child, then so be it.'

A cold shudder racked Katherine's body. A moment passed before she could breathe again.

Chapter Sixteen

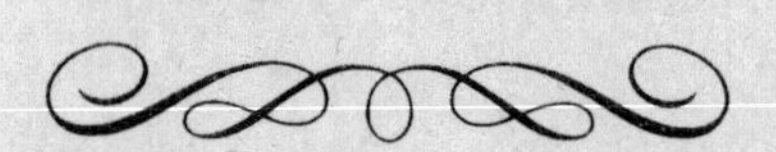

The sound of Katherine's gasp filled the room. Even in Augustine's care, she'd been protected somewhat. She wouldn't fare the same with Fillmore as a husband. He couldn't let him have her.

'Brandt...' Her voice whispered into the room. 'Tell me what your brother meant about your courtship?' she asked. She moved away, lowering herself to the pallet.

He looked to the bed, only able to make out the barest outline of her body.

'Mary worked for my family, and Adam discovered I was leaving my room in the night and visiting Mary's. He pretended illness so he could stay home from Sunday services and, while the house was empty, he nailed Mary's window shut from the inside with enough nails to build a small house.' Brandt looked at the motionless mound on the bed. 'I pretended the same illness the next Sunday so I could pry them loose.'

'Your parents suspected nothing?'

Her voice reminded him of the way a woman might speak to a frightened animal to calm it, but he didn't need the compassion. It wouldn't change anything of his memories.

Stretching his legs, he leaned against the chair back. 'They were concerned with making sure Adam conducted a proper courtship. Adam had fallen in love with Ione. He was chaperoned every moment he was near Ione and could not as much as steal a kiss. He endured endless conversations with her grandmother. I wasn't courting and, since I was younger, my parents weren't concerned because I hadn't shown interest in attending any events to dance or speak to women. I spent a lot of time dozing in my room. My parents thought I was reading constantly and might be interested in the clergy.'

He stopped twisting the rope and let it fall to the table while he remembered the stolen moments with Mary. 'After a picnic, Adam was being chided for sitting too close to Ione and I snickered. He didn't take it well. My parents were shocked at what he said. If I hadn't charged across the room, trying to punch him senseless, they *might* have believed my innocence.' He shook his head, remembering the tussle and his father shoving them apart.

His father had furiously forbade any more nighttime trysts and Brandt became determined to wed Mary.

'Mother said if I waited until I was nineteen, and Mary was seventeen, and courted properly, she would see if she could convince Father we should marry. They didn't want my wife to be a servant, but didn't feel right not letting me marry her—especially when they guessed I'd spent a considerable amount of time in her bed.'

Her head turned and her voice faded. She sounded far away.

'You obeyed your father?' she asked.

He shrugged again. 'Not willingly. In the wintertime, her window froze shut. It was a cold winter except for the few times she managed to get past the others and make it to my room.'

Brandt remembered trying to keep snow off his boots so he wouldn't leave tracks in the house, trying not to leave tracks in the snow and still not being able to get the window open.

'After I married,' he continued and felt himself smile, 'Adam told me he'd overheard our parents and they knew I'd changed the time of my visits to Mary. I crawled in her window before first light and she pushed me out when she had to start the fires. Father agreed to the marriage because he was tired of Mother asking him if Mary looked to be increasing.'

She sat, tucking the covers tightly under her arms. 'You loved her a lot.'

He didn't speak right away. And he didn't feel the need to. Because he felt Katherine understood. Or at least, understood as much as someone could who hadn't been in the same situation.

'I cannot imagine loving anyone else as much as Mary.'

'Did she know it?'

He let her words rest in his mind a moment. 'I suppose she did.'

He waited, thinking she wouldn't speak again, and then she said. 'I almost envy her.' She spoke with more force. 'I do envy her the love she had.'

'Mary deserved more.'

'She would be angry with you for staying in the sadness.' The words were soft—not accusing. 'And the way you've spent your time in the tavern.'

She spoke in such a gentle tone, he felt nothing but an awareness of her thoughts. No blame.

'Where else can I go late into the morning?' he responded, not feeling the need to justify himself, but to explain. 'When all I can think of is her face, and Nathan's laughter? And how I let her down. I long for the touch of Mary's hand so much I feel the hunger as pain. She has nothing of her left behind.'

This time he filled the silence. 'The tavern folk don't care about my problems. They laugh and cry about their own woes. Their voices drown the thoughts in my head and, with ale added, I usually don't think of the past. Better than being alone where all I can hear is the memories.'

He'd fallen into his words so much, he didn't realise she'd crossed the room until her hand touched his shoulder. 'You have brothers. A whole family. And they care for you. Doesn't that ease anything?'

He put his fingers over hers. 'No.' He gave a dry chuckle. 'It doesn't. Because I had something else. Something golden. Separate from them.'

He stood and, with one arm, pulled her against him, letting his face rest against the silk of her hair, smelling of lavender. Comfort flooded into him.

'When you were gone, I went into the house.'

His body tightened. 'You did not.'

She turned, moving away, and pulled out the tattered book she'd taken and put it in his hands.

Then the fury clogged his mind. Part of him distanced itself and felt amazement Katherine had managed to get into the house. She'd looked into the upper floors. Rooms he'd not been in since he'd left for London with Mary. She'd walked in Mary's house.

He'd had his brother handle the servants and close up the house. Board it, so no one could go inside again. The house was Mary's. Her castle. Their happiness.

And without a by-your-leave, the moment his back was turned, the uppity duke's granddaughter had somehow found a way into the house and looked at the world Mary had left. 'I can't believe you did such a thing. I can't believe you would betray me so.'

She stepped back, palms flat against the door behind her. 'Yes.'

He slapped the book on to the table and she jumped a step back. 'What right did you have to go to the upstairs?'

'None,' she said.

'You had no right to touch this book. You went to the family rooms. I didn't leave the servants' quarters,' he sputtered. 'How dare you? I was going to have all her things removed before I let anyone step foot in it.'

He heard his voice and heard the anger. And pain. 'I built it for her. Mary and Nathan. And the little girl Mary wanted so badly.' He turned his back to her. 'I should never have brought you here. Never.'

'I shouldn't have done it,' she said. 'I wish I hadn't. But I saw inside her heart and saw how much she loved you.'

'There's never been any question on that.'

'Marry me,' she whispered. 'Please. I can't let the man Mary loved die for me. I can't.'

He stood. 'Don't follow me.'

* * *

He'd been gone for a time when she heard the first creak.

She crept to the outer door, looking about. Nothing moved, except a few rustles from Apple and Hercules. They were both in their stalls, so Brandt remained.

She heard the creak. Boards being removed from the house in the darkness. The thuds as they hit the ground.

Katherine crawled back to her bed, imagining the grief he carried with each step. Wishing he would return. Leaving the lamp on.

When she heard the door open, she didn't move, but then the silence engulfed her.

He stood by the pallet, his back to her, and unbuttoned his shirt. He slipped it from his shoulders and tossed it lightly on the back of the chair. 'I took the boards from the door away.'

She heard the thump as he tossed his boots to the side.

'If I were in London,' he spoke, 'I would not even be thinking of bed. Half the night is gone, but I would not be any more ready to sleep than if it were afternoon.'

He leaned back, resting his head on the wall. 'I would probably be at the Hare's Breath and the boy who plays the piano would have played a song he calls *Brandt's Buttons*.'

'The tavern sounds entertaining.' She kept her words gentle, willing them to work as a balm to Brandt and to keep him talking.

'Sometimes by morning I have dozed a bit at the table. Then one of the women would wake me. When I walk home, I can see the sunrise and, for some reason, I often am irritated at the sun shining through the fog. I am thankful there are so many foggy days and so much soot in the air.'

She didn't think he'd have spoken so easily except for the darkness.

She heard a sound which could have been called laughter. 'I am alone. Or at least I consider it so. Yet I surround myself with people. Even as I'm walking in the morning, others are about their business. I may not know the name of the rag men I see, nor the coal boys or the pickpockets, but we often share greetings when the air is clear. Sometimes I help with their work—except the pickpocket, of course. He just tells me of the things he learns about the people he steals from.'

He reached to straighten his boots, standing one beside the other, lining them up just so.

'After I lost those I cared about most, I couldn't have silence about me. Every time I was alone, I could hear memories of their voices, taunting me with what was gone for ever.'

'You could find other ways to hide from your thoughts besides a tavern.'

'Not at four in the morning. I had to get away from all who knew me. Their sadness and sympathy—I couldn't look them in the eye.'

'Surely there are more important things for you to do than to spend your nights with dissolute people.'

'No. I am fond of them—even Rose. Except when she gets a few drinks—she has the most vile mouth I've ever heard on a person.'

He stretched out on the pallet, clasped his hands behind his head, the muscles of his forearms showing in the darkness and a darker shadow under his arm.

He took in a deep breath.

'We were in London,' he spoke. 'Nathan had wanted to ride in the coachman's seat and I let him. But he stood and the horses bolted and he fell, hitting his head on the cobblestones. He died the next morning. Wednesday morning. My wife died on a Thursday night, two days before her twenty-fourth birthday. One day after she watched her son die.'

She heard the sound of his breath expelled. 'I'd had the modiste make her a new ball gown, with ribbons to match Mary's eyes. The dress arrived Friday morning when I was getting the box to bring Mary back home. Wednesday.' He raised his fingers, tapping his thumb against a finger with each word. 'Thursday. Friday.'

He pushed his fingers through his hair. 'She hadn't been able to sleep a moment since Nathan's accident. I had the physician treat her. But the medicine made her ghastly ill and she couldn't catch her breath. He gave her something to ease her breathing, but it only made it worse. Too much worse. She'd always been susceptible to fits of gasping for air, but this time, she couldn't ever catch her breath.'

She shuddered. 'When Mother died, I sent a maid to wake my stepfather's valet so he could be told.' She shrugged. 'I didn't hear from him until after his morning meal, when I heard the crash of him throwing her chair at the window. He was furious she'd left him.' She met Brandt's eyes. 'He felt no grief, only fury. His wife had found a way to escape.'

Brandt spoke, his voice rigid. 'He may have felt the sadness in a deep place he couldn't show.'

She couldn't let her stepfather be found innocent. 'I

would believe such grief of you, of almost anyone, but I saw what I saw and it wasn't any kind of melancholy. He raged so many hours, but showed only a few moments of mourning, and those when callers arrived.'

'You can't be so positive of his true thoughts.'

'I'm certain. You never chuckle over the loss of someone you love when you take her jewellery to be sold.' She clasped her right hand over the knuckles of her left. 'What happened to your wife's gems?'

'I suppose my brother has them for safekeeping. I told him to do as he must, but I did not want the house changed. I wanted it to remain just the way it had been with us. For ever.' He shook his head. 'Which isn't possible.'

Katherine sat on the mattress, watching Brandt.

'You're really not alone, Brandt.' She might as well have spoken to the ceiling for all the acknowledgement he gave.

'You have a whole family that cares for you.' She pulled a thin cover around her, but not for warmth. 'And the people in the tavern.'

'I'm sure they care for me and I care for them, and we go along the same as always.'

'Your mother loves you.'

'And I tell her the joys of life in my letters and I'm sure she sees through it, but she appreciates the flowery words and I appreciate her pretending to believe them. And she has written to me that I am her worrisome child and she wishes I would come home so she could feel her family is together, but she understands that I don't.'

'Can't you?'

He turned to her, face expressionless. 'I can take

the boards off the house, but they're there to stay in my mind.'

She waited, watching his face for emotion. 'Just open a window.'

'But I have no windows to let the light in.' He shrugged. 'They were there once, so I know what it feels like.'

'Make new ones.'

His lips turned up, but the smile didn't reach his eyes. 'No glass panes. No opening to put them in.' He shook his head.

'Get a different carpenter.'

'I have had helpful carpenters all about me and I do not even care to see what kind of windows they might make. I can imagine broken panes and windows trying to overlap, and the beauty of the day outside twisted through warped glass, and winter winds coming in.'

She shook her head. 'Perhaps your mother really meant you're her child who thinks too much and should just settle into a pleasant life. You *do* have a family that can take you in. I don't.'

'And you have windows inside you, Katherine, and they let light in of all different colours.'

She pictured the windows of cathedrals. 'Stained glass?'

'Un-stained glass. You have no idea.'

'Perhaps that makes me seem bland.'

'Bland is good.' He sat up and looked down at her. 'You planned a kidnapping. If we *were* going to discuss you, you're definitely a bit cracked.'

She adjusted the covers at her chest. 'That's not a nice thing to say.'

He huffed out a breath. 'Have I ever claimed to be nice?'

'You're a cad. A layabout. I forgot. But your family likes you.'

'Mothers lean towards liking their children because they birthed them. My father and I never saw eye to eye and my brothers and I keep our distance so we'll get along. Now go to sleep.' He paused, waited a long breath. 'You do seem to rattle a bit when the wind blows the slightest amount.'

'My pardon.' She stretched out her elbows and bumped him.

'You're supposed to say that after you jostle someone—accidentally, and not before.' He touched her elbow and slowly pushed it back against her body.

'Planning ahead.' Katherine turned. 'Or trying to make a spot for the light to get in. Marry me. It would make so little difference in your life and so much difference in mine.'

He rolled over and his arm draped over her as casually as if he circled a pillow. An awareness shot through her body, jolting her into a wide awakening. 'I accept your proposal, Katherine. I'll get a special licence tomorrow. You're right. It will be easy enough to do and won't mean anything to me. But do not expect any windows of light to suddenly appear and do not expect me to live with you in Mary's house. I'll be leaving as soon as I get you settled. You will be protected with a world of people around you. You'll have respectability, but never a true husband. I can't live here. It's no longer my home. Perhaps it never was. Now I realise that's why I took Mary away. It was for me. Not her.'

He pulled her closer, kissing the side of her neck. 'I fit among the mismatched people of the tavern.'

'You could fit among your true family if you wanted.'

He snuggled in closer. 'But I don't wish it. I don't need the Sunday dinners and the world my father planned out for my brothers and me. The soot suits me better than the summertime roses in the vases and the winter evergreens for luck.'

'You prefer darkness over light.'

'Shadows. The shadows you can see through and not the harsh sunlight that demands a clean-shaven face.'

'You can't hate shaving that much.'

He pulled over her so that he could brush his chin against her cheek several times, creating a friction that warmed her. He settled behind her.

'I don't hate it at all,' he said. 'For the right reason.'

Even as the new sensations flooded her, she clenched her jaw and forced her body immobile and held her breath as best she could. 'You're awfully close.' She spoke softly.

'My pardon.'

He had a smile in his voice and something else, something that drew her in as snug as his arm.

She was lying with her backside against him. She knew he had to be feverish, as she could feel the temperature flaring inside her own body where they touched.

She had no idea how he could lie so close to her and actually sleep with the storm of pulsations flickering between their bodies—or at least bombarding her.

Brandt reached up and brushed back the hair that

wisped at her ears. 'Are you comfortable?' His voice rolled over her, a rumble of masculinity cloaked in a whisper surrounded by darkness.

'Yes.'

'I've sworn never to have children again.'

She didn't ask what that had to do with her—because she had a feeling she knew.

'I understand.' She spoke into the pillow.

Again he brushed at the hair at her temple. 'Is Gussie enough for you?'

'Most certainly. She is a handful sometimes. Without Mrs Caudle I would be lost.'

His thumb moved down the side of her face, traced her jawline and each fingertip trailed over her lips.

'You are a bit misguided. But I can feel your compassion for me. It's different than anyone else's. You care, but it doesn't matter to you because today is all that concerns you.'

'That sounds selfish.'

'Or like someone who has been worried for some time what her future is going to hold, and is more concerned with survival than anything else.'

'I do so want Gussie safe.'

'She will be. And so will you.' His words stopped on a whisper.

He took his time, exploring the feel of her skin, brushing her hair back, first with his fingers and then at the back of her neck with his lips.

Sensations of warmth exploded inside her. She could feel her skin, all of it. The bits of her that he didn't touch, didn't know they weren't being caressed. She shut her eyes, all the energy of her body floating away, and she rested in his touch, letting him explore the innocence of her skin while she savoured the sensations he gave her.

She heard and felt the movement all at once. He propped himself on one elbow and rolled her towards him before settling them against each other. He slid her so that her head rested in the crook of his arm and grasped her leg and pulled it over his, bringing them closer.

Before he stopped moving, his lips rested against hers, caressing, floating against her. The kiss connected them and he pulled her close against his body, his hand slowly sweeping down her back, fingers splayed, holding her into him.

He took his time, unbuttoning her shirt, moving it aside, replacing the cloth he'd pushed back with his lips.

Moving back to cup her breasts, he kissed them, holding his face against them, his hair swirling against her neck, tickling her with pleasure.

Her palms roved over his chest, feeling the taut skin, resting only long enough to take in a stronger perception of his body.

The maleness of him washed over her and, when he removed her shirt, he pulled her against him. He kissed her and she tasted a soft hint of cinnamon, and perhaps brandy, but mostly the male power of him.

He had no trouble removing the rest of their clothing, never stopping his exploration of her as he did so.

She lay against him, his hardness pressing against her, and he took his time, moving back to brush his lips over her face.

In the dimness, she couldn't see his expression as much as she could feel the intensity of it. His breathing. Now she understood. It had changed. All of him had. He wasn't the same person she'd seen naked on the bed. This was a different kind of bareness, one that went beyond skin, deeper into the heart of a person. A raw power of feeling that intensified with each brush of the hand against the body, the skin against skin, and sparking a different power of feeling.

Then he held her close and cradled her, and when his hands roamed her body, he didn't stop until she gasped in pleasure.

He touched her, moving her gently so he could rise over her and slid himself inside her, but when his body tensed, he pulled away.

In the quietness that followed, as her heartbeats slowed, he held her close.

Then with even more care than he'd used undressing her, he helped her pull her clothing back on, giving her soft kisses through her clothes as he fastened them in the darkness.

She opened her mouth to speak, but nothing seemed important enough to break the moments between them.

He tucked her against him. 'It doesn't seem quite so dark in here now.'

She pulled away and turned back to him so that she could run her hand along where he'd shaved. 'You never seem dark to me. Just scratchy.'

Chapter Seventeen

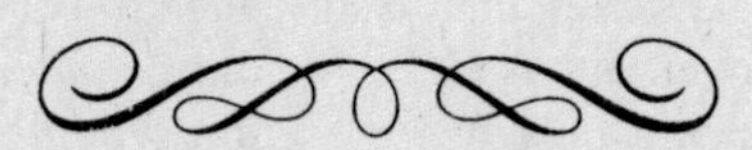

'Brandt isn't as bad as I thought.' Katherine leaned across the table in Brandt's boarding room. Mrs Caudle didn't make a noise, just continued the slow shake of her head at every word Katherine spoke. 'He doesn't seem to gamble. He talks of the tavern women no differently than sisters. He doesn't even seem to care for his own money. I'm marrying him. Gussie will be safe.'

Katherine reached in to give Mrs Caudle another hug. She savoured the scent of baking which always hovered around the governess. Brandt waited outside while she dressed in the fresh clothing Mrs Caudle had brought. The laundress's son had managed to get into Augustine's house, but Mrs Caudle was not allowed to leave the premises with Gussie.

'I warned you.' Mrs Caudle straightened her necklace. 'The problem is that you let the kidnapper breathe all over you.'

Katherine nodded, movements slow. 'All the time.' She tilted her head to the side. 'But it doesn't matter to me any more.'

'Why do you wish to take—? Oh, child…' Mrs Caudle reached to grasp one shoulder of Katherine's so she could shake her.

Mrs Caudle's eyes narrowed and she tapped Katherine's shoulder. 'You have to keep using your hands to push it out—especially after you marry.' She gave Katherine a worn look. 'Once you've got a babe on the way and he's been drinking—that elixir fades fast.'

The governess sighed. 'The only weapons we have are the ones we use before we marry and they're our downfall.'

'What are you talking about?' Katherine asked.

'Men can't hardly say no to a woman they aren't married to. Particularly if she sidles up against him some. They have their elixir to use and we have our weapons. We can move in closer and give them those little touches to weaken them just enough, then we fall right into their trap. We think we're sweetening them up and they're leading us right to that mucky spider's web that traps us for ever. For. Ever.'

Katherine flicked the words away with a turn of her head. She stood, lifting the dress to her own shoulders that Mrs Caudle had brought. She even held the silk against her face, pleased at the thought of leaving the trousers behind for good.

At least she had some choices this time. One more than last time.

'I don't feel right about this.' Mrs Caudle shook her head.

'Well, we will be hopeful.' Katherine placed the dress on the bed while Mrs Caudle undid her laces. 'I've been wearing a man's clothing and I must say, it's changed my view on the world.'

'Thinking like a man might not be a good thing,' Mrs Caudle said, moving by Katherine and helping her pull the chemise over her head. The governess pulled down the hem of the white skirt until it flowed around Katherine's knees. 'In fact, I can't remember a time I've seen a man think.'

'Mrs Caudle…' Katherine paused, raising her hand to her lips. 'Maybe I do think like a man and that is my problem. A man decides what he wants and goes after it, not caring what happens along the way.' She stood still while Mrs Caudle worked with the laces. 'I see no reason to change until after I get what I wish for.'

'You're about to get more 'n you wished for though.' She muttered a grumble.

Mrs Caudle finished dressing Katherine, both silent.

Katherine looked in the mirror. She leaned down to see better. 'This is not a fashionable bodice. I wished to be married in a better bodice.'

Mrs Caudle shook her head. 'I would have travelled with you,' she grumbled, 'but I knew Gussie needed me. That daft maid who's watching her now is no smarter than Gussie. And that tavern fare corrupted you.'

'No, he didn't.' Katherine tugged a bit at her dress.

She turned to Mrs Caudle. 'We may have a weakness where men's elixir is concerned, but…' She took a deep breath, filling her lungs with air. 'It all somehow ties together.'

Mrs Caudle gently brushed at the frazzle of hair around her face. 'I will never understand—' She looked at Katherine. 'Before she died, I promised your mother I'd see to her girls. If she'd thought how my own turned out, I dare say she'd have asked me to stay away from her babies.'

Katherine turned away from Mrs Caudle's face. She knew why her mother had died. Augustine had pecked her to death.

He had watched her mother, day after day, looking for tender flesh to pick at. Her mother's face was puffy or her dress was too tight or her hair straw or her books foolish or her hands wrinkled. He lived to find fault. And he flapped around like a greedy buzzard when he nipped a particularly vulnerable spot.

'I will marry, Mrs Caudle. I will not let Gussie grow up to become a prisoner to him as I was.'

Mrs Caudle folded the clothes Katherine had given her. 'Child. I cannot believe what's become of you. I've failed to protect you.'

'I have some of my father's blood as well. So, don't blame yourself, Mrs Caudle.'

Katherine smiled, satisfied with the dress she would be married in.

'You can change your mind.'

'I have no intention of changing my mind,' Katherine said. 'It's better to go forward or sideways, than to go back to Fillmore.'

Mrs Caudle looked at Katherine, her words slow and speculative. 'Child, are you sure you know what you're doing?'

'I will do what I have to do,' Katherine met Mrs Caudle's gaze with her eyes steady and she took a slow, deep breath.

Mrs Caudle shut her eyes and lowered her head.

'Rot.' She opened the door and waved Brandt in. 'I will get back to Gussie.' She rushed by them.

'Everything is ready?' Katherine turned her attention to Brandt. She pressed her lips together when he shook his head.

'It will be an hour or so before the bishop is able to prepare the special licence for us. I suppose I must have new clothing.' He looked at his sleeves. 'This one is worn through. Go with me. We must see you're pleased with the purchase. I'm afraid my tastes might run to last year's fashions. I've a tailor shop to visit.'

When he raised his eyes to her, she could see the distance in them.

'A wedding to prepare for,' he added, much in the same way he might have said a last meal to have.

Katharine walked to him, and put a hand on his arm, and could feel the tension in him. 'I appreciate what you're doing for me and my sister. I know my stepfather may not release her, but I think he will. It is better for her to live with me than for the world to know his natural daughter is in a madhouse. He doesn't want anyone to believe his blood is tainted. That is the thing he fears most, a madness in his veins.'

'I'll see that he lets you take her,' he said.

He stepped aside, opening the door, and the scent of good soap wafted along behind her. He shook his head, watching her move past.

He examined how she'd dressed to be married. Without even realising it, she'd dressed like a fashion plate from *La Belle Assemblée*. Her bonnet had a bow bigger than his fist. She had no idea of the stamp society had left on her, even if she didn't go to the events around her. The lightskirts at the tavern had once spent three shillings for a copy of the periodical and spent the evening making up jests about the superior noses of the women portrayed in it.

They were a fine couple.

He stared at her bonnet a moment. She reached up to pat it.

'It's fashionable,' she said.

'I think you mistake excess for fashion.'

'This—from a man who has worn the same waistcoat for how many years?' She took the threads apart with her glance.

'I do not claim my waistcoat is a bit more attractive than your bonnets. In fact—' He stared at the concoction on her head. 'I would rate them as quite similar in style.'

'I'm a duke's granddaughter. Even when I was on the shelf, it was the very top shelf.' She shook her head, staring at his clothing. 'And I should dress the part, particularly if I am to challenge Augustine and Fillmore. It would not do to show up in rags.'

'Well, I agree. I should have something new to wear since I have been so *fortunate*—' he stopped talking for a moment '—to marry a duke's granddaughter.

She tugged at her gloves. 'It was necessary. My sister is not going to grow up with Augustine as her only parent. I had my mother to protect me from him. She only has me.'

'Couldn't you have just visited an apothecary?'

She shook her head. 'It would have been noticed. Dukes' granddaughters do not buy poison for vermin.'

'No. You hire someone to kidnap you in front of Almack's.'

'It was a good plan.'

'It was a disaster waiting to happen. As it did, anyway.'

'Obstacles didn't stop my forebears.'

'I would assume they had their obstacles shot.'

She turned to him. 'Or engaged others to do it for them. But I am peaceable. I don't wish for you to kill Fillmore or Augustine, but neither do I wish Gussie to be raised by them. I'm all she has.'

'Heaven help her.' He rubbed a hand across his beard and met her eyes. She blinked.

Shortly after they walked along the street, he saw a hackney and put two fingers to his lips and whistled loudly enough to hurt her ears.

Immediately the cab, paint glistening so fresh it could have been applied that day, pulled to a stop.

When Brandt sat beside her in the carriage, the leather seat creaked and scented the interior.

She bent closer to him. 'I hope you can find something dark and menacing. Fillmore is rather bold.'

He turned his head slowly until his eyes locked on hers. He laughed, but the sound was aimed at himself.

His face changed. He shut his eyes and shook his head. 'Only the granddaughter of the Duke of Carville would be so straightforward. You should have been the duke's firstborn son, Katherine.'

'I don't particularly like my uncle.'

'No surprise there.' He chuckled. 'My elder brother has known him for years and he doesn't particularly like him either.'

'My mother's brother has had nothing to do with us since my mother married my father. I have never even met him and wouldn't be allowed in the door. Mother hated him for not accepting my father.'

'Your father was—'

'Elan Wilder.'

'Really?' He stopped, looking again at her. 'I've heard of him.'

'My mother adored him, but—'

'But he gambled.'

'A bit.'

'Just like his daughter, I would say.'

'I've never played a wagering game in my life.'

'Oh, heavens no. Not something so mild for you.' He laughed softly.

She froze, just watching him. He looked so different when he laughed. Not exactly trustworthy. Not at all trustworthy, but he must have breathed out a full barrel of elixir and it hit her stomach and swirled around.

The carriage rolled to a stop and he helped her down. Then he looked at her bonnet and grimaced again. 'Don't ever choose my clothes.'

Her chin went up. 'Obviously I haven't.'

He grinned, then put her arm around his elbow and gave her a tug.

When they stepped into the tailor shop, a tall man bustled out from the back. The sombre cut of the tailor's clothes contrasted sharply with the white cravat which seemed to burst into flower at his neck. The man had cropped thinning hair, which curled slightly in a tousled look.

His eyes took them both in, but darted to Brandt's clothing, then he squinted. His face soured. 'How can I be of service?'

'Royce,' Brandt said, a flash of recognition in his eyes.

The man's eyes did a quick appraisal of Brandt. His head snapped back and he wrinkled his nose as if he couldn't believe his own words, 'Brandt?'

Brandt nodded. 'I am to be married.' He indicated Katherine with a nod. 'She's determined I improve my appearance.'

'You married?' the older man asked again, uncertainty still in his eyes. Then he caught himself, bowed briefly and took a step aside. 'If you'll step to the counter, I have fabric samples for whatever you might wish.'

'I believe you once told me you could make me a gentleman—' Brandt stood before Royce '—but I'm sure you thought you'd never have the challenge. I'll leave all the choices to you—just no blue and yellow.'

The tailor raised an eyebrow. 'Brandt. That was a dashing style.'

'No. You had leftover cloth,' Brandt said.

The tailor grinned. 'I did.' His lips pouched a bit and then he raised his chin. 'I can make anyone look like a gentleman.' He held his head high. 'But you'll be easier than most.' He sized up Brandt's clothes. 'Those are not worthy for a tavern,' Royce continued, eyes glinting with humour. 'And the buttons?' he asked. 'Would you like to choose them?'

'No. I trust your judgement. And you'd best use your proprietor judgement and not your tavern judgement, or you will not be paid.'

'Fine,' the tailor pretended to grouse. 'I will not sew any shut.' He waved his arm to indicate the back room. 'If you'll let me take a few measurements, we'll discuss what you would like. I even have a few things on hand which would come close to fitting.'

Katherine sat, arranging her skirts to keep them from wrinkling while she waited. She could hear the rumble of voices from the back and one yip of pain from the tailor and a complaint that Brandt best stand still or the next pin would go in him.

Almost an hour later, Brandt chuckled as he emerged from the back of the shop. The black coat he wore could have been made for a peer.

'Royce is getting us a carriage,' he said.

'How did he manage to get you clothing so quickly?' she asked.

He shrugged. 'We're near the same size. He sent someone for some of his own and let out the trouser legs. He had a staff member exchange more expensive buttons to a coat he had. He can tell it is not a perfect fit, and I can tell, but it will suit the purposes of the day.'

'I cannot imagine him in a tavern.'

Brandt didn't answer immediately. 'Royce isn't a regular at the Hare's Breath. But he made my clothes for me when I was a lad—and later—and he once recognised me when I was walking to the Hare's Breath. And he's been by a few times to see—how I'm faring. They welcome him because I know him.' He gave a wry smile. 'I guess I am one of the patrons of the Hare's Breath now.'

He took her elbow. 'It seems everyone has an opinion on how I should live my life. Always have since I have been a very young man. Do you get the same advice?'

'Not really. Augustine has so much control over me that no one else had any say in the matter. Or even thought to speak.'

'Well, perhaps I should like to give a bit of advice to you now.'

The carriage arrived, Brandt thanked Royce and they walked out. She turned back to see Royce watching them leave, but with a smile on his face.

Brandt helped her into the carriage and he followed, sitting with a bit of a bounce before he settled against her side. Thumping the carriage top, he alerted the driver they were ready.

She saw a slight scar at the corner of his temple. 'What advice might you give?'

'I discussed what kind of dresses he might suggest for you.' Brandt's lips parted a bit and she saw his eyes move to her body, and he gave a tiny swallow before he spoke. 'The dullness, you know. I think you should wear happier colours.' Then he reached across her, tugging the shade closed, and leaned back to pull the one on his side. With the outside fog, and the dimness inside, he'd enveloped her in a cocoon. He looked at her and her skin began to tingle.

'I told the tailor you wish for fashionable clothes and I asked if he might recommend a colour.' Brandt touched the faded brown sleeve of her dress, frowning. 'Royce said your skin would glow bathed in a pink shade.'

He bent forward a bit, reached into his waistcoat pocket and took out a square of fabric no bigger than half his palm—and the hue a light rose. He stared at it and then held the swatch to her cheek, so close the fibres brushed her skin.

With his eyes intent and the closed quarters, she tensed. She could only feel the merest edge of the cloth, but she could sense the material with her whole body.

Brandt studied the scrap, attention focused. Katherine could feel him thinking of her skin.

She moved back against the leather squabs.

'Hold still,' he spoke softly, letting the fabric remain against her. He leaned closer, eyes determined to make the most of the soft light. 'Lovely. Perfect for a fashionable bodice.' He brushed it down to where the fabric of her gown ended near her neck, then frowned.

With his free hand he reached around her, surrounding her in a layer of his own warmth and the scent of a tart shaving spice. He undid several hooks more quickly than any lady's maid. She felt the brush of his fingertips as he pushed back the shoulder of her dress.

She couldn't protest. She put a hand against his chest to push him away, but he took it as encouragement, moving closer to her, as if the touch heightened his own senses.

'So.' He brushed the fabric at the soft skin just above the top of her exposed chemise. She felt the tickles of the silken cloth, causing ripples in the rest of her body. 'To go with your fashionable bodices, I think you'll have to get some new chemises, as well.' He shook his head 'Can't have them showing above your dress.'

He put the fabric to his lips, securing it between his teeth, and then took both hands to brush the shoulders of her chemise away, leaving a décolletage a whisper away from scandalous.

He didn't speak at first, but took the silk from his lips. She almost couldn't hear his words above her own heartbeats, but he finally spoke, his eyes still resting on the skin above her chemise. 'I agree with you. Very much. About the bodices.'

She felt the fabric stroke her again, damp from where his mouth had wetted the cloth. She swallowed. He dragged the fabric up her skin, to her neck, her chin and fluttered it across her lips. 'What do you think?' he asked. 'About the colour?'

She nodded and her fingers covered his wrist. He stilled a moment, but she didn't push away, just held on.

Her eyes rested on his face and she knew his thoughts. Whether or not he was hers, she was his.

Brandt watched her study him. He was bound to Katherine. Even before the cleric said the words, he'd already been tied to her. Not by marriage vows, but because he could not watch her struggle without wanting to rescue her.

He didn't take his eyes from her. Katherine—not Nigel now, he supposed. But for him, he wasn't sure her real name fit her. Nigel. A safe name. Katherine—a woman's name.

A man could walk away from a Nigel. And a Nigel's breasts were just— He looked again. Those, he would have to say, belonged to a Katherine.

And they would look so appealing with a dress of the cloth Royce had given him. They were fine even covered in a tired undergarment.

Beyond imaginable—

Something he shouldn't think about, or she'd have him captured. Truly captured.

He reached under her breast, to her side, and gave a delicate pull so more of her skin showed. He took the fabric and then brushed it against the top of her breast. He let the cloth rest there a moment.

'This would do, I think,' he said of the swatch.

She twisted in the seat, still gripping his arms. She had taut muscles in her body and the darkness in her eyes.

He dropped the scrap, letting it flutter between them.

He traced his finger along the very edge of the chemise poking from her dress. 'He suggested a rich sable as well, to match your hair.'

His hand splayed, keeping the dress between himself and her skin, but didn't stop until he rested on the corset under her breasts. 'Holding you here, with the stays, is not much different than touching a knight's armour, yet it seems I can feel every beat of your heart, every breath, and even the blink of your lashes seem to flutter against my skin. Can you even feel my touch, Katherine?'

She nodded. He let his hands slide to her waist, feeling the ridges of boning which trapped her body, letting his fingertips imagine so much more.

'I suppose I should have got more samples of fabric,' he whispered. 'It's hard to know just how the other colours would look against you.'

He bent his head down, not touching her neck, but he felt her move—not away.

'Soap. You always smell of soap. Not a soap a man might use. Not one used by a woman scrubbing away her sins. But one which brings to mind meadows and breezes which soothe the soul.'

His lips lingered against her neck, his hands still

at her waist. 'But not all of the scent is soap, some is the sweetness of your skin. The warmth of it tumbling about my face, reminding me of what could get even better as I touch more of you.'

He raised his eyes to hers. 'Did you like the pink colour? I wonder if we should select a slightly brighter shade?' He heard his voice, as casual as if he discussed a carriage wheel, but he'd begun to feel the touch of her which his fingers couldn't quite manage enough of through the garments—but he felt too much.

'Would that be fashionable enough for you?' He watched her face.

She didn't speak, but she answered what he didn't ask.

He backed away, but his eyes didn't.

'You're right about the fashionable bodices and I know...' His hand brushed down, fingers splayed, over the dress bunched at her waist, touching her stomach. His lips came to hers and his teeth nipped her bottom lip. He held her firm, not letting her push herself against him. He didn't raise his voice above a whisper at her ear. 'Sweet, I will miss you.'

His forehead touched hers and his nose touched hers, and his words were spoken almost into her mouth.

Brandt's lips fell into the hollow of her neck, his teeth grazing her skin.

She reached out, clasping the tendrils of his hair, holding him close, and he let himself mould her back into the seat. His tongue swirled on her skin and he blew against her, letting his breath heat the trail his tongue left behind.

The carriage pulled to a stop, and he heard the

creaks and felt the carriage jostle as the man moved from his seat to pull down the steps for them.

Brandt reached to the door handle and his fingers tightened, holding it to prevent opening. He leaned back in the squab, against the corner, putting his arm along the back of the seat, never releasing her from his gaze.

His eyes roamed to the places his lips had touched. 'I will miss you, Katherine. But understand it's for the best…'

He pressed a kiss against her neck, lips moving a trail that touched deep inside her. She clasped him close, but he pulled back, his exhalation warming where his mouth had been.

His shoulders moved with his breaths. His arm fell from around her and he took her gloved hand as he moved away. He kissed her glove and released the door. 'The closer I get to you, the more I remember the pain, the loss and all the darkness.'

'You don't have to love me. I wouldn't care.'

'I would. Care. And that would be too much.' She sensed rather than felt him lean in towards her. 'Wear the bright colours. Live a life that brings you peace.'

'What of you?'

'I will be doing the same in London.' He leaned closer and, instead of a kiss, he touched her back. 'You have shown me that I belong among the plain folk, the ones I have been near the past few years. The tart-mouthed, ale-soaked folks. I always have. I just hadn't realised how much it is true.'

'But—'

He put two gentle fingers over her lips, silencing her.

Chapter Eighteen

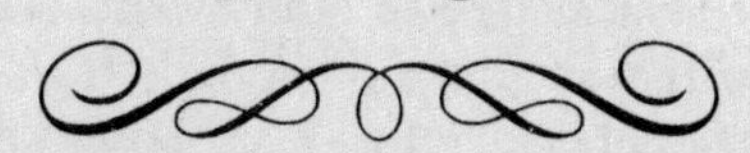

When Brandt heard the cleric speaking the words, he paid no attention, until he heard her name. *Katherine. Katherine Louisa Wilder. Katherine Louisa May Radcliffe.* He'd given a different woman his last name. Not Mary. He'd taken Mary's last name away from her.

He let out a loud sigh and looked at Katherine. The cleric stumbled over a word and Brandt stared at him. The man spoke faster.

Katherine elbowed Brandt.

He raised his head to look at the ceiling—it needed fresh paint. He firmed his jaw and turned, seeing Katherine's pale face. He leaned to her. 'Take in a deep breath, Katherine. It is only a marriage.' He spoke softly. Then he looked at the cleric and the man's eyes opened wide when he saw Brandt's face. 'I do—to that question you're about to ask.'

The man paused. 'Please wait until I've asked it.' He continued speaking, then he paused and looked at Brandt. 'You may give the correct answer now.'

'I will.'

At least this didn't feel like a wedding or a marriage,

and the thought eased Brandt's mind. He'd not realised marriage could be such a simple act. He'd pleaded and promised and fumed to marry his first wife.

First wife, he scowled at the thought. If Mary would have lived she would have been his *only* wife.

His father had promised to disown him, saying if he wished to marry a servant then he could become one as well and said he certainly would not send him to university now. His mother had cried. Mary and her mother had been let go and he'd followed them. Finally, he'd married and things had slowly returned to normal.

This marriage, he'd merely showed up. No one seemed to have noticed his presence particularly.

He'd lost one wife and now he'd gained… He paused. He'd gained a Nigel.

He'd refused to think of courting and certainly not marriage ever again. It would have been making light of the first one, of his wife's death, and erasing that it had ever happened. In fact, he hadn't given marriage much thought the first time until after the window had lifted so easily.

He couldn't help that part of him had died with her, buried even before the first shovel of dirt covered her coffin, and had decayed into dust long before the grass had covered her grave.

By no means would he become a husband.

Because this wasn't to be the same marriage he'd had before.

He could leave when he wished. He'd made her no promises or no real vows. He'd stood up with her and the only tie of their wedding was that they were bound together for ever on a special licence.

He shut his eyes and imagined Mary and thought of her watching him get married, and crying into her handkerchief.

As the sun set, Katherine found herself on the steps of her old home, Brandt's hand at her elbow. She shivered and his clasp tightened.

But it was worth it to get a family. And if Brandt didn't want his, that was fine. She'd take them. Gussie would have another grandmother besides the governess. Uncles. Aunts. A world of family that Katherine had never had.

When she looked at the house, she couldn't move forward. Her father and her mother had died in the house. She'd been born there.

'Tell the house goodbye, Katherine. It's best.'

She looked at the house—staring at the ivy growing up the filigree. When she raised her eyes to the next level, she saw the window at the end which was her stepfather's. She looked up to the third floor, where she sometimes escaped to find peace.

The house had been tainted. She could leave it behind. She only wished Augustine had not gained it by marriage.

Weddle, the butler, opened the towering door and Katherine saw his lips curl into a sneer before he stepped back and maintained the perfected disinterest.

'I do believe we must speak with Augustine. He is not expecting us, but I wouldn't want to hurt his feelings by passing by.'

Weddle's snowy mane never moved and his pinched eyes never stilled.

Brandt turned, his body shielding her from Weddle, and offered his arm to her.

She didn't want to step inside. She'd tasted freedom, savoured it, and now, with a few steps, she would be returning to where she'd been a near prisoner. But she would be with her sister.

Brandt gave her a nudge, while standing close, becoming a protective barrier. She stepped over the threshold. The polished wood and the lingering scent of lemons almost welcomed her, but Weddle dispelled any pleasant feelings she might have without so much as a bobble of his chin.

She looked at Weddle. He stood like a stone monument to himself. He'd worked for her father, then her mother and then her stepfather. His loyalty had been given to whoever allowed him the most time in front of a mirror. His hair was his glory and his livery never creased.

'I will let him know you've arrived.' His eyes smirked, even when his voice remained pleasant.

She turned. Brandt studied the area around him. Every surface gleamed even in the dim light and nothing had an apparent nick or look of use.

'I don't believe he likes me,' Brandt said. 'Might there be a footman about who can be trusted? We will need someone to carry your things to the vehicle.'

'I believe there is a younger one who has a good heart. He's helped Mrs Caudle and me when we've needed him.'

'Tell me where I might find the footman.'

She pointed him in the direction of the man's quarters. 'I'll ring and send someone for him.'

Brandt arched a brow and turned to her. 'I am comfortable with walking into the servants' quarters. If they are not comfortable with it, they may speak about it amongst themselves afterwards.'

He took her arm and they walked downstairs. After finding someone to complete his request, he asked, 'Where might Augustine be?'

'His library.'

They took the servants' stairs and moved back to the main quarters.

This staircase stretched out like a goblin's mouth, ready to take them in. She touched the banister and began her ascent. With each step she took, she felt Brandt behind her and his strength surrounded her.

She didn't knock at the door to the library, but whooshed it open.

Augustine sat at his desk, a pen in his hand, and looked up as she walked into the room. The gloom of the room enveloped him and she could smell spoiled greens. He raised his eyebrows a bit when he saw her, but otherwise showed no surprise.

Augustine spread his fingers, letting the pen clatter to the table.

Fillmore stood at Augustine's shoulder. 'You've returned to me.' Then he frowned, looking at Brandt. 'Goodbye.'

'My husband. I wanted you to meet him.' Katherine stood beside Brandt as he entered. 'We married today by special licence.' She looked at Augustine. 'You should reimburse him for it. A dowry of sorts.'

'Ha.' Fillmore stepped from the shadows. His eyes hardened. 'Augustine doesn't have enough funds to do so.'

'The money my grandfather left my mother.' Katherine raised her chin.

'He's spent it. All that your father didn't gamble away,' Fillmore said, shrugging. 'Without me, he wouldn't be able to pay any servants. He'd have to empty his own chamber pot.'

Augustine stood, his mouth as bland as she had ever seen it, his eyes slits under droopy lids. 'Katherine, you'd have been better off with my choice.' He appraised Brandt. 'Much better.'

Fillmore's smile oozed on to his face. 'Not really.' His eyebrow arched.

Brandt put his hand on her shoulder and the touch was as protective as any shield.

Fillmore stopped. 'Did you know I had you followed, Katherine? Many times. I just couldn't figure out what you were doing to visit a person's lodgings who was barely able to stand.' He pulled his hand up and examined his fingernails. 'I just didn't think you such a quick worker and I didn't realise you'd get someone to take you in the night. My mistake, but again, you'll pay for it.' He paused. 'But I wouldn't have waited if I'd known how slippery you could be. That sister of yours will be in the madhouse before nightfall.'

'Gussie is my child,' Augustine said. 'I make the decision on when she goes to the madhouse.'

'No, you won't,' Brandt said. 'We're taking Katherine's sister. She leaves with us.'

'You can have her, Katherine. A wedding gift from me,' Fillmore said. 'But you have to stay here to keep her.'

'Collect her, Katherine. Now.' Brandt's stance widened and firmed.

Katherine paused.

Fillmore stepped closer to Brandt. 'You think you have Katherine, but you don't.'

Brandt and Fillmore's eyes locked and in the same moment Fillmore reached into his coat, Brandt moved forward, shoving him against the wall, Brandt holding Fillmore's wrist. He'd not taken the knife from the sheath.

'I spent the last years of my life in a tavern,' Brandt said to Fillmore. 'Not a month goes by without a blade flashing.' Then he spun Fillmore around and shoved him, knocking him into Augustine's desk.

Augustine had a drawer open, and was reaching inside. Brandt lunged forward, still moving towards Fillmore, and grabbed him, slinging him across the desk and on to Augustine. A pistol clattered to the floor.

He still ploughed forward, shoving the desk, and then turned sideways, reaching for the gun on the floor, glancing at it. Augustine had finally learned to clean his guns.

'You won't shoot me,' Fillmore said, standing. 'You'd hang for it.'

Brandt handed the gun to Katherine, then stepped forward. 'Don't have to shoot you.' He reached out, grabbed Fillmore by the throat. Fillmore clasped the knife handle. Brandt grabbed Fillmore's wrist, slamming him into the wall. The knife clattered to the floor.

Fillmore spoke from between clenched teeth. 'You can kill me, but you'll hang. And if you take Gussie, you'll be charged with kidnapping.'

'Sounds like an easy solution to me. A slow death

for you. A quick end for me. But there's something else you should know. I've had my elder brother contact the Duke of Carville. While he and Katherine may not be acquainted, he's even less fond of anyone who might try to harm her. If you wish to continue to do business in this town, I think it best for both of you to keep your distance from her. Or face his power.'

'Take Gussie,' Augustine shouted, pushing himself up from the floor. 'I'm getting rid of her anyway. She's my child. Katherine can have her. Better with her sister than locked away. The little nuisance bothers my humours. I never intended to send her away anyway, but it kept Katherine in line.'

Brandt looked over his shoulder. Katherine turned to Augustine and had her finger on the trigger. The pistol was pointed at his head. She held the gun with both hands and she cocked the hammer.

'Katherine. Katherine,' Brandt said her name. She didn't move.

He shoved back from Fillmore, toppling him again, and secured the knife in his own waistband. The intensity on Katherine's face stilled Fillmore and Augustine.

Brandt stepped gently towards her. 'I'll take that,' he whispered. He put his hands out and with his left hand under the gun, and his right hand above, he put his forefinger between the hammer and the flange.

'Katherine. If you pull the trigger, it's going to pinch my finger like blazes.'

'He's not going to hurt you or Gussie.'

'No,' Brandt reassured her. 'Remember, I have two

brothers and one has a pack of dogs. You'll be safe. We'll all be safe.'

'Just get out of my house and take the brat with you,' Augustine said. 'I never want to see either of you again.'

She looked up at Brandt. 'I must get Gussie.'

Chapter Nineteen

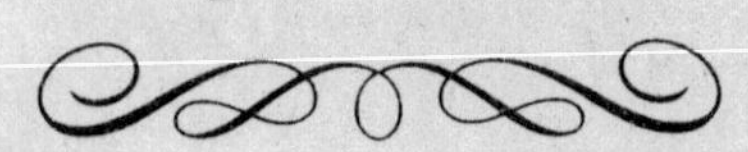

Katherine ran up the stairs to the next storey and flung open the door to the old nursery. She put one hand on the frame and leaned in. 'Mrs Caudle, get Gussie. Take her to the carriage outside now.'

'I've already packed a satchel for us,' Mrs Caudle answered, turning, her skirt swirling at her ankles. 'Gussie. Come here.'

The door wobbled of the adjoining room and, with a slow creak of opening, a small face peered around the wood.

A squeak hit the air and a bright-eyed child ran into the room. She bounded forward and threw herself against Katherine, squeezing with all her might.

Katherine's heart thumped. She took Gussie's arms and knelt down to give Gussie a cheek-to-cheek hug.

Gussie squirmed free and reached up and gave a pinch to Katherine's nose and pretended to hold it in her hands. Katherine reached out, grabbed the imaginary nose and wiggled it back on to her face. Gussie laughed.

'I missed you. Did you miss me?'

Gussie nodded vigorously, her braids bouncing.

'Now you are going on an adventure with me. We are going to live in a different house. Mrs Caudle will go with us, too.'

Gussie listened.

'We shall take your dolls as well.' Katherine rose. Gussie smiled, nodded her head once more and gave Katherine another hug and took her hand. She rested her forehead against Katherine's side.

With Gussie's hand in hers, and with Mrs Caudle behind them, Katherine ran downstairs, catching up with the footman carrying the trunk of clothing. Brandt stood in the doorway of Augustine's room, still holding the weapon.

After they jumped into the carriage, Brandt followed behind a few moments later. He walked to the shrubbery and pulled the trigger, discharging the weapon, and then followed them into the carriage.

As the vehicle rolled away, Katherine used her free hand to indicate him. 'This is Brandt,' she said to Gussie.

Brandt stared at the little child. He took in a breath to calm himself.

'Gussie.' Brandt gave her a nod. 'You have a beautiful smile.'

She frowned and shook her head.

He didn't want to ask the question in his head. He didn't want to hear the answer.

'Fine.' He shrugged. 'You look meaner than a snake.'

Gussie looked up at Katherine, a question in her eyes.

'Pay him no mind,' Katherine said. 'He's had a rough day. But he's taking us to our new home.'

'Do you speak, Gussie?' Brandt asked.

She shook her head. If she didn't speak, she couldn't answer him. 'How old are you, little one?'

She held up her hand, fingers splayed.

Nathan would have been five on his next birthday, if he had lived.

Brandt waited for the blackness inside him to fade enough so that he could see, then he reached behind him and opened the carriage window. He shouted to the driver to take them to a livery.

He had to get another horse because he was not riding all the distance to his house in the same carriage as the two women and the child.

Besides, he'd need a way to return to his room.

When the carriage pulled up in front of his mother's house, Brandt jumped from the horse and handed the reins to one of the carriage drivers. The dogs were barking loud enough to stir anyone from miles around.

He opened the door and Katherine stepped out.

Katherine turned back for Gussie.

'No,' she squealed. 'No.' She turned back, burying herself in Mrs Caudle's arms.

'Gussie. Come out. We're going to meet your new family.'

Katherine pried from the front. Mrs Caudle pushed from the back. He watched, refusing to enter the fray. Nathan would never have acted so. Never.

'She's nervous of the dogs,' Mrs Caudle said.

They got Gussie out of the carriage and Mrs Caudle held her. Gussie's legs dangled, far too big to be carried.

'Bear. Bear.' Gussie hugged Mrs Caudle's neck, crying.

Harlan came out of the house. He called to the dogs and they quieted. He moved his hand and they sat.

'Bear,' she said and sniffled.

Katherine shook her head. 'It's not Bear.' Eyes apologetic, she turned to Harlan. 'Our neighbour had a dog he called Bear. It chased Gussie and it scarred her leg where it bit her.'

Harlan reached down, patted the dog nearest him. He pointed behind the house. 'Barn.' The dogs trotted away. Harlan stepped forward. 'You don't have to worry about my dogs. They are smarter than they look.'

Gussie quieted and Mrs Caudle sat her down.

His mother stepped out of the house and moved down the steps. 'I didn't expect you back so soon.'

'Things have changed, much more quickly than I expected, and I thought to keep you informed.' He turned to Katherine. 'We were married today. She, Gussie and Gussie's governess will be living in my house.'

His mother's eyes widened and her hand crimped the fabric of her skirt at her hip. 'You're married?' she asked. 'I thought—'

'Could you send servants to pack up Mary's things today? It's time they were given to—to someone who needs them.'

'Of course.' She reached up and tucked a strand of hair behind her ear.

'Would you oversee it with Katherine, Mother?'

'All of Mary's things?' The words moved slowly from his mother's lips.

He thought of the house and the things he remembered. 'I'd like to keep the drawings she did, but pack them away for later.'

She sniffled louder than the little girl had. 'Of course.'

He moved forward and touched her shoulder. He couldn't tell her that he would only be living in his house temporarily. She would have been crushed again.

'I loved Mary, too.' She sniffed again, then turned to Katherine. 'And I'm so pleased to have you in the house. It needs a family. Houses do.' She sniffed. 'Just like mothers.'

He reached out, putting an arm around his mother's waist. 'Mother, you always have family, even when we aren't here.'

'I know.' She patted him. 'Now I've some work to do. If you will excuse me.' She turned to Harlan. 'Send the stable men on horses. We are going to have a few chores to do before nightfall. I'll ride in the carriage.' She paused, a finger to her chin. 'Linens,' she said. 'Linens.'

Then she looked at Harlan. 'And have the men pull a cart around to the back. I'm going to need a few things to take with us.'

Then she smiled at Katherine. 'We'll have you settled in no time.'

Brandt's mother had stripped the linens from the master bedroom, had the men move the furniture around and exchanged some of the prints on the wall with ones from her house. Katherine knew she'd not wanted her son to step back into the world he'd lived before.

Now Katherine sat in Gussie's room, with Mrs Caudle asleep on top of the covers, the house empty except for the few servants his mother had instructed to stay.

Gussie had the wooden rabbit. 'Hop. Hop. Hop.' Then she looked at Katherine. 'Moo.'

'Rabbits don't moo,' Katherine said. 'Cows moo.'

Gussie looked at the rabbit, and laughed. 'It pretends…it's a cow.' She hopped along with it. Then she growled and held the rabbit up. 'Bites…bears. Bites bears hard.' She growled and hopped closer.

Katherine raised her head, realising Brandt stood in the doorway, watching, face grim as any undertaker's.

Gussie's white muslin dress had its familiar smear of jam at the shoulder where she always had to be reminded not to wipe her face when she finished eating.

Brandt watched.

Certainly he would see how dear Gussie was.

'You need to read to me, Angel Eyes.' Katherine put her arm around the thin shoulders and pulled Gussie against her, stilling the little one from flitting around and slipping the rabbit from her sister's hands. 'I read to you last time.'

Gussie's head slanted to lean against Katherine. 'Sleepy.'

She lifted the book. 'You will read the first page to me,' Katherine negotiated. 'You read the first and I'll read the rest to you.'

Gussie shrugged in a way that dismissed Katherine's plea.

'You talk too much.' Leaning to her, Katherine squeezed Gussie's shoulders again.

Gussie looked at Katherine, scrunched her face and then reached to pull Katherine's head to hers. Katherine felt a tiny kiss on her cheek.

Then Gussie clasped the book with one hand and held the book in front of Katherine's face and turned the pages.

Surely Brandt could see how dear Gussie was and how happy she was to be in her new home.

Once they were all settled, she'd make them a family. She looked up, hoping to see something in Brandt's face that let her know he was accepting them into his life.

In the seconds she looked at him, his eyes changed, returning to the present, but not softening. He had the same look of a beast not wishing to be tamed, of waiting until just the proper moment when no one watched and he could glide quickly and silently away.

He nodded to her, no life behind his eyes, and he left her sight.

Brandt sat in the study. The air suffocated him and it had the stamp of the past on it, but still he preferred it to the little girl's exuberance.

He moved to the desk, propping himself against it. He picked up the globe and twirled it several times before sitting it back in place.

Again, he spun the globe slowly, watching the markings go by. The worlds. The days. His other life had spun away. Taking the best of him with it. Taking all of him, leaving only his shell.

Katherine would not be a bad sort to reside with.

Her look pleased him—better than any tavern woman. Or any woman, he supposed. And, with all her ways, even wearing those sad trousers—he found himself aware of her.

But, the globe kept spinning and nothing stopped.

Not for happiness. He'd had his, for the time he could have it.

His finger pressed into the orb and rested over a patch of blue. Where no one resided.

The door opened, giving a soft creak. 'You do not have to stay here if it pains you. I understand. I don't want you to be miserable. It won't do anyone any good. The tavern folk will be pleased to see you.'

He turned. 'Mrs Radcliffe, you're generous with others' opinions. What if the poor women would tell me I should be home with you?' He stood and strode to the window and pushed the curtains wide and gave a little hoist to raise the frame, hoping the fresh air wouldn't kill him.

She darted her eyes up. 'Would they?'

He turned back to her. 'I'm sure they would think it. They're quite romantic, you know.' He stepped in front of her.

'The—'

Her words stopped with his clasp of her waist.

'Yes.' He moved a breath towards her and leaned in. 'Yes. The women are quite certain husbands should be at home with their wives. They secretly sneer at the married men giving them coin—knowing the women at home would be pleased with a new dress, or better food to cook for the children.'

'You were there often?'

'I was, but my coin only went for the ale. Not the women. Yes…' he took her arms and gently unfolded them, keeping her hands in his '… I suppose, though, as I would find it hard to lie with a paid woman knowing she might be wishing me to the devil, on my wedding night I should stay home with a wife who might do the same.'

'Will you stay?'

He moved so his forehead brushed against hers. He ignored her question, answering it without speaking. With her hands captured, she could only lean back. He pulled her ringed finger to his lips, but after glancing at it, he turned her fingers down and kissed the back of her hand.

He turned away, adding space between them.

'Brandt. You cannot be as cold as you say.'

'My heart might be gone, but I've still eyes in my head.' He knew nothing showed in his face, though. 'And my hands work and the rest of me as well. Only the heart is gone.'

He looked around the room. 'Feel free to take any room you like. It's nothing more than bare walls to me. The same as the rest of the house.'

He stood. 'I'm going to the tavern. It's not as fine as the Hare's Breath. It's just a room that Abernathy has set up to be a place to drink into the night. But it will suffice.'

Chapter Twenty

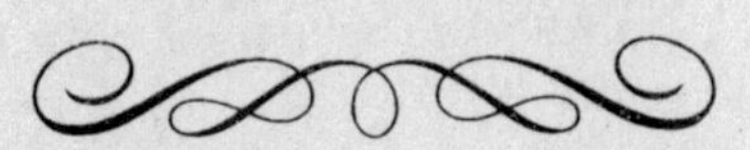

Abernathy's had stunk worse than a barnyard. He'd not been able to stay for more than one mug. He preferred the Hare's Breath with its more motley visitors.

He moved up the stairs, holding the lamp they'd left beside the front door for him. A few servants had stayed.

Katherine hadn't chosen Mary's room. She'd chosen the smaller one at the end of the hall. Hardly more than room for the bed. He knocked briefly and opened the door without waiting for a response.

Sitting the lamp on the table, he saw two wine glasses, one empty. He dimmed the light and lay beside her.

He yawned again, leaning back on the bed and propped his head on his arm. His eyes wanted to close.

He made a decision. He'd leave the next day—Nigel or no Nigel, wife or no wife, he'd find another town further from London. And this time he might really change his name. He chuckled at the thought of calling himself Nigel. He looked less of a Nigel than she did.

He'd make sure he had a well-sprung carriage to

travel in. He was not riding any horse. Ever again. Never. No more saddles. And no more wives.

'Rose and Mashburn will be making wagers on how soon our ways will part.'

'How could they even know you've married?'

'The carriage driver. Or the man who gave me directions to the bishop. Or Royce.'

'I don't see what the opinion of a few tavern folk matters to you.'

Her words hit him in a way he couldn't have imagined. He considered his speech as he spoke. 'I've sat with them most nights for years. It's not as if they're strangers. They have been like blood to me. I've listened as the ale spirited their words and their eyes teared.' He'd never known the truth of it before. He'd thought he'd left all family behind him, but he hadn't. He'd merely moved to another place and grown another sort of relatives around him.

'It's your choice, I suppose.'

He leaned over her. 'You've seen where I've lived. Where I chose to spend my nights.' He moved closer, the softness of her earlobe brushing his face. His lips stopped at her skin.

Then he sat up and left the bed. He went to the curtains and spread them wide, letting the moonlight reflect into the room.

'I took Mary's innocence as easily as I might take a kiss from you.' His voice seeped in the air, a rumble. 'She bore my son. And then she died. They were taken. And I lost more than I ever knew I had.'

'We may feel love strongest when it's taken from us.'

'I felt it even while she lived. I just didn't know

I *was* the stranger in the house, not her. As a child, I would sneak away and spend time with the field hands. I worked with them. One was my age and, if we could finish his chores together, then he would go fishing with me. My father knew. And one day, my friend had to leave suddenly, because a man showed up to offer him a job. My father said he refused to stand in his way and sacked him.'

'Your father didn't like him.'

'It all came out later in the tussle for Mary's hand. In his rage, my father told me he'd always seen that I was a servant at heart. I agreed and left with Mary and her mother. I was sturdy even then and I had already had a good share of work in the fields. I knew I could support them.'

If not for the deal his mother had secretly made with Mary's mother during the winter trysts to see that her daughter would have a fine house, it was unlikely they would have ever returned. But Mary's mother sent messages to his mother and, when tempers cooled, both mothers pushed and pulled them back to the estate.

'Mother kept after Father to make good on her promise to me and we were wed. Very quietly. My father was kind to Mary, not so kind to me, and they accepted her and made her a part of their lives and she loved it. I still helped the field hands and Father never again said a word about it. I think, at the end, he admired that I could.'

'Perhaps working in the field is what you need.'

'The blisters?' He held up his hand. 'I finally have the soft hands my father wanted me to have. I lead a life without physical labour, just as he wanted. And he was right. It led me into bed with a duke's granddaughter. I can now sire children with the best of blood and the worst of parents.'

'It would mean Gussie could have a sister.'

His chuckle was low and dark. 'I don't think it is a good idea for us to bring children into the world.'

'I don't know that it's a good idea for anyone to bring children into the world.'

'But now—you think I will have no choice but to sire children.' He stepped away from the window, each move deliberate.

'So tell me, Wife, did you take my gentleness with you as weakness?' His voice was soft. 'Did you take my preference for the tavern as a mark of insensibility? Did you think I would let you make me into nothing more than a mate to service you?'

He put his right hand on her shoulder and, with a grasp of iron, pulled her so she moved into the circle of his anger. 'You won't make a pet of me.'

'We are married.' The words sounded forced.

He smiled and his jaw firmed. 'My lovely wife. Say that as many times as you wish. It doesn't change a hair on my head and it doesn't free you.'

He took his finger and touched the tip of it to the bow of her mouth, then traced each side. 'It's not I who is the prisoner. It's you. You wove this web and now the insect you caught is not small enough for you to hold or devour. I never kidnapped you. I never once planned to ask for a ransom. It was easiest to let you believe it until I could unlock the door of my house and let you inside. I planned to let you live here. But not with me.'

She moved to shake her head, but with their eyes as one and the tip of his finger against her mouth, he held her still.

The loss of his family had seared something into him she'd never seen in another person. He had a brittleness, and perhaps the same strength as someone hardened by battle. She supposed after soldiers had buried their dead, and stepped over fallen friends and enemies, they lost their own fear of dying because life was a battlefield.

'Marriage.' He smiled. 'Never, ever again…' He laughed softly. He dropped his hand and turned away. Raising his hands up as if surrendering to the irony of life.

'Brandt. I told you. People marry, and, well, do as they wish.'

He took a step away. 'All people who marry do as they wish afterwards. Some wish to live together. Others apart. But I will not risk children. They are like tiny flower buds,' he spoke rapidly, 'and then they burst open and you cannot believe the beauty in them.' He stopped. 'And then…'

He picked up the wine glass, feeling the heat from where it had been close to the lamp, and then he emptied the glass and sat it back on the table. 'Why *do* you have such colours in all your clothing?'

'I was in mourning, first for my father and then for my mother. I saw no reason to buy new later, as I wasn't to attend any events.'

'We've both been wearing dark for a long time.'

He moved closer to her, then reached out a hand and folded Katherine into his arms.

'I would like it if you cared for me,' she said.

His kiss took her thoughts away. And in that moment, she no longer thought about whether his heart was hers or only his body. She would take as much as he could give.

Chapter Twenty-One

After the kiss, he took her into his arms and pulled her against him, cradling her and rocking her gently. He soothed her tremors and soaked in the feminine feel of her. She wasn't stained glass. Perhaps some kind of unbreakable porcelain.

They must have lain close for an hour when he felt a push at his chest and she moved to stand beside the bed.

Her hair looked even more frazzled at the edges. He liked her that way, looking as if she'd just taken a tumble into the bed.

A wonderful thing about the female body. It had been arranged so pleasantly.

Their eyes locked.

She swallowed. Took a breath. 'Truly, do you wish to continue this?'

'I would not miss it for the world,' he said. His movements were languid and he moved across the bed and, with one leg on the floor, he reached out, securing her in his arms and lifting her as easily as he might a flower, and kissed her before he tossed her to the bed.

He moved above her, crouching, and even though they barely touched, they were locked together.

His eyes searched hers. 'I have you to consider now, Katherine. I didn't wish it. You blasted into my doorway.'

He shut his eyes and brushed their cheeks together.

He felt her palm flat at his chest, but her other hand reached upwards, to his face.

Her touch started at his ear and he felt the line she traced, down his jaw, his neck, his shoulder, his chest. He let her fingers trail until she extended her reach, and she didn't miss much.

He savoured the womanliness against him. She smelled of unsoiled sheets and pleasing warmth.

He let himself fall to his side and she propped herself up on an elbow, and again her hand began to trace his body. Gently putting her palms at his chest, touching the curves and contours above the muscles.

'You know—a fashionable bodice is not quite as fashionable in the bedchamber as no bodice.'

She didn't answer, just rested her hand against him.

He shut his eyes and he could hear the tavern piano in his head. Brandt's buttons were no longer sewn shut.

He let his lips fall open and he breathed out softly. He forced his hands to remain still.

If he could only seize on to the feelings and lock out everything else in his mind, he could feel complete.

Already he anticipated the pleasure of sinking into Katherine, of feeling her against his chest and both of them lost in passion.

He ran his hands the rest of the way down her arms and then his fingers traced up the line of her body.

He pressed, letting his fingers slide along the construction. 'No, I do not feel a Nigel.'

With her wrinkled chemise, mussed hair and wide eyes staring at him, he responded with the force of thunder and lightning taking the sky.

Dropping his face into the curve where her neck met her shoulder and resting against the soft fabric, he breathed in. 'These chemises you wear,' he whispered. 'I like them.'

He let his breath heat her skin and her skin teased his lips. He saw her eyelashes flutter closed and he felt the essence of her moving through his fingers and into his own body. With only small touches, he felt joined to her.

'Oh,' she whispered.

He met her eyes. 'Yes.'

He gave himself a moment so he could take in the vision.

Her nose nudged his ear. Her tongue—tentative, barely brushing.

His fingertips trailed down her back, slowly enough so he could linger over each rib, until he stopped at the swell of her backside and pulled her closer.

He rolled her on to her back, braced himself on his elbows and held himself above her. He feathered his lips to hers, overwhelmed.

'Katherine.' He moved back and saw her half-opened eyes. She waited.

He spoke. 'I just wanted to hear your name.'

She shut her eyes and he bent again to her mouth, tasting her lips, but being very gentle with his tongue.

He nipped her ear and felt as her hand touched his chest, exploring.

His mouth savoured the saltiness of her skin from their exertion and his lips moved against her neck, as if she were a morsel and he needed to relish each taste. He truly wanted her.

He pulled himself from her arms, allowing himself a long glance at her body. And then he caught what he was doing. Memorising her body so that he could remember her after they parted. Instantly he stopped those thoughts. It would do him no good to be thinking of how she'd looked after he'd left her.

Now her lips caught his attention and he kissed her.

She tasted of chocolate and wine, and she had a wanton pull in her lips. When he backed away, she followed, refusing to let him ease from her touch. He let himself fall back into the bed, only lightly holding her with his arms, and she moved up, looking down at him.

He could feel each of her fingers pressing into his shoulders. And he could tell she had no complaints of his tongue. He moved back, breathing in her sweetness.

She touched him delicately and the softer she touched him, the more he craved her. The softest flutters of her bolted heat into him. Stirred his blood through his veins.

When he felt her hands leave his shoulders and run across his chest, he almost let himself burrow her back into the counterpane. Her head was buried in the hollow of his neck and he had to push her hands back.

He rolled her into his arms and saw the look in her eyes. Swollen lips and a hunger he hoped he could fill.

Brandt draped a leg over her to keep her settled.

He could not keep his face from hers. She whimpered in protest each time he pulled back and her distress caused a reaction in his body so strong he could barely control his needs.

Cherishing the smoothness under his touch, he held her breast and then touched her stomach. He wanted to feel the whole of her, capture her in his memory.

He pressed himself into her thigh, her leg a balm to his manhood.

His hand slid the length of her, to touch her and give her pleasure. He had to, or he was afraid between the two of them they'd never get the act done properly, or as he preferred, improperly.

He kissed her bottom lip, keeping her close and waiting, feeling her tense against his hand, and this time, instead of whimpers, he felt the gasps from her throat.

Brandt didn't want to give her time to completely return to herself and he pushed above her, raising her knees, and began his descent.

He whispered her name again, for the sound to soothe his own ears.

But he couldn't risk another child. He could not.

He was barely able to breathe when he pulled himself from her and collapsed beside her. He'd been so close to losing himself completely, risking a chance of a child. Unforgivable.

It seemed the only part of him which could still function was his eyes and his lungs.

He lay there, taking in the tangy air, the feel of the room cooling, and his heartbeats returned to normal. He'd let himself get carried away in the moment and he could not risk it happening again.

She mumbled at him and she raised an arm and let it fall against him. He sat up, moving the covers, blanketing them together, and then he slipped back beside her, their bodies relaxing.

The room slowly got quiet. His senses were so alert and the room so still, he thought if a mouse had wiggled a whisker he would have felt the breeze.

He put his lips to her hair, wanting to hear an endearment from her. And when she didn't speak, he nipped her ear.

She jumped, giving him a half-hearted nudge away with her elbow. 'Bran…' she mumbled, slapping at him.

'Near enough,' he whispered, beginning a gentle caress of her hip and stomach.

She moved so her lips nearly touched his chin as she spoke.

She had a look about her which caught his eye so easily. He would have to keep himself a little further from her.

Something ripped into his body and took him by the senses and pulled him straight to her. He couldn't live like this.

Katherine couldn't tell if Brandt was asleep or awake. He lay at her side and they weren't touching.

She ran her fingertips along his arm, feeling the underlying strength. His breathing changed, stopping, then continued as it had. He didn't speak. He didn't roll away.

No matter. He had chosen to spend the night with her. Surely it meant something to him.

She looked out of the corner of one eye to see the

open window. She'd not realised the air was moving, but she felt coldness.

She was closer to him than she'd ever been to any other person and they might as well have been in different rooms. In different houses.

Marriage had made her feel more abandoned than ever, and the closer she moved physically to Brandt the further she felt him retreat.

She looked at his eyes and the line of his jaw. He wasn't thinking of her.

He rolled to her, pulling the covers around them.

'I'll leave instructions with the banker and the man of affairs to let them know my wishes.' He spoke quietly. 'They will be told to follow your words as carefully as they would my own. And, the man of affairs will send reports to my brother and he'll see I'm informed—although I have no problem with how you spend the money. Just do as you wish.'

'And you?' she asked, trying to keep her voice even.

'I'll live somewhere else.'

'You don't wish to live in London and live the life of a gentleman, or a tavern rug?' If he were at the Hare's Breath, or his room, he would not be far. But, he sounded as if he wished to disappear.

'No. I don't wish to go back there.'

'Brandt. I won't follow you. I won't. And it would be so much better, for your mother, if you were to be close.'

'I will not tell her where I am. She'll think I returned to the old place. She never has to know. And you can tell her that I will return eventually. And the hope will keep her happy.'

'She'll not believe it.'

'Perhaps she will.'

'I must thank you, I suppose. For giving us a home. And freedom. And a family. I will do my best to spend many days with your mother and we will keep each other company.'

She tugged at the top edge of the cover, not because she wanted more, but because she wanted to discomfit him.

'If you have need of anything, I'll see that the man of affairs can send a note to me.'

'Will you visit?'

'It's possible.' The bed creaked and he moved over her, and even as she tried to ignore the movement, she couldn't erase the nearness of his body, the hint of skin brushing past her eyes, the scent of a man and the way he made her feel as if she were half the size of him. Surely he couldn't be that much larger than she was. But when he was naked, his size increased.

'Do you feel any caring for me at all?' she asked.

'I care for you. Of course. How could I not?'

'More than you feel for Hercules?'

'I hate his sorry hide. Bit my ear. Hard. And nickered like he'd won a race. So, it's not much to say I care for you more than Hercules. But I do.'

She met his eyes. 'You're more generous than I.'

She rolled from the bed, attempting to pull the cover with her, but the cloth didn't move with her. She looked back. The bedclothes were caught in his fist quite firmly and he'd raised an eyebrow.

'I still have not thanked you for opening my door when I was naked and showing my backside to Mrs Caudle.'

'We're even now,' she snapped and threw her side of the covers over his head and reached for her chemise.

She heard his movements as he pulled the counterpane from over his head.

'I cannot wait for you to leave,' she said as she tugged the chemise in place. Then she stepped beside the bed, picked up her corset, examined it, then tossed it to the wall.

She turned back to him. 'If you don't wish to live with me, I understand completely.'

'Good.' He stepped to the washstand and splashed the water on his face with both hands.

The action irritated her.

She'd never had a man in her room—in her actual sleeping quarters—before—except, of course, him. Mrs Caudle was right. He did have a pleasant elixir. And every place on his body seemed to waft it into the room.

But he didn't care.

'I can't father a child and think, *well, must be on my way.*' He turned, eyes darkened. Changed. Almost not the same man. 'No. Children are much more to me then little weeds who pop up after a rain. You cannot ignore a miracle and you cannot walk away with a backwards yawn and a fresh brandy. And even when you stay you cannot save them from fate. Do not think with sweet whispers you can talk me into the risk.'

'I talked you into the kidnapping and now I'm free of Augustine.'

'You see how well it's turned out for me when I listened to you. Practically had a pistol in my face and nearly had to choose between hanging or a marriage.'

Katherine couldn't help herself. She tried a different vein. 'You are what a woman needs in a father for her children. A caring man. And we have the benefit of marriage.'

He turned, pulling her close. 'Nigel, that sweet mouth of yours isn't going to be able to talk me into a child.'

She felt his lips near hers. The warmth seeping into her. His tongue brushed against her lips, dipping softly into her mouth. Pulling back, and then he kissed her softly.

'Katherine,' he whispered. 'You're as tempting as any woman in the world. A precious jewel, but you're made of flesh and bone, not stone. And all of this can end in a second. It's not good to have a heart involved.'

His words stayed in the air when he backed away.

'Yes, I have a heart,' she bit out the words. 'For what it's worth. So perhaps I should use it. I suppose I should care about someone other than Gussie or Mrs Caudle. I am just not certain I know anyone worthy of my highest esteem.'

'If I could love anyone, Katherine, it would be you.'

He stopped and his voice softened. 'You're truly a fine woman, but I am not your husband.'

In those seconds, she saw nothing in his eyes she wanted to see.

His words crashed into her skin. 'A marriage has never made any man a husband who did not wish to be.'

She turned her head away as the door closed softly behind him. She didn't want him to see her face.

She jerked herself upright and moved to a chair at the table, sat and put her face in her hands.

Brandt meant what he said. She knew.

Her heart felt a shudder and she wondered if its coldness seeped in from the ring on her finger. Once it had been her mother's. The one from her first marriage and it hadn't done her well, either.

Chapter Twenty-Two

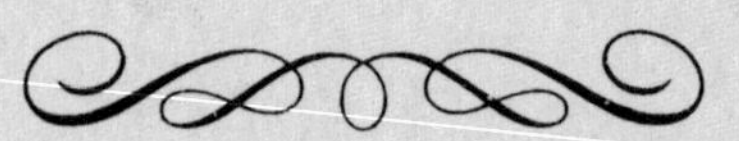

Brandt grabbed his clothing and moved to the adjoining dressing chamber. He did not want to speak with her. He had to leave quickly.

He pulled on his small clothes and took his time dressing, tying his cravat carefully.

When he opened the door to her room, he ignored her grunt and the hairbrush that flew by his head. He was too drained to wish for anything but his clothing.

Bad enough she stirred him—even now, with her clothes on. That couldn't be helped. She had been made too ripe for his hands, too perfect for his eyes. And his eyes. Keeping them from her took all his strength. He'd felt such a physical pull once before, but this time, he was a man and he wouldn't let it ensnare his heart. Katherine was a beauty. He loved the feel of her hair. The way her body moved when she simply walked across the room, or the way she carried the tepid tea as if the cup might burn her hand.

Even when she sneezed at the dust in the carriage house, she did little more than emit a squeak. His lips turned up. Then he felt the heat begin to stir in him.

Blast. He would speak with her again and wish her well, and he would leave to a new tavern in a new town.

Brandt strode into the study. He had to leave.

He saw a rag doll on the floor, and picked it up, staring for a moment at the embroidered eyes before sitting it in the chair.

He didn't even take the time to sit at the desk, but pulled out foolscap and readied the quill.

The door burst open. Katherine walked in and put her hands at her hips. 'Brandt—your mother needs you. You have lost a son. Don't take hers from her.'

'That was a bit low, even from you, Katherine.' His eyes darkened. 'You know nothing of my grief. The marrow is removed from your bones, replaced with grinding ache. Breathing pulls the sorrow into you deeper.'

'You lived through it.'

He grunted. 'That was not living. I breathed. I drank. I ate. I sometimes slept. I could have been in a gaol. It made me no difference.'

He spread extended fingers over the desk and tapped them against the wood, almost as if he played pianoforte. 'Katherine. This is not a choice I made. It's how I'm made. I lost so much, including a part of myself. The part that loves died with them. Children are so fragile. They fall from wagons. They get consumptive. They die. I know everyone dies, but when it's a child in your care and you've failed him, then you are not given a second chance. Children die. They die, and while you watch and you can't make them breathe again and you can't make their eyes open again or take the pain from their lips as they fade away… No matter how much you have—you have nothing any more.'

'Brandt. It doesn't mean—'

'Katherine. I saw Nathan's breath stop and I waited for the next one, and waited, and he had no strength to breathe again and I had no strength to beg his ravaged body to work harder than it could. I kept waiting and waiting. He didn't breathe again.'

He let himself look at the worthless things on the desk. 'Children leave so easily. More easily than you can imagine.'

'This is not the way you should feel. I want you to feel differently.' She leaned forward.

'It would be pleasant for me to feel *differently*,' His words slashed out. '*I would like to feel differently.* But I don't.'

'You still have something in your heart.'

'I cannot find my heart, Katherine.' He sat at the desk and steepled his fingers, resting his hand against them. 'It died.' Then he spoke so softly she almost didn't hear. 'Gone.'

Katherine didn't move and Brandt stood. He turned his back to her.

'Katherine. Mary lost a baby girl. I don't know why. Stillborn. Mary couldn't stop crying. This was the second lost baby. The first time wasn't so difficult. Mary had barely known she was going to have a child and then she lost it. But the second…'

She heard the intake of breath and saw him put both hands to the wall and lean into it.

'I insisted I could make her better. We must go to London, I said. London. We'll buy you pretty dresses and it will be good for Nathan to see all the buildings and people. We'll have a nice visit and it will make everything better and then we can come home.'

'Brandt.' She reached out.

'Leave me, Katherine.' He dropped his head even lower, outstretched fingers raking up through his hair. 'I hadn't even thought of the children growing older. It was all so new to me. The family. The home. I knew all children leave home eventually. But then they left me alone. Nathan. My son. Almost five. Like Gussie. And he was gone. They were all gone for ever.'

Katherine turned. The spirits of Brandt's family didn't walk the earth. They lived inside him, trapped by his memories and his heart.

Maybe his family was in heaven looking at Brandt, but she doubted they watched. How could you leave someone behind and bear to see him suffer? If heaven were a place of comfort, Mary could not be watching Brandt and be in peace.

Katherine walked to Brandt. She touched his back, letting her hand rest a moment, and turned away.

When she pulled the door shut, the sound hammered into her heart, then left a silence. He could stay in the room or leave. She couldn't control his actions or his heart.

When the door shut behind Katherine, Brandt felt the deadness seep into his soul.

'When?'

The little voice was less than a whisper and it shuddered as if blown about by the force of the earth.

He looked, and saw the girl, Gussie, sliding her thin frame from behind the curtain. She grabbed her doll from the chair. Her brown eyes bit into him.

'When?' she repeated, stronger this time. 'Bedlam?'

'No.' He took a step backward, his palm outstretched. 'No. You're not leaving. This is to be your home.'

Solemn eyes stared at him.

'Not you. My children,' he said. 'They had to go away.'

He saw the sideways shudder of her head—the disagreement in her eyes.

'Gussie. I was talking of my children.'

Her face didn't soften. 'Papa said Bedlam for bad children.'

He knelt on one knee. 'You're not a bad child and neither were mine.'

Her face didn't change. 'You want me to go.'

He saw the eyes, accusing.

'Gussie…' He put his hand on her shoulder, surprised by the thinness underneath her shift.

She stepped back from his touch. 'You're ugly.' She ran to the door, darting through it.

He stood and walked to the window, seeing nothing but Gussie's frightened stare.

This wasn't his world. His life. He hadn't meant to be here. He should be back at the tavern. But it felt as closed to him as his house.

What kind of man was he that every place he found solace became impossible for him? He made both hands into fists, knowing raging did no good. If it had, his wife would have returned to him, and his son.

Raging did nothing. Tears did nothing. *Nothing.*

He turned to the door Katherine had first shut and then Gussie had closed as quietly as a tick of a clock.

This time was different.

'Gussie,' he called as he half-ran.

He went to Gussie's room and found it empty. Then he turned and ran to the governess's room, banging his fist on the door. Almost instantly the barrier opened, and the woman, with sleepy eyes, stood before him.

'Is Gussie with you?' he asked and saw her step back.

'She's asleep. I read her to sleep almost a half-hour ago.'

He shut his eyes slowly, opened them and turned from her.

'Gussie,' he commanded, shouting out. 'Gussie. Come here.'

'What is the matter?' Katherine stepped into the hallway. 'You're shouting the house down.'

He clenched his jaw. He would not put this into words. 'I need to see Gussie. She is to be in bed and she slipped away.'

'She's not a prisoner. She's a child. If she wakes—she finds something to play. She isn't troublesome.'

'Katherine...' His voice was slow. 'Find her and bring her to me. I must—'

'Must what?'

He turned his face from hers. 'She's a babe. I do not want her to carry the scars I carry.'

'No one can, Brandt.' Her whisper-soft voice reached into his soul.

He turned to her. 'I cannot risk it.' He took a breath. 'Gussie.' The loudness doubled with each word.

'Hush, Brandt,' Katherine walked to him, putting a hand on his arm. 'No one would come to you when you speak so harshly. I'll find her and bring her to the study.'

Brandt gave a sharp nod and went to the study, and

lowered himself into the chair he'd sat in a thousand times before.

He watched the doorway for the little girl.

Katherine brought Gussie into the room, almost dragging her.

Brandt faced the tear-stained eyes.

He stood and walked in front of them and knelt down.

'Go away.' Gussie's voice quavered, her long hair tangling around her shoulders. 'I want home.'

Brandt knelt in front of her. 'This is better for you.'

'No.'

Gussie looked at her sister. 'I… Home.'

'Gussie.' Katherine turned her sister so she could stare into her eyes. 'We'll make a new home here.'

'This is Bedlam?'

'No. It's not. You will learn to like it here,' Brandt said. 'You can build a bonfire at night and watch for shooting stars. And you can ride horses and play outside.'

She turned her head to him, chin raised. 'No.'

'You're a stubborn child,' Brandt said.

She nodded her head.

'Almost as stubborn as I am.'

'I don't like horses,' she said.

'Neither do I.'

'She doesn't usually act this way.' Katherine ran her hand over the little girl's hair, smoothing it back in place.

'I do.' Gussie looked at Brandt. Her chin rose high. ''Cept when I'm worse.'

'My Nathan was a good child.'

'I threw Papa's papers in the fire.'

Katherine gasped. 'You did not.'

Gussie stared at Brandt. 'I did. They burned.'

'She's just tired,' Katherine said. 'We've had a long day. I'll take her to bed.'

Brandt followed behind them, watching as she tucked Gussie into bed. When Katherine left the room, he waited outside the doorway.

'You didn't tell me she was so wilful,' he said. 'She is nothing like my son.'

'She is a ray of sunshine in my life and Mrs Caudle's.'

'Then you have a lot of sooty days.'

Brandt returned to his room, and settled into a chair. Nothing looked the same as it had. Even in the darkness, he could tell that. In the past, it had always had the scent of gardenias, but now it had more of a mixture of fresh stirred dirt and lemon. It almost reminded him of the tavern when the women had cleaned at night.

He relaxed into the chair and shut his eyes, trying to imagine somewhere along the road north to Scotland that would take him in. He'd forgotten how much he'd enjoyed the fields in the summer and the movements of ploughing, of caring for the cows. Of honest sweat tiring him and the sudden change of jumping into a standing pool when the work was done, and stepping out with a feeling of having earned the right to sit by a fire.

He never knew when he fell into a slumber, but the sudden clattering thump of wood hitting his head caused his eyes to dart open. Morning light streamed in the window.

A little girl in nightclothes stared at him. Nathan's rabbit lay on the floor by his chair. He reached up, feeling the spot where the rabbit had connected with his head.

'I'm ready to go to Bedlam now,' she informed him.

'Then go and get Katherine. I'm not taking you. And get out of my room.'

She walked over, picked up Nathan's rabbit and hugged it close.

'Katty is asleep. You're not.'

'Perhaps I should take you. But I'm going, too. I've my own journey to take.'

'You're leaving?' she asked, rocking the rabbit.

'Yes. Today.'

She looked around his room. 'I like this room. I will stay here.'

He rose to his feet and strode to the door. The rabbit hit the wall beside the facing as he went outside.

He walked down the hallway and into Katherine's room without knocking.

'Katherine,' he muttered, opening her door. He shut it firmly behind him. 'Why did Augustine not like Gussie?'

'Well...' She sat up, eyes half-closed, running a hand over her face to remove the hair that had escaped in the night. 'She might have poured treacle into his clothes.'

'Did she ever throw things at him?'

'Oh, no. Never. But she hid under his desk and almost tripped him with a cane.'

'Where is Mrs Caudle? Does she not watch her?'

'Of course she does. But Gussie is generally such a good child that Mrs Caudle doesn't always watch her close.'

'Do you ever punish the little—?' *Monster* was the first word that popped into his mind. 'Girl?'

'Well, when she misbehaves we give her tarts to settle her down and we talk about what she did wrong.'

'If I misbehaved and someone gave me a bottle of brandy every time I did, I doubt I'd stop.' He waved an arm.

She snorted. 'Well, that's what you did. You went to the tavern and had crateloads of brandy.' She tossed her head and had the same rebellion in her eyes the little one had.

'Do not be humorous. The child is a little hellion and she has planned to take my room when I leave.'

'Well, what is wrong with her taking your room?'

'She is a little girl and it is the master's chambers.'

'She's growing up soon and won't want a room with Mrs Caudle. She'll have to sleep somewhere.'

He walked to the mirror, looked into it and touched the red bump on his head.

'She lost her mother so young,' Katherine said, sliding out of the bed and slipping into her nightrail. 'Her father shouted at her every time she came near. Mrs Caudle and I care a great deal for her.'

'Perhaps too much.'

He left the room. He heard the door open and close behind him and Katherine's footsteps following along.

He walked by the doorway to his room where Gussie glared at him. She hurled the rabbit his way. He reached out and caught it.

'You will not be allowed to play with this any

more.' He held the rabbit shoulder high for emphasis. 'Ever. Again.'

'You're leaving. I don't care.'

He shrugged. 'Neither do I.'

But he looked down at her and could see her growing up and searching taverns for a kidnapper or a gambler.

'I'm putting this away where you can never play with it again.'

She charged him, hitting his legs.

'No, Gussie.' Katherine pulled her back and Gussie tried to escape, flailing and kicking.

'Let her go,' he said.

Gussie wriggled free and charged at him again. He took her thin shoulders and held her at arm's length as she struggled to hit him. He turned his head towards Katherine. 'What does she like more than anything in the world?'

'To be read to.'

'Gussie, if you do not be good—' he held her firm '—we will take your books.'

'I don't care,' she said, stepping back. 'I have my doll.'

'The next time you misbehave, the books will go away for a day. If you misbehave again, the doll will go away for a day.'

He looked at Katherine. 'Below stairs there is a place where the silver was stored—you should find it soon and be prepared to put her books and doll in it.'

'I hate you. I want Mrs Caudle,' the child shouted.

He released Gussie's arms and she ran down the hallway and to the stairs, going out of sight. He turned to Katherine and chuckled softly. 'She hates me. And

I really, really don't like her.' He shook his head. 'And I don't see that changing any time soon.'

'But she's a sweet child.'

He tilted his head sideways, question in his eyes.

'But a bit wilful,' Katherine said.

Brandt turned to her. He reached out, took the rabbit and, with his other hand, his fingertips trailed the delicate skin of her cheek.

'Katherine. It feels too much for me. The worry. But I have a feeling I might worry more about you if I leave than if I stay.'

She reached up to take his hand and held it.

'Brandt. You believe you're more than you are. You're a man. Even with your strength, you're only strong as one man.' Her fingers tightened on his. 'You can't lift more than three men. You can't change the course of the world.'

He pulled her tightly against him, shutting his eyes, and the rabbit clattered to the floor. He let himself truly feel what he had around him. 'But if I lose you, Katherine...'

'Then you should remember how much you gave me.' She moved back, gazing into his face. 'Stop looking to the door and counting the steps.'

He let out a deep breath. 'I want to leave so badly. But I need to stay. You would let that little girl rule the household.'

'You can't protect us from everything, Brandt.'

'I know that well. But I can protect you from her.'

'You don't control life and death. You're here, now,' she whispered. 'Live with us. Not with the family you've lost.'

'It always comes back to my mind.' He pulled her

back into his arms and let his chin rest in her hair. He realised Katherine had seen all sides of his life, yet she'd chosen him for a husband.

'Does it return as often as it did before?'

'Not since I've met you.' He shook his head. 'You've kept me busy.'

'Is it the grief which captured you? Or the guilt?'

He stilled. 'I wronged Mary in life by not thinking her good enough. And if I had not felt the things I did, I wouldn't have been so quick to take them to London. I didn't want to wrong her in death.'

'Don't you think she would have forgiven you?'

He laughed, a low sound. 'Not soon. She carried a grudge for ever.'

'Well, it would have been a convenient thing for her to hold over your head if you had a shouting match then.' She took in a deep breath. 'And should we get in a shouting match, I think I will throw that back in your face, on her behalf.'

'You may. It would have made her happy to have a woman raised in society defending her.'

'Then I shall.'

'I will hold you to it.' He kissed her, a soft lingering kiss, running his hand along her back, pulling them close.

'Are you sure you just aren't willing to let Gussie have your room?'

'It is out of the question.' He paused. 'I will happily let her hate me. And I'm not going to make any overtures of friendship to her. She will have to come to me if she wishes us to be acquainted, but if not, that is how it is.'

'That sounds harsh.'

He shook his head. 'It worked for the lightskirts.'

Katherine's mouth fell open.

'The little one is making me feel right at home. A few blisters on my hands will be next. It's not always an easy path, Katherine. In fact, it never is. I can't escape problems or troubles. I've tried. It's time I accepted that grief and regret and mistakes are a part of life, and settle into this world. You, Gussie and I are misfits. But together, we'll fit into our own lives and our own family.'

'Maybe that's what marriage is meant to be.'

He smiled. 'I suspect it is what our marriage was meant to be.'

He rested his head against hers and his shoulders relaxed. He just held her and felt her breathe against him, and it seemed the breaths she gave moved into his own body, filling him with a peace he hadn't felt in a very long time.

Pulling back, he looked to her fingers. He saw the ring she'd handed him during the marriage and that he'd slipped on her hand during the vows. 'That is your mother's ring?'

She brushed her fingers over the simple band, her eyes on the ring. 'Yes.'

He took her fingertips and pulled her hand so he could see the ring. He didn't speak as he examined the band.

She could see the sweep of his lashes and beyond the hard planes of his face. He gently turned the ring on her finger. Then he pulled her hand to his lips, and kissed the ring. 'I love you,' he spoke, his voice little more than a gravelly whisper.

'I'm not surprised,' she said. 'After all, we did run away together.'

He raised his eyes to her and then straightened. 'I truly wouldn't have chosen to marry again. But I hadn't met a woman who looked so fetching in trousers and a waistcoat. And if I let you from my sight, I'm afraid what you might do to some poor man should you decide to replace me.'

'You're irreplaceable, you scoundrel.'

He savoured the warmth he felt in her arms. 'Katherine. You are the scoundrel. You barged into my door and nestled yourself a place in my heart, kidnapping me. I said *I do* to a woman who woke me in the midst of a deep sleep. The sleep I lived each day of my life. And you would not let me continue my life of slumber.'

'I am not a scoundrel,' she said.

'Well, be that as it may,' he said, 'I'm so fortunate you woke me.'

He felt her body relax into his.

He opened his mouth to tell her of his love again, but she interrupted. 'Brandt, should we have children, how will we tell them we met?'

'The truth is best—except leave out the part about the kidnapping.' He let his cheek rest in her hair.

'I believe I will tell them how their father was so entranced by me, he could hardly let me out of his sight.' She let her fingertips trail through his hair.

'And I will tell them we met at a surprise soirée and I was so taken with the way your eyes took me in, I swept you away.' He nipped her ear.

He could hear the smile in her words when she spoke again. 'And I took one look at you and could barely speak.'

'Well, an unmarried woman isn't supposed to speak to a man without a proper introduction.' His arms tightened around her. Brandt shut his eyes and shook his head. 'If we do have children, Katherine, I think that I might be the one to instruct them more than you and Mrs Caudle.'

She laughed.

The sound was pure. Clear. The haze that had deadened the sounds of all happiness had faded.

Katherine was the answer to the quest he'd not allowed his heart to take and now she was nestled there, snug and secure.

He looked at her and, in the way of knowing a truth that is secret to the rest of the world and is generated from forces stronger than the ones creating air, he knew they would be together long into the lives of their grandchildren.

* * * * *

If you enjoyed this story
check out these other great reads
by Liz Tyner